AND THE WHOLE MOUNTAIN BURNED

AND THE WHOLE MOUNTAIN BURNED

A War Novel

RAY MCPADDEN

CENTER STREET

New York Nashville

Copyright © 2018 by Ray McPadden

Cover copyright © 2018 by Hachette Book Group, Inc.

Hachette Book Group supports the right to free expression and the value of copyright. The purpose of copyright is to encourage writers and artists to produce the creative works that enrich our culture.

The scanning, uploading, and distribution of this book without permission is a theft of the author's intellectual property. If you would like permission to use material from the book (other than for review purposes), please contact permissions@hbgusa.com. Thank you for your support of the author's rights.

Center Street
Hachette Book Group
1290 Avenue of the Americas, New York, NY 10104
centerstreet.com

twitter.com/centerstreet

First Edition: November 2018

Center Street is a division of Hachette Book Group, Inc. The Center Street name and logo are trademarks of Hachette Book Group, Inc.

The publisher is not responsible for websites (or their content) that are not owned by the publisher.

The Hachette Speakers Bureau provides a wide range of authors for speaking events. To find out more, go to www.HachetteSpeakersBureau.com or call (866) 376-6591.

Map pf Afghanistan by John Barnett, 4eyesdesign.com

Library of Congress Cataloging-in-Publication Data
Names: McPadden, Ray, author.
Title: And the whole mountain burned : a war novel / Ray McPadden.
Description: First edition. | New York : Center Street, 2018.
Identifiers: LCCN 2018021696| ISBN 9781546081913 (hardcover) | ISBN 9781549117336 (audio download) | ISBN 9781546081920 (ebook)
Subjects: LCSH: Afghan War, 2001---Fiction. | LCGFT: War fiction.
Classification: LCC PS3613.C5865 A53 2018 | DDC 813/.6--dc23
LC record available at https://lccn.loc.gov/2018021696

ISBNs: 978-1-5460-8191-3 (hardcover), 978-1-5460-8192-0 (ebook)

Printed in the United States of America

LSC-C

10 9 8 7 6 5 4 3 2 1

*To all the infantrymen, and to my daughter
Lupine—don't marry one of us*

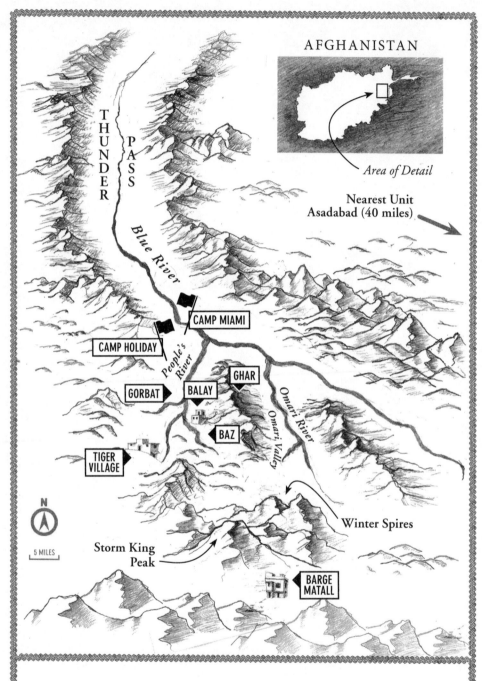

AFGHANISTAN

Area of Detail

Nearest Unit
Asadabad (40 miles)

THUNDER PASS

Blue River

CAMP MIAMI

CAMP HOLIDAY

People's River

GHAR

GORBAT

BALAY

Omari River

BAZ

Omari Valley

TIGER VILLAGE

N

5 MILES

Winter Spires

Storm King Peak

BARGE MATALL

AND THE WHOLE
MOUNTAIN BURNED

NEWT PLATOON
HEADQUARTERS

Platoon	RTO	FO	Platoon	Medic
Leader			Sergeant	
LT. Dillon			Vasquez	Doc Soto

1ST SQUAD

ALPHA TEAM   BRAVO TEAM

Squad
Leader
Martinez

2ND SQUAD

ALPHA TEAM   BRAVO TEAM

Squad
Leader   Austin   Bloome

3RD SQUAD

ALPHA TEAM   BRAVO TEAM

Squad   Cassidy   Shane
Leader
Burch

MACHINE GUN SQUAD

GUN 1   GUN 2   GUN 3

Squad   Kopeki
Leader

PROLOGUE

Eastern Afghanistan—2002

R anger Nick Burch carried a 240B machine gun during the invasion. He once fired from the hip just to say he did. Most nights he fell asleep on his gun with rocks in his ribs. Shivers woke him before the ambush patrols set out. It was hard living among the fleas, stones, and sharp-eyed mountain people. But there was something in the Hindu Kush, a life force felt but unseen, like static in a storm. Today, Burch was sure of it as he eyed the roaring cataract in the Blue River.

Burch's Ranger platoon held a house with cracked mud walls. He was sitting behind his 240B, voice hoarse from the last gunfight, broken glass under his boots. A fly fresh off the dead landed on Burch's knuckle and eagerly rubbed its front legs together. Swatting it away, Burch surveyed the cratered slopes above the river.

He spotted an Afghan kid named Sadboy romping toward the house with a bag of potatoes swinging in his hand. Sadboy was ten, or about that age. One couldn't be sure with the Afghans. Burch's platoon called the kid Sadboy because of the tear-shaped birth-

1

mark under his eye, and because his real name, Habibullah, was a mouthful. Today, Sadboy wore homemade sandals and a skullcap. A green parka issued by the U.S. Army hung from his shoulders down to his knees.

Burch strode into the courtyard to meet the boy. "Sadboy, how's it hanging?"

Sadboy defended his Afghan name. "Habibullah, Habibullah."

Pointing at the boy's spruce-root sandals, Burch said, "I gotta get some of them go-fasters."

Sadboy nodded and announced he was going to make *chipas*—Pashto for "french fries."

Burch said, "You really shouldn't be here," and gestured like he was firing a rifle.

Sadboy said, "*Chipas* quick."

Burch said, "How much?"

"Two dollar."

"That's a dollar more than last week."

Sadboy drummed his fingers on a rock.

Burch said, "Listen, we might go knuckles up here in a minute. How 'bout I just give you two bucks and you piss off?"

"Then I'd be a beggar. No good."

"Your English is coming along."

"Thanks," said Sadboy. "I learn from you—skin flute, meat curtain, pooh-see."

Burch said, "Thatta boy. Start cooking."

Sadboy unrolled his green blanket, revealing an iron skillet, a rusty knife, a lighter, and a vial of grease. He then weaved up the hillside and returned with kindling. The boy set up in the courtyard, sitting on his haunches near a low stone wall.

Sadboy's potatoes sizzled and popped. Burch paced over the boy, one eye on the hills. The wonderful perfume of french fries wafted into the main room of the house, where Burch's squad pulled afternoon watch, their elbows resting on stacked sandbags. The scent drifted into another room, where the squad on night ambush rustled in their sleeping bags. The scent curled into a third room, where a fire team sweated on their cards playing Texas Hold'em. As the winnings moved between men, the sun set pink behind a mountain, throwing shadows up the valley's east wall. A granite reef seemed to catch fire for a moment in the fading light. Night's black hand touched a rib on the east side.

Just then, the staccato sound of machine guns erupted from the hills. Enemy bullets mushroomed on the house walls. Rocket-propelled grenades came in like comets. Burch's cell membranes were screaming *Flee, flee* as he ran headlong for his machine gun. His ears stung from gunfire and explosions. Echoes bounced off the valley walls and spun together. Burch couldn't tell incoming from outgoing. The bedlam of a mountain gunfight was upon him.

The muzzle of a heavy machine gun flashed from a ridge at eight hundred yards. The gun was tucked between two rocks that looked to be gargoyles. In came plunging fire on the Ranger platoon. The house courtyard was horribly exposed. It became a magnet for 12.7 mm rounds, which pinged and cracked and bounced about. The house protected the Rangers. They had hard-baked mud and sandbags for cover. Burch thought of Sadboy in the courtyard. Perhaps he had reached one of the rooms. Burch imagined Sadboy jumping through a window with cannonball velocity.

The hills kept on sparkling with fire. The Rangers kept on pumping bullets at the enemy. Finding his nerve, Burch went turbo with his machine gun. He was scared for himself, his friends, and Sadboy. Faces swirled through his mind, but he soon forgot them. Burch became intoxicated as his 240 shook his brain. The violence was grand. He didn't expect a gunfight to feel so good, and now a single glorious image ruled his awareness—he saw a burning zeppelin. And down it went in brilliant flames.

Burch fired in six-to-nine-round bursts. His special technique for controlling the gun's rhythm was saying *Die motherfucker die* in his head. Finishing the phrase, he eased off the trigger to reset his aim. Then he mashed down the trigger again. *Die mother-*

fucker die. The barrel was glowing. A pile of brass clinked at his boots.

The Rangers used rifle-mounted grenade launchers. *Thump… thump… thump.* The grenades leapt from the tubes but kept falling short. The ridge was just out of range. Three Rangers wrestled AT4s off rucksacks and yanked the safety pins. "Backblast area clear." The first antitank round vaporized a granite statue. The next split a boulder. Another splintered a tree. The enemy ran for defilade.

A ringing quiet came over the hills. Burch remembered Sadboy. Running for the courtyard with his temples thumping in his helmet, Burch envisioned what he would see when he rounded the corner: Sadboy in a pool of blood, with lifeless eyes, his pan and *chipas* flung about, his cooking fire smoldering. Sadboy would be light when Burch picked him up—just a boy, a hungry little boy.

But when Burch actually rounded the corner, Sadboy was on his haunches, tending his *chipas*, just as he had been before the fight. He flicked his wrist. The sizzling *chipas* flipped in the pan. He did it again. The *chipas* flipped higher. Burch realized Sadboy wasn't going to run off in a panic and piss away his investment. This little dirt-eating kid was nickel-plated.

Sadboy looked up, showing Burch the tear-shaped birthmark under his eye.

He chirped, *"Chipas? Chipas?"*

Spring 2008

1

Eastern Afghanistan
Day 1 of tour

I n the Hindu Kush range, the snowline was fourteen thousand feet. The forest started at ten thousand. Everything below that was battlefield. The all-seeing peaks of this range were the tail of the Himalayas. The bellies of the mountains hid wheelbarrows full of jewels—wild topaz, rubies, emeralds, and aquamarines. Snow leopards weaved through cliff bands on snowshoe-sized paws. To the east were the titans that bewitched climbers from around the world, peaks such as K2 and Buni Zom.

It was April 1 when a Chinook helicopter chugged over these mountains with the forty-three men of Newt platoon riding in back. The Newts were mountain commandos. They fought on foot, and on skis if need be. The Chinook carrying them flared over a lone flat spot in the terrain.

The youngest trigger puller in the platoon, Pvt. Danny Shane, sprung from his cargo net seat. Shane was splinter thin but wore his uniform well. He mustered a half smile at the others. Inside he was thrashing like a hooked trout.

The bird touched down and Shane hustled over the ramp. He had the honor of claiming first one on the ground. It was something he'd been waiting for. Shane ran for a copse of pines fifty yards distant and dropped to a knee. At that moment, he was a mere fleck in a valley that ran north–south for fifteen miles. The valley mouth was at the north end; so was the Blue River. On the south end the terrain rose sheer to peaks over eighteen thousand feet. Steep ridges walled in the valley on the east and west. Altogether, it was a jagged culvert lying sinuous among giants.

The Chinook throttled up. Downwash blasted Shane. The rucksack he wore almost matched his body weight. He teetered backward, arms windmilling, and fell over a downed trunk. Lying on his back, he flailed to get up, all the while thinking, *Stupid, stupid.* After struggling to a knee, Shane glanced at his squad leader, hoping he hadn't seen.

Sergeant Burch was shaking his head.

A minute on the ground and you've made a fool of yourself, thought Shane.

Four more Chinooks landed. They carried supplies and two more platoons. The full 145-man company was on the ground in three minutes. They had just been injected into the heart of the Hindu Kush. The company's mission was to subdue a ferocious tribe.

The Newts had the honor of a special mission: Kill an Al Qaeda commander who'd for many years evaded Western pursuit. His name was Abdul Rahman. Everyone called him "the Egyptian." He'd married the daughter of the tribal chief and now called the valley home. Back in '02, the Egyptian rose to prominence after leading an ambush on a Green Beret patrol. His guerrillas killed six and captured one. On video, the Egyptian took a scimitar to the prisoner's head and sawed it off in a spurting mess. And so began the manhunt. Later the Egyptian orchestrated a rocket attack on Bagram Airfield that killed a gray-haired two-star. The brass shit their pants. No opponent had killed a U.S. general since 'Nam.

Shane leaned into swirling dust and ferried crates of bullets and batteries from the choppers. Going back for more, he lugged tuff boxes brimming with snowshoes, ropes, webbing, carabiners, nuts, cams, and hexes. He shouldered nylon cases holding Rossignol powder skis.

As the din of the last chopper faded, Shane again looked to Sergeant Burch, who lifted his goggles. Dust powdered Burch's face, save the rings around his eyes.

Burch said, "We won't be wearing those skis anytime soon." He knifed the tie on a bundle of sandbags and passed them out to his squad, saying, "Alpha team, drop your kit. You're digging first. Bravo pulls security."

Shane loosened his helmet and body armor. He tied a snakeskin across his brow and unfolded a collapsible shovel known as an e-tool. Shane commenced digging, the e-tool clanking against crumbly gray earth. The veins in his forearms were blue-green ropes. Overhead, a rock formation jutted from the hillside like a ship's prow. Seams and dikes of quartz had zigzagged across the prow at a time when all was molten. Shane's eyes wandered over the face, landing on three black streaks running down. They could have been the claw marks of a prehistoric beast.

The clatter of tools bounced off the prow. Shane hacked away, his e-tool vibrating with each bite into the slanted earth. One by one Shane stacked sandbags at his feet. His snakeskin headband glimmered in the sun. Salt ringed the collar and armpits of his brown shirt. Forty sandbags were now piled by his hole. He'd bested the others by at least ten bags. He kept close count.

Sergeant Burch strolled by with an M4 slung across his chest. The gun was tricked out with a scope, laser, and suppressor, and painted with tiger stripes for camouflage.

Shane had painted the same pattern on his own gun, but it didn't look nearly as sexy.

Burch looked at the stacked sandbags beside Shane's hole, then said, "Slow down, Shane. We got fifteen months left. Don't blow your wad on the first day."

Shane said, "Roger, Sar'nt."

Burch asked, "You got any more deer jerky?"

"Roger, Sar'nt."

"Break me off a plug."

Shane had made the jerky himself back home and brought five pounds to the Stan. To oblige his sergeant, Shane dug into his pack, ripped off a piece the size of a ham, and handed it over.

Burch asked, "What's that shit wrapped around your head?"

Shane removed his headband and kneaded it in his fingers. "This is an eastern diamondback rattlesnake, Sar'nt. I hit it with a twelve-gauge shotty under the steps of my trailer. I was ten at the time...no wait, nine. This skin is my warbonnet. And I'll tell ya, if you want to see if a man's got grit, have him crawl under a trailer in Tupelo, Mississippi, in mid-July. You've never seen so many creepy-crawlies."

With a mouth full of jerky, Burch said, "Keep it on the down low. If Sergeant Vasquez sees you wearing it, I'll be sunk."

"Roger, Sar'nt."

Shane was a cherry, meaning this was his first combat tour. Assigned to Newt platoon nine months before the deployment, Shane had reported for duty wearing a Bart Simpson shirt and clicked his heels in front of Sergeant Burch, who had been sitting over a disassembled machine gun in the barracks. Burch looked up and went ghostly white, his bottom lip quivering for a long second. Then Burch bolted from the room.

It was the damnedest thing. Shane was still getting his head around it.

The morning sky was stained glass on day number two. Shane lined up for his first patrol, radio intercept. It was simple enough because the enemy communicated with unencrypted walkie-talkies.

The patrol would range south to get the enemy talking. "Stir shit up," was how Shane understood it. Perhaps they'd hear the Egyptian, and they could start collecting on him, building a profile so they could later strike with a capture/kill mission.

Standing at the camp perimeter, Shane turned on the walkie-talkie clipped to his shoulder. His stomach was tight, his eyes alert.

At the perimeter, Burch inspected the squad, giving orders around a cigarette clenched in his front teeth. When Burch came to Shane, he pointed, saying, "Drop this, this, this, and this. The side with the simplest uniform wins."

Shane nodded and ditched his crotch and neck armor, Oakley sunglasses, kneepads, and gloves. Then Shane jawed a twist of tobacco so big he couldn't close his mouth.

"Move out." The squad set off, nine soldiers passing the wire one at a time, each taking his position five yards from the next. They followed a southern azimuth toward the heart of the valley, snaking past the gnarled boughs of holly trees. Shane moved in back of the column, halting every so often to scan the flanks. Up front, the point man picked through a maze of boulders, probing here and there for a route, sometimes backing out and starting over. Progress was painfully slow, and Shane felt exposed, naked. He cussed the point man for his route selection. "Stevie Wonder's leading this fuckin' patrol."

After a few minutes they found a break in the maze. The squad surged ahead. They had just reached checkpoint one when they came upon a broken slope of granite. A narrow ledge offered passage down to a landing. From there it looked to be easy going again.

One by one, the squad boys balanced onto the ledge. Shane brought up the rear, sidling with one hand on his gun, the other gripping rocks at his shoulder. Down Shane went, grabbing tree roots when he could. He was still on the ledge when the first fire team reached the landing. They called up to the rest of the squad, saying, "You're good to here."

Those still on the ledge began shuffling faster. The man in front of Shane, a SAW gunner named Cassidy, pulled loose a rock the size of a microwave. It rolled twice before going airborne. "Rock," yelled Cassidy, and the team below dove for cover just as the rock crashed by. "Assholes," called someone from the landing.

Cassidy turned round with pleading eyes and said to Shane, "Don't tell."

Shane said, "I won't," and Cassidy pressed on.

At that moment an image popped into Shane's mind: the Egyptian on a ridgeline observing the patrol, laughing himself silly.

At last, it was Shane's turn to finish the descent. He checked handholds, then downclimbed, ladder style, and soon touched down beside the others.

Nine men sat panting on a strip of rock above a cliff. It had taken a half hour to cover three hundred feet, and they'd walked into a dead end. There was no doubt in Shane's mind that he could do better walking point. But a cherry had to bide his time. Left of Shane, the squad boys were searching for a way off the landing.

Shane examined the options: They could downclimb a vertical slab for thirty feet to easy ground, or go back the way they came. There would be no going back. Shane was sure of it. After all, the others at camp would have much to say if the squad had to retreat and start over. Shane dug in his pack for a hundred-foot coil of climbing rope. Then he doled it out and doubled the line.

Smacking a holly trunk, Burch told Shane, "Anchor it here."

Shane knelt. Pointed holly leaves matted the ground, stabbing his knees as he wrapped one-inch webbing around the trunk and finished the anchor with a water knot. Using a carabiner, Shane secured the climbing rope to the anchor. The squad began rappelling in the Dulfersitz technique, where the rope was wrapped around the body in such a way that no climbing gear was required.

With the first team safely down, Burch grabbed the rope, threw it over a shoulder, and threaded it under one leg.

Burch told Shane, "Good work setting the rap. Steady hands will serve you well."

Then Burch muscled over the ledge.

When Burch was out of sight, Shane whispered "*Yes*" to himself. Then Shane followed, the rope burning his skin as he inched down the rock face with his gear jangling. Minutes later Shane pulled the rope, and they put the first obstacle behind them.

Ahead Shane saw gullies fluting the rises on both flanks. He hopped rills and climbed up a boulder train. Under another cliff, little blocks were lying here and there, as if the cliff had vomited. Shane picked through the blocks, blowing sweat beads off the tip of his nose.

Enemy radio chatter kicked off. They spoke in code. Shane could hear a dozen different voices saying things like, "The children are here." "They're in the place." "Bring the donkeys up." "We're beside the bend." *At least they aren't laughing*, thought Shane, but there was no mention of the Egyptian.

Shane kept marching, sweeping around the shoulder of another cliff band and polishing off his first canteen. All around, the land was raw with crumbling schist, wind-tortured ridges, and dashing streams. This was the adventure Shane had been waiting for. Here was the home turf of a formidable Afghan tribe. The barbarous terra isolated these natives. At the center of the universe, they called themselves the People. And somewhere in their smashed terrain, they hid the Egyptian, a man chased for so long that the chase became an end in itself.

The Kush sprawled farther than the eye could see. He saw a collage of mountain figures: some table-like, some pyramidal, some shaped like horns, turrets, and dragon tails—and not a flat spot anywhere. Storm King Peak was the patriarch of this land, marking the southern terminus of the valley. Gilded by glaciers, Storm King was ancient, solemn, and shining down on everything. Spindrifts curled off its ridges. On the north face, a patchwork of polished walls and cirques stood testament to the genius of some mad architect.

Shane's patrol kept on their southern azimuth, climbing upslope most of the day. But the ascent was more like tunneling; they were going deeper, away from everything. The valley got tighter. The streams got swifter. The peaks built up while the forests crept down.

Twelve hours later, Shane and the others returned to camp with sunburned faces and dry canteens. Shane hadn't seen a lick of action nor heard a whisper from the Egyptian, but the mountains rang through him. He wanted more. He asked himself why. The answer was jumbled in his mind. He strained to decipher it. In the hills, there was freedom, a world unconfined, and something else. Just beyond Storm King was a thing he could not name, something hungry.

The days slid by. Shane lived on the ground and under it, smearing it on himself. They burrowed day and night. Bunkers, earthworks, and trenches took shape around the camp. Shane fought to straighten his fingers. He could not make a fist—too much time swinging that damn e-tool. Day number six passed slow and sweaty. Evening came on. Blue shadows marched across the valley.

Shane ducked into a bunker for sentry duty and sat down on an ammo crate. He squinted into his rifle scope and saw feathers of smoke rising from village flues. About then, the company radioman came over the Newt frequency. "We have a signal from 110 degrees. Two voices. One said the Egyptian put the rockets beside the meadow. The other said it's ready."

With a thumping heart, Shane pulled the compass from his vest and shot an azimuth of 110 degrees, all the while thinking, *Killing them isn't so hard.* All Shane had to do was identify a meadow along the 110 azimuth and call for bombs. He scanned. High above the foothills, a ridgeline bristled with pines. The trees broke only for a single meadow. Shane studied it from left to right. A band of talus split the grass. This was probably it. Something flashed in the talus.

A single spark came forward in slow motion.

Shane wondered what it was. The spark cleared a rib and a creek and kept coming. Shane got to thinking that he should duck. He had time. The spark closed in. His knees still hadn't dropped. *You've got to duck*, he thought. A banshee shriek registered in his mind.

The world turned burning white. Sandbags tumbled over. Shane fell in a heap. Smoke burned his lungs. He pushed a sandbag off his head. He could move no further. The terrible weight of sandbags robbed the air from his chest. He was buried for a long time, sucking for breath.

There were confused voices and bootfalls on gravel.

Someone yelled, "The bunker is blown to shit."

Then came Burch's steady voice, "Our man's in there. Start digging."

They got to it.

Shane's breathing came easier as the Newts dug and cussed one another somewhere above him in the dark. Then headlamps shined through the haze. The Newts lifted sandbags off Shane's chest. Someone stepped on his hand. He groaned. They pulled him from the wreckage. Shane was on his feet. The others patted him down for blood. All was dry.

Burch was there smiling. He smacked dust from Shane's fighting vest and squared his helmet. "Look at you, not a scratch."

Shane smiled back with dirt in his teeth. "What was that?"

Burch said, "A rocket. Probably a 107."

"Not cool."

Their mortar crews shelled the meadow until well after dark, then called it a night.

———————

In the morning Shane woke to the sound of the platoon battle flag snapping in the wind. He unzipped his fart sack and climbed out and smacked dew off it. The tangerine globe peered into the valley. Light came in arrows through the teeth and cols of the east ridge. Shane hustled to the bunker where Burch was marshaling the squad. Two fire teams of dusty men formed a half circle. They all stood spitting and scratching.

Shane figured this was news about the mortars the night before. *Had they hit the Egyptian?*

Burch had his thumbs hooked in his belt when he said, "We've got the green light to name the camp. Any bright ideas?"

So no Egyptian. Shane fiddled with the camo netting on his helmet, thinking it best for a cherry to keep quiet. He shifted in his body armor. *Someone else will speak up*, he thought. No one did. Then an idea came to him. It was ironic. And they all liked the ironic.

Shane ventured, "Camp Holiday."

With officious looks, everyone agreed.

Burch said, "That'll do," and the matter was settled.

Burch pivoted, cast an arm at the mountain mosaic, and said, "Camp Holiday is our middle finger to these fucks. And this is no contest between machines. Terrain and weather have stripped away the robots, engines, and rotors. The might of the mountains is on full parade." He aimed a finger at the rusting hulk of a Soviet Hind on the valley's east side. The rocks beneath it were stained orange. Further uphill, a Chinook helicopter lay in rubble. One rotor blade was still lodged in a conifer.

"Some say the Egyptian can't be caught." Burch held up a grainy black-and-white picture of Abdul Rahman. They'd all seen it before. The fuzzy image could have been anyone with a beard and dark eyes.

Burch went on, "I know, this picture ain't worth much. S2 says the Egyptian has a limp, a gift from us during the invasion. So we listen and we track in these hills. I say, no hobbled man can beat an aggressive small unit taking well-aimed shots. Audacity, boys, that's how we get him."

Having finished, Sergeant Burch fixed his eyes on the hills.

Burch was Newt platoon's senior squad leader, responsible for eight men, including Shane, who would have it no other way. When on the move, Burch glided on long legs. The squad boys said he could outrun an escaped convict. They had to keep up, so they hated his legs. Out of earshot, they plotted to go "Tonya Harding on his ass."

Burch had deployed to the Kush in 2002 as a private in Second Ranger Battalion. He snatched a black scarf during the tour. Burch now wore the scarf every day. He pulled it up to his eyes when trouble was brewing, like a bandit robbing a bank in the Old West. Shane pondered on the scarf's origin. All the boys did. They had a pool going on who was right.

At 1100 they worked on their defense. More sandbags needed filling. Shane hustled toward the prow and took up his e-tool. The handle was already stinging hot from the sun. Shane poured canteen water over it and stabbed at the rocks. Burch jumped into a hole next to him and shoveled away. A lone cumulus passed overhead. A bulb of shade fanned over them. The sun seemed to notice the challenge and burned away the cloud. When the sun returned, Burch had carved a T-shaped machine gun position. His pile of sandbags dwarfed Shane's pile. Shane paused to draw his bayonet and lance a blister in his palm. He wiped the ooze on his pant leg.

Midswing with his e-tool, Burch said, "Girl hands."

Shane dug faster.

They dropped their e-tools around 1400 and paused for lunch. Nine men pressed together in the shade of one holly, where two fat crows gripped a branch and stared at Shane with dead, black eyes. The hot wind offered no solace. As the sun moved, so did the shade, and Shane kept scooting with it. Burch stayed put and flipped his black scarf over his head. After spooning the last of his ration, Burch wiped his mouth with the scarf. That was when Shane came forward with it.

"Sar'nt. Did you get that scarf here?"

Burch sat back on both elbows. "What's it to ya?"

"We'd like to put it to bed, square some bets."

"Bets, huh?"

"That's all."

Burch took his time. "I got it during the invasion, not far from here. We were chasing the Egyptian."

"What happened?"

Burch looked far, far off. "A girl gave it to me."

"A girl?"

"Leave it alone."

Shane did.

———

Early the next day, the wind spent itself and the valley stood still. A few crows cawed from the holly trees that dotted Holiday. Shane waited at the camp perimeter, thumbs hooked into his belt like Burch. Burch took notice and shook his head.

Shane tucked his thumbs in a little deeper. The squad boys came down in twos and threes and readied their kit. Today's mission was radio intercept again. The objective was a horseshoe hill two miles south. From there, they would listen for the Egyptian. This time they had a direction-finding device. A few intercepts would allow for triangulation of the Egyptian's location. Then they could strike.

At 0630 they stepped out in a file formation on a goat trail, spread at ten-yard intervals. They ranged over slants and talus and slabs, avoiding the terrain that smoked them the first time out. Far below, the growling river slashed toward the valley mouth. Shane caught peeks of the foaming ribbon here and there. Vapor still clung to the watercourse in patches, just come down from the high tributaries, giving the valley bottom a sinister finish.

Up ahead the hill came into view. The squad split in two. One team took an overwatch position while Shane's team climbed to-ward the shark-fin rock that crowned the hill. They advanced in a line, then in short rushes across the last stretch of open ground. When they reached the shark-fin, they called up the team in overwatch. In the shadow of the rock, Shane took cover and studied the valley through a spotting scope.

He spied a colony of sandcastles, guarded by a flying buttress. The houses were equipped with outer walls, slit windows, and parapets. Around the village, he saw the People going about their trades. Down low, farmers hunched in their terraces. Higher up, shepherds swatted their goats, and higher still, woodsmen swung their axes. And somewhere out of sight, where the clouds met the ridges, perhaps the Egyptian camped in the crags.

The sun climbed to its zenith. Shane shifted on his belly to find relief from the hot rocks. Sand fleas were having his shins for lunch. There was chatter on the enemy radios. Most signals were from the south. Nothing indicated the Egyptian. Shane glassed a village, looking for a man with a limp, thinking, *I'm looking for a hobbled man among people forever at war. That doesn't exactly narrow it down.*

In a splatter of hollies beside Shane, Sergeants Burch and Vasquez traded off behind a spotting scope. Sergeant Vasquez was the platoon sergeant. He was big as a tank, and the only one with more combat time than Burch. The two vets seemed to shine for each other. They played cards in absolute silence, sometimes for hours. They hid rocks in the lieutenant's ruck and salted his canteens. And once in a while, they got teary-eyed watching Disney's *The Lion King*. Shane had thought on that for a long time. He hadn't figured it out.

Shane could barely hear the two sergeants whispering.

Vasquez asked, "How's the squad?"

Burch said, "Hard as woodpecker lips."

Vasquez asked, "How about whats-his-nuts, uh, the cherry?"

Burch said, "Shane's coming along. It's a little weird."

"Why?"

Grimly, Burch answered, "He reminds me of my little bro."

"The one that drowned?"

Burch said, "Yeah. Shane looks like him, walks the same—you know, up on his toes. The day I lost my bro, he had on this Bart Simpson shirt. Wore it so much the pits were yellow." Burch stopped and laughed before turning serious again. "No joke, the day Shane reported to us, he was wearing the same shirt. I thought he was fucking with me. But how could he know?"

Vasquez said, "If this is messin' with your judgment, I'll move Shane to another squad."

Very quickly, Burch said, "No, no. I want him."

For a while the two were quiet, wiggling on their stomachs against the rocks with the valley below gray and hot and sharp.

Vasquez asked, "This place look the same?"

Burch said, "I think the mountains got bigger."

Vasquez said, "You probably got friends in that village."

Burch said, "*Friend's* a strong word."

Vasquez said, "I wouldn't put it past you to have sired a few kids last time. For all we know, they're maneuvering on us now, all full of hate 'cause they never knew Papa."

"I was here for a time. But tell you what, coming back don't feel right."

"How's that?"

"I've invaded two countries," said Burch. "We won by my account. I got more stripes and moved up the heap. Now here I am, back in the same place with my rifle." Burch caressed the tiger stripes on his M4. "Don't get me wrong, gunfights give me a hard-on, but everything I've done, well, it just brought me right back here. Hell, it's almost like I'm supposed to be here. Then I get to thinking…maybe I'm not supposed to…" He trailed off.

Vasquez said, "I'm gonna make this easy for you: Take care of the boys, and slay every bad guy you can along the way, Egyptian or not. You do that and you'll be right by me. And for God's sake, don't get weird on me. I ain't got time for it."

Burch said, "Affirm. I just couldn't say what side of the wire is the wrong one. Not for sure."

Vasquez gave Burch a sidelong glance. "And about that hamster wheel: I'm on it right beside you. I've been running longer than most anyone. But who's keeping score?"

Burch said, "Affirm."

At that moment, Burch seemed to notice someone listening in. He cocked his head and glared at Shane. "Hey asshole. Are you glassing your sector or eavesdropping?"

Shane rolled back onto his belly and buried his eye in his spotting scope.

———————

A few hours later they bagged their optics and made for camp with nothing to report. During the return march, Shane thought on how it had gone so far. Shane had expected to drop into the valley and start kicking ass. They would patrol aggressively and collect intel, first rolling up the Egyptian's crew, and soon enough, Shane would have his boot on the Egyptian's neck. It had not been that easy.

The days that followed were a blur. Shane volunteered for every patrol, anything but digging. Sunrises and 'sets came and went, colored scarlet, copper, and gold. Shane devoured each one. Time melted into something primitive. No more calendar. No Presidents' Day or Columbus Day or Prostate Cancer Awareness Month or Taco Tuesday or whatever the fuck. Light and dark mattered. So did the lunar cycle. That was about it.

It was getting dark when Shane took his rifle to the prow for guard duty. He stayed low in the hole, scanning for the flash of another rocket. He'd duck this time, right when he saw the flash. No sitting there gawking like a newbie. In the distance a group of natives had gathered in the arcade of a white mosque. More than once, they pointed to the new American camp.

The uplands turned blue in the dying light. Village cooking fires soon glowed against the slopes. Sitting there, Shane could almost feel the beating heart of the enemy. The closest American unit was forty miles away. And although winter had gone, snow still mantled the passes and washouts choked the roads. Any help would be a light-year by ground. Other units had been this deep on short ops, but no one tried to *live* this far back.

The crux was supplies. They could scrounge food from villages and water from streams to survive short periods, but bullets and batteries were different. A manhunt without bullets and batteries was a lopsided game of hide-and-seek. Bullets and batteries couldn't be grown in fields and wouldn't fall from the sky in the next storm. Their success, and survival, hinged on a supply run from a CH-47 Chinook, the Army's workhorse helicopter.

The following day, Shane's squad drew work detail for the first run. A proper helicopter landing zone was the order. Shane chopped hollies and spread rocks to keep down the dust. Eight others did the same. Then they lounged on a basalt plug and eyed the northern sky. All was still for a time, just a few holly leaves skipping through camp on a light wind and the boys speaking of women they'd never get to bed. Then the radio antennae on the command bunker got to swaying. The wind grew restless, shifting this way and that.

A cloud bank marched in from the north, spilled into side valleys, and rolled the ridges. Off in the distance the high peaks were black islands in a sea of mercury. First came rain, then trembling thunder. Lightning forked a dozen ways and jousted between clouds. Golf-ball-sized hailstones bounced off Shane's helmet. Two hours dripped by. The chopper pilots stayed on the ground in Asadabad. They wanted no part of the storm. They promised "tomorrow." That night, Shane put his feet into his sleeping bag with a pang of hunger in his stomach.

Clear skies followed. Chinooks came in two-day intervals, dropping all manner of crates, pallets, and connexes. Shane counted each arriving chopper. Six had come, each like the one before, nice and easy from the head of the valley.

Shane pulled guard duty for run number seven, watching for the bird as day protested night with a last blaze of red in the west. He rested his elbows on the foxhole brim. Burch was next to him. They were little more than shadows, tucked in the hollies near the river, just inside the Holiday perimeter. A low thumping sound came from the north. Burch turned his radio to the air freq. They listened. The bird had just crossed the valley mouth and was now flying nap of the earth through the river cut, never silhouetting itself against space. The chopper's reverberations grew bolder. The bird was now a half mile out, still tucked into the bottomlands.

All at once, enemy machine guns barked from a knob on the river's far side. Tracers streamed through the dark. Supersonic rounds raced down the chopper's axis of travel. It was enfilading fire. Then the enemy volley fired RPGs. The knob itself protected the enemy from the guns of Holiday. Even Shane recognized the enemy positioning was perfect.

The chopper nosed up from the bottomlands and lumbered away, bleeding smoke.

Burch told Shane, "Two-oh-three on my mark," and lasered the tip of the knob. "Right behind there."

Shane tubed a frag grenade in his rifle-mounted launcher. He planted the buttstock in his shoulder and squeezed one off. The frag arced over the knob. Shane heard the explosion but couldn't see the impact.

"Again," said Burch.

Shane tubed another frag and out it went. *Crump.*

"No, like this," said Burch. He ripped the gun from Shane's hands. Making a crease with his hip and elbow, Burch nestled the buttstock into it. He pinched the windage on the front sight post, fired off three frags, and turned to Shane. "Elbow in the hip, not out to the side. Act like you've done this before."

23

"Roger, Sar'nt."

The sound of chopping blades had just faded when Burch looked at his watch and said, "Shit."

Burch leapt from the foxhole and ran toward the command bunker. *He's quick to move on*, thought Shane. A few minutes later, Burch returned with a satellite phone in hand. He lowered himself into the hole and pressed the volume button all the way up.

Burch said, "I can't hear too good these days. Don't mind me."

Remembering Burch's previous insult, Shane said, "I'm no eavesdropper."

Burch pressed a couple dozen digits. The screen's green light illuminated his smiling face. Burch turned to Shane. "Gotta check in with the old lady. Forgot about the time difference."

Shane turned away and pretended not to listen.

She answered, "Nick."

Burch said, "Hey, gurl."

She said, "I knew you'd call. I felt that phone about to ring. Ain't that crazy?"

Burch said, "I don't miss birthdays, now do I? What you doin'?"

"Mom's coming over."

"I got you a little something. It's in the garage. Open the footlocker. You'll see the wrapping."

"What is it?"

"Now what's the point in telling? Go see."

After a long silence, she said, "It's beautiful, Nick. I'm putting it on."

Burch said, "You tell everyone I found it for you myself. It ain't store-bought."

"I will." She drew a slow breath. "It feels good to be back home. Hanging around the base isn't much fun without you."

"Nothing to do there except gossip, and that never helped anyone. How's the boy?"

"He's good. Mrs. Priestley is getting on him. Says he isn't up to par or whatever. He's a grade level behind on reading. "

"She's an old bag. Told me the same when I was his age. Don't let her get you riled."

"Mark Fuller's been by. He's recruiting for the Broncos."

"That sumbitch is recruiting for Pop Warner football?"

"Says he'll start the boy at tailback and corner."

"Let the boy decide." Burch tugged his black scarf. Silence followed. Then he said, "How you doing, gurl?"

"Just fine."

"Really."

"Hanging in there, I suppose. Vasquez's wife called a couple times. She's so steady you wouldn't think she had a heart."

"She's probably happy he's gone. Mean old bastard."

"You'd think this would get easier after a few go-rounds."

"Don't you worry. This'll be the last."

"I've heard that before."

"I mean what I say."

"Are you safe?"

"Yeah. We got an easy mission."

"That's not what I heard."

"Some got it rough, but I'm mostly in the wire these days. I'm getting caught up on sleep and everything. Now don't you lose none. I'll talk to you soon. Happy birthday."

Burch set down the phone.

Shane leaned over to Burch. "What did you get her, Sar'nt?"

"Nosy, ain't you?"

2

Camp Holiday
Day 30

Word around Camp Holiday was the chopper pilots landed that evening and refused any further runs into the People's Valley. The brigade commander acquiesced. Two days on, headquarters pulled the plug on the helicopter runs to the People's Valley. Instead, the Air Force would fill the supply gap with a more elaborate scheme. They would deliver supplies into the People's Valley by parachute using a C-130 cargo plane, the airborne semitruck. For now, the manhunt was on hold. The focus was on the supply line. Some said the Egyptian was dictating the fight.

The first airdrop was in-flight the following week. Shane couldn't wait. Burch called it the must-see event of the season. Jumpmaster had taught Burch a thing or two about airdrop physics, and he imparted that knowledge to Shane. The cargo plane pilots had to factor wind directions and speeds, bundle weight, aircraft speed, and drop zone size, as well as air resistance created by the parachutes. The pilots would have a sound plan if aiming for a calm open area, but they were dropping supplies into a narrow valley with complex winds. The target was Camp Holiday, a flat spot smaller than a football field. A jumble of rocky slopes girdled the camp perimeter.

Raising his hand against the sun, Shane looked to the horizon. The Newts were gathered at his left and right, all staring into electric blue sky of spring in the Kush. The aircraft's hum grew and grew. The Newts squinted to find the plane, tight shoulders and clenched fists to the man. In the distance, Storm King Peak thrust up, its pointy summit looking to stab the sun.

Burch stood to Shane's left, twirling his black scarf and whistling "(Sittin' on) the Dock of the Bay." The buttstock of his M4 rested in the crook of his arm, the barrel toward the sky. Burch wore full battle rattle. The weight was spread across front and back just right so the pull forward offset the pull backward, and the burden was only on his legs. Shane copied the configuration with his own fighting gear.

The cargo plane streaked over the valley with turboprops thrumming. Car-sized bundles poured out the back of the bird. The parachutes deployed. Supplies floated in a mile-long line. Each bundle weighed hundreds of pounds. The parachutes strained under their weight.

After a minute in the air, the bundles smashed into sun-bleached hillsides and ravines. The contents exploded and rolled down slopes in yard sale fashion. Two bundles landed inside the tiny American perimeter. Both contained water. The odds were impossible.

Shane declared, "That pilot hit the G-Spot."

The squad boys cheered.

The Newts had plenty of work. Ten more bundles were hidden outside the camp. Patrols stepped off in three directions to recover what they could. Shane's squad hiked south for an hour, worming up and down the wrinkled bottomlands, scrambling, sometimes losing each other, then bunching up again. In the distance, Shane saw the farthest bundle splattered in the rocks near the river. They threaded hollies and crossed into reeds on the riverbank and fanned into a wedge. Shane was walking flank, barrel at the ready, when he heard slithering in the grass.

A king cobra sprang into strike position, flashing its hood. The cobra had the girth of a man's forearm. The tail rested somewhere unseen in the chest-high grass. Vertical pupils radiated fire and precision. It flicked a forked tongue at the invaders. Shane took a bead.

Burch yelled, "No. No. No." He plowed through the reeds and leapt in front of Shane, three feet from the cobra. The viper waved back and forth, displaying two black rings on its hood. Burch stood frozen in a wetland, his boots ankle deep in mud. Burch's hands fell from his piece and dangled at his hips. He soon moved in rhythm with the snake. As Burch swayed, his feet sunk into the morass. Rising bubbles left no doubt.

Shane wrestled his own feet from the mud and plodded to a little rise above the reeds. He pointed to the hillside. "Sar'nt, the bundle's over there."

Keeping eyes on the snake, Burch didn't respond. Burch's desert boots were now subsurface. The muck wet his shins. The snake kept flicking its tongue.

Shane said, "Sar'nt Burch, you're sinking."

Burch paid no mind.

Shane yelled, "The bundle."

Burch remained hypnotized.

Shane whispered to the others, "We're starving and 3-3 is playin' with Jake the Snake."

———————

Two hours later, the squad returned to Camp Holiday with everything they could carry. Burch hobbled in with one boot and a mud-caked sock.

From there on out, the Air Force stuck with the airdrops. Shane had a spring in his step on drop days, and not because his platoon was desperate for supplies. His attention was on the pilot who hit the G-Spot. The pilot was female, and armed with a sexy voice. It didn't take long for Shane to dub her "G-Spot" because of her aim. All the Newts took to calling her that.

The fourth time G-Spot flew over the valley, the squad boys huddled around the radio to hear the erotic voice. Standing in the center, Burch held up the hand mike for everyone. Shane pushed his way closer. The others shoved each other for real estate. No one touched Burch.

G-Spot reported in the cool, detached manner of all pilots, "My ramp's down."

Shane gaped and bit his knuckle.

G-Spot said, "I'm coming in hot."

Shane yelled, "Goddamn right you are."

The squad boys swooned and blew kisses at G-Spot flying high above. They ripped off their sweat-stained shirts and flexed their biceps and pecs for her. One pleaded, "Take me with you." They hadn't seen a woman for weeks, and they wondered what G-Spot looked like.

Shane couldn't be sure, but he was certain she wore edible underwear beneath her flight suit.

He told the squad, "I'd crawl through broken glass to watch her pee into a canteen cup."

Then they patrolled for bundles.

———

They returned in the evening. Shane wolfed down beef stroganoff and reported for guard duty. He ducked into a bunker and found Private Kopeki manning his 240B machine gun. Kopeki was an odd soldier with lifeless blue eyes, which were hidden behind Army-issued glasses with coke-bottle lenses so thick they could focus the sun and set a barn ablaze. The Newts called his glasses birth control goggles, because a guy would never get laid while wearing them.

The light died in the west. A ceiling of stars came on. Shane raised his thermal optic and studied a hill in the distance.

Kopeki whispered to Shane, "I have a proposition for you."

"Okay."

"I'd like to buy your soul."

Shane set down the thermal optic. "What's in it for me?"

"Twenty-five dollars, cash."

"What do I have to do?"

"Just sign this bill of sale." Kopeki reached into an ammo pouch and unfolded a piece of card stock, the classy kind used for wedding invitations and such.

Shane opened it and read:

I, {insert name}, hereby sell my soul to the great William Kopeki for all eternity and anything further. His power transcends all borders, continents, universes, and physical dimensions. I shall seek no restitution for any events that may transpire as a result of this sale. All sales are final.
Signed,

{insert name}

Shane asked, "All I have to do is sign, and you give me twenty-five bucks?"

"Yes."

"Has anyone else done this?"

"Yes. I now command the souls of fifteen men."

"Deal." Shane signed the bill of sale and Kopeki handed over the $25 immediately.

Kopeki held the paper like it was a precious scroll and dropped it in a plastic bag and pouched it in his vest. "Welcome to my army."

In the morning a call came over the camp radio, "Airdrop number five is on the way." By that time, everyone knew the drill. Shane shouldered an empty rucksack and topped off his canteens. The squad gathered around Burch, who cranked the volume on the radio. G-Spot approached at 150 mph. The boys whistled and waved and grabbed themselves.

Cack-cack-cack-cack. A hush swept over Camp Holiday. An antiaircraft gun had come to life deep in the valley. The sound was that of a Soviet Dushka. It was two ridges back, maybe three. The enemy positioned it where they could fire at the slow cargo plane but avoid counterattack from foot soldiers. They aimed to sever the American umbilical cord from somewhere unseen.

A glowing stream of tracers zipped past the plane. The opening volley was close, but G-Spot stayed on her approach. *Cack-cack-cack.* A second burst zipped by her right wing. *Cack-cack-cack.* Big bullets punched through the tailfin. A wisp of smoke trailed the plane. G-Spot dipped one wing, banked, and leveled once more.

Cack-cack-cack-cack-cack-cack. The enemy must have smelled blood. Their tracers stitched half the sky. G-Spot disappeared in the armada of clouds ringing Storm King. She didn't make the drop. And then she was gone.

Shane kicked the dirt up in disappointment. "I was hoping they'd shoot her down, so we could go save her."

On the next drop, G-Spot raised the altitude of her plane. Approaching from the north, she was little more than a humming dot in the vast sky. Out came the bundles one at a time. A green parachute popped above each one. The bundles swung beneath. All looked well, but the altitude of the drop widened the spread as the bundles drifted down.

When the supplies landed, Shane found himself on a treasure hunt through miles of rotten terrain. A three-hour hump brought his squad to a ravine. The descent was an undignified affair. Shane heel-plunged through scree, glissaded the steepest parts, and twice fell headfirst. The rocks slid away with each step and crashed into more rocks. Those rocks found friends and down they went together until the whole slope was one quivering mess. Shane landed at the bottom and sliced a cluster of pines and there was the bundle.

Afghan boys were crawling all over the supplies. The kids' faces were sticky from candy in the rations. One had a belt of 7.62 around his waist. Another boy wore the parachute as a cape. Shane paused, waiting for his squad leader's cue.

Burch told Shane, "The caped boy's the ringleader, I'm thinking. When I say *draw*, pull your pigsticker and make like you're gonna stab him."

Shane nodded agreement, though he was unsure what Burch's game was.

Burch stalked toward the boy with the cape, who was suddenly aware he'd been caught. The boy took off sprinting. He cleared a rise, but the parachute followed him for another thirty feet, like the long train of a princess' gown.

Burch stepped on the parachute and clotheslined the boy. The caped looter groaned and rose and ran again. This time Burch kicked the boy in the butt. His face burrowed the dirt. Burch curled his fingers around the boy's skinny neck and squeezed. The boy thrashed and coughed, eyes flooding with red.

Burch pointed at the supplies, "Mine," then ripped the batteries from the boy's arms and issued stiff smacks across the boy's head.

Burch switched to Pashto with the boy: "Where's the Egyptian?" The boy shook his head.

Burch squeezed the boy's neck harder. "Where?" Burch's fingernails pierced the skin, drawing drops of blood. Burch pointed at Shane and told the boy, "This one here's a maniac. Best talk or he'll get to cutting." He whispered over his shoulder, "Draw."

Shane drew his bayonet and stomped forward, doing his best to look menacing. He drew back the knife for a stab.

The boy's eyes widened with fear.

"Don't, don't," rasped the boy in Pashto. "The policemen know." The boy pointed north, toward the valley entrance. "Police."

Burch held the boy in a choke for a few more seconds, then let go. "Keep the chute."

The boy got up, rubbing his neck, and set off running again with the parachute fluttering behind him.

Shane asked, "Police?"

Burch said, "Worth a try."

3

Camp Holiday
Day 50

Camp Holiday was eight weeks old. Pinched supply lines put the Newts' manhunt in doubt. They still had not intercepted communication traffic from the Egyptian. Over the radio, the division commander gave the Newts a pep talk that turned into an ass chewing. "Pissing it away," he said, then, "Maybe we'll send in Marines."

Without signals intelligence, the Newts had to hunt the Egyptian the old-fashioned way, by developing human sources of information. Tonight all forty-three Newts would move north to the valley's V-shaped mouth. From there, they would make contact with the local police. The S2 shop believed some of the ragtag cops moonlighted as fighters for the Egyptian. The boy with the parachute had confirmed it. The officers called this corroboration. Now the Newts would feel out the local police for intelligence.

At midnight, Shane donned his night vision goggles. Green static cloaked the world. He slipped past the wire of Camp Holiday, five steps behind Burch. The rest of Newt platoon followed, three full squads, each with a machine gun team attached. The tritium in Shane's compass pointed north. A GPS jiggled in his cargo pocket, but the compass was never wanting for batteries, so the compass was his tool. That was what Burch insisted.

Shane kept five steps behind Burch. A half hour into the march, Burch halted and hissed over his shoulder at Shane, "Quit riding my ass. What are you—scared of the dark?"

The words came sharp, as if fixed to an arrow. With a hurt smile Shane said, "My bad, Sar'nt." Walking again, Shane decided Burch was the one who was scared of the dark.

The movement lasted six hours. The sun and moon were sharing the sky when they arrived. At the entrance, the renegade river that cut the People's Valley swirled into the Blue River. The water from ten thousand peaks massed at this confluence. A hill stood over the junction. Bearing three rocky spines cut by three gullies, it looked like an eagle talon. After gaining the top, the Newts pitched a hasty camp. They named it Camp Miami because they wanted to be on a Florida beach.

Shane settled into position on the hill's north flank. He was just offset from a road trace that corkscrewed to the hilltop. Kneeling there, Shane stacked rocks for cover, one by one, minding the tan scorpions in the crevices. By lunch he'd built a wall three feet high. It wrapped his flanks and had two notches so he could fire without silhouetting himself. Shane couldn't help his smile. He shopped for a final rock, found one the size of a football, and placed it on top. With hands on his hips, he admired his work. The stone wobbled and, without warning, his wall collapsed. Shane cussed the sky and flung the stone downhill.

Burch was on him at once. "What's this Mickey Mouse shit?"

"My wall collapsed, Sar'nt."

Burch dropped to a knee and picked up a rock and then another. Stacking them again, Burch said, "You need a bigger base."

They rebuilt the wall and then sat cross-legged, overlooking the terrain below. Tributaries braided the land. One artery, the Blue

River, united everything. The snowmelt surge had passed and the river ran well below the banks. The wet, organic scent off the water was new to Shane. A shoal of cobblestones hugged a bend. Over the shoal, a bridge with red trusses was pocked by bullet holes. Water swirled in eddies behind the bridge's concrete pylons.

Burch pointed across the river, saying, "Back in '02, we had a position in that house there. About dark, this Afghan boy comes up and starts cooking me french fries. The boy was sitting in the courtyard when we got hit from two sides. I'm talking RPGs, heavy machine guns, all kinds of shit. The boy didn't blink, just kept right on making them fries. He would be about your age now."

Burch stroked his black scarf for a time, taking in the terrain. "Not much has changed since then. The land looks the same, maybe a couple new war wounds is all." Burch pointed once more, this time to a village far downstream. "See that village? The night after we got hit, we raided the compound on the west end."

Shane saw a compound with mud walls twenty feet high. Its corrugated metal gate gleamed in the sun. Passages and canals fanned out from it in a winding network.

Shane asked, "Were you after the Egyptian?"

"Yeah. Intel made it seem like he was in every house." Burch flashed a murderous smile. "No moon that night. I was in a rock pile outside the house. Had my 240 pointed down a corridor. Around a bend, I heard a door creak open. Someone called out to me. It wasn't English, wasn't Pashto, either. The voice was soft. It had a secret to share, a secret as old as time. A secret lost on the world. I got up and took a few steps, and then thought better of it. It beckoned me, but I didn't want to know what the voice knew."

"Sar'nt, you okay?"

Burch laughed and slapped his knee. "I'm messing with you. But we need to keep clear of that village."

———

Shane woke the next day after three hours of shut-eye. He thumbed the crust from his eyes and rolled up his sleeping mat. It fit nicely on his ruck but offered no comfort against the rocks. Snapping open his e-tool, he leveled his sleeping spot, determined to quit sliding downhill while dozing. After finishing, he watched two squads gathered round Vasquez and Lieutenant Dillon, who they called the "LT." The LT was the only officer in the platoon, and as such, he gave the mission briefing: He was leading a patrol to find the police chief. They'd be gone for two days, maybe three. Shane's squad would remain in Camp Miami.

Minutes later, the LT's patrol lined up and set out. Shane examined the route as the patrol corkscrewed down the trace and crossed the bridge and disappeared behind a hummock.

Burch was now the ranking man at Miami. He moseyed by, swinging his arms, and parked himself next to Shane. Side by side, they watched geese in chevron flight through the valley. Just east, the river wrapped a little peninsula. Floodwater on the land shined right back at the sun. On the tip of the peninsula, a boy with a bulging stomach threw his fishing net into the river and pulled it in hand over hand.

About midmorning, two Afghan policemen approached the camp. They wore gray wool uniforms and black eyeliner. They held hands. *Funny thing*, thought Shane, *the Newts have gone looking for the chief and here come two of his men.* Maybe they had something to say that they didn't want their chief to hear. Or perhaps they were looking for a spot to do some necking. Shane covered for Burch, who met the cops in the shade of a lonely cedar. There was much butt sniffing. Shane kept his rifle on the bigger cop. Money changed hands. The cops jogged down the hill.

Burch dusted off a rock where he then sat waiting with a cigarette. Thirty minutes later, the two cops reappeared on a motorcycle, racing up the corkscrew path. As they bounced over stones, the one on the back hugged the driver tight. Shane figured these people weren't so tough. The driver soon kicked the stand

and handed the motorcycle over to Burch. The cops trotted away on foot.

Burch grabbed the handlebars and examined the bike, then waved at Shane to join him.

Shane obliged.

"I need you locked and loaded for a classified mission."

"Whatever you need, Sar'nt."

"There's a bazaar upstream, about one valley west. The coppers said the Egyptian stops in once in a while. We can use this bike to look around."

"Just the two of us, Sar'nt? Sounds risky."

"Affirm. I've been to this bazaar, back in '02. If nothing else, they got all kinds of animals for sale, and we need a mascot. Every great fighting unit has a mascot. It's good luck." Burch kicked the tires on the bike. "We had a beagle my first time in the Stan. He was batshit crazy. His favorite thing to do was crap on our woobies, but he saved our skin one night when he heard the Taliban sneaking up a creek."

"Roger, Sar'nt. Why don't we hump it to the bazaar, bring all the boys with us?"

"Take a half a day on foot. Everyone will see us coming." Burch pointed to the police motorcycle. "We'll be there lickety-split on this Afghan chopper."

"Ain't this area crawling with bad guys, Sar'nt? What if we get in a pinch?"

Burch flashed a nicotine-drenched smile. "Audacity, Private, audacity. We haul ass on the bike at first light. We're in and out of the bazaar before the enemy knows the score. Maybe we'll come back with the Egyptian thrown over the seat."

"But—"

Burch stuck his chin in Shane's face. "Here I am, offering you commando status, and you're fussin' like an old prostitute. Take it or leave it. It's all the same to me."

Shane thought on that and decided he didn't want to be an old prostitute. He said, "I'm in, Sar'nt."

———————

Light came bit by bit in the morning. Shane switched off his night vision and high-fived his replacement on the north machine gun. An engine cranked on the far side of camp. Burch was straddling the little motorcycle with chrome trim and a dent in the gas tank. The bike was a toy under Burch's long legs.

Burch waved at Shane. "Grab your piece and mount up."

Shane slung his gun and cinched his snake headband tight over his brow. He threw a leg over the cracked seat behind his squad leader. The cycle's frame creaked under their weight and almost touched the tires. Burch pulled his black scarf up to his eyes, saying, "Hells Angels ain't got shit on us."

The clutch popped and they tore off, full throttle, the high-pitched whine of the engine reverberating off the slopes. Shane held on to the seat, supposing it better to fall off than hug another man. They sped down the trace. First they passed the boy with the fishing net, who again worked from the riverbank. They rounded a bend. Burch leaned into a turn, his knee skimming the gravel. The olive trees lining the road zipped past. Gravity pulled at Shane's stomach. The wind desiccated his eyes. He blinked at the speedometer: The red needle was maxed out.

One gallon later, they arrived. The Afghan bazaar was a shanty-town of matchbox huts, split by a dirt path. The place was busier than a beehive. Hundreds of natives milled about, wearing vests and flowing garb, every last one with a blanket over a shoulder. Some were shouting and pushing carts, some hawking goods from stalls and truck beds.

Shane tailed Burch into the throng of people. It didn't take long for Shane to stray. He saw red rugs with dazzling prisms. Next to the rugs, bobcats, falcons, and camels were on sale.

"You buy camel, falcon is free," said the handler.

Shane stood on his toes and craned his neck. Down the path, a shopkeeper sat on his heels, cleaning his teeth with a miswak.

Another shopkeeper shuffled rupees. Just behind them was Burch, a ways off, but still in shouting distance. Shane went back to shopping. A few huts down, he strode past Afghans cooking food in black cauldrons, unleashing a riot of aromas.

Shane wandered into a rookery of huts. Scrappy kids rallied and followed him. They had muddy feet and jutting collarbones. One kid was shirtless, and Shane could count his ribs. Others danced and whooped like Injuns. As the kids frisked about, Shane handed them candy. More kids gathered round Shane. They yipped and laughed and groped Shane's equipment in wonder. A smiling kid extended one innocent, little finger and touched Shane's rifle. Another did the same.

Shane jerked his gun away. Things were going too far. He looked up.

A crowd of men had boxed him in. They sneered and moved in closer. Dozens of dirty hands reached out. The men chanted in angry Pashto and shouted at each other, and at him. They smelled of woodsmoke and sweat. A Makarov pistol appeared in the crowd. The mob shifted. The pistol disappeared. Shane's adrenaline spiked. He figured this was what it felt like before a man's heart exploded. He pulled his rifle into his shoulder. The mob reeled and surged forward once more. He saw the man with the Makarov again, holding the gun casually at his side. The man didn't look like the others. There was something foreign in his light complexion. Shane thumbed his selector to semi, yelling, "Burch. Burch. Help," while the mob swirled around him.

A revving engine and peeling tires answered his call. Burch tore into the mob on the motorcycle with a little gray monkey on his shoulder. Using one hand, Burch aimed his M4 into the mob, looking like he would enjoy gunning them all down. Just then, Shane realized his own mistake. *One had to look sure of himself.* Burch grabbed Shane by the bulletproof vest and threw him across the seat.

Burch said, "I think we've worn out our welcome."

Burch popped a wheelie that nearly dumped Shane off the back of the bike. The monkey screeched, holding tight with furry hands. Shane almost wet himself. They hit Mach 1 again. Shane looked back at the mob shrinking in the distance. The man with the pistol was gone. Shane asked himself if he had just seen the Egyptian. If he told Burch, the crazy bastard just might turn back. Shane convinced himself, *He couldn't have been.*

As they traversed up a hill, Burch yelled over his shoulder, "Let this be a lesson to you. You stick with me and you'll survive. If you do your own thing, these people will fucking eat you."

Shane said, "Roger, Sar'nt. I'm sorry."

Burch said, "No sweat. Oh, and don't tell Vasquez about this."

"Roger, Sar'nt."

They rounded a river bend and saw Miami. The monkey hugged Shane tight. The primate's big black eyes asked, *Will you be my friend?*

Shane had a new buddy. He named the monkey George. The exotic little creature fascinated him. Back in Mississippi, Shane had taught dogs to bird-hunt. Now he used his dog-training skills on the platoon mascot. By week's end, the monkey could throw smoke grenades and fetch supplies. Shane fed the monkey and took him on patrol. The damned thing had tactical discipline. Shane gave the monkey a bayonet and taught it to stab and slash. The monkey fancied himself a real ass kicker with that blade. He pulled guard duty on the Miami perimeter and flashed his steel at everyone who walked up.

4

The days were long at Miami, the nights little more than a blink. Past, present, and future ran together under the greedy sun. During snatches of sleep, Shane dreamed, his mind spooling out scenes from before the tour, mostly of his girl-friend, Candy. The most vivid dream was of them in Savannah. Shane was sitting beside Candy on a bench in the square, under some oak trees. The lightbulbs strung between the branches were swaying with the Spanish moss in the Atlantic wind. Candy leaned in close, put her hands on Shane's face, and said he was brave, as brave as anyone had ever been, and she knew he would take care of her. *Always*, he said.

It was first light when Shane woke from his nap in the dirt. Shane tied his boots. He'd napped with them on so he could be ready, but his socks never dried that way. Maybe this "always keep your boots on" thing was one of Burch's jokes.

Shane fished into the pocket on his sleeve and pulled out the photo of Candy and him on the bench in Savannah. He held the photo in his dirty hands for a long time. Burch glided by, and upon seeing Shane lost in the picture, stopped and grinned.

"Who's that?" asked Burch.

Shane answered with pride, "My girl Candy."

"She's purty. Hometown girl?"

"Negative, Sar'nt."

"Where'd you meet?"

"Treasures."

"The Columbus strip club?"

"Roger, Sar'nt."

"Fuck, dude. You got the stripper disease."

"She's different, Sar'nt."

"How's that?"

"Her dad was in the Army."

"Right," said Burch. "Answer this: When you got orders to the unit, did she ask to leave Benning with you?"

Shane was slow to answer. "Roger."

"And now where is she?"

"I got her an apartment off post."

After a long whistle, Burch said, "Them Benning girls are ticks, Shane. They'll hitch a ride, suck you dry, then bounce. Please, please don't tell me you're getting married."

"When I get back."

"If she's still around," shot Burch. "In the meantime, check your bank account." And Burch glided on, shaking his head as he scouted the line.

Shane deposited the photo back in his sleeve pocket.

After stand-to, the squad boys took turns shaving and scarfing chow. Using parachute cord as a leash, Shane tied George to a tree beside his hooch. He settled in behind his rock wall and laid his rifle beside him. He took a razor to his face for a dry shave. Off to the left, he heard two soldiers in a loud exchange. One was Kopeki, the soul-buying private. At the moment, he was purchasing the soul of Private Raker. Shane heard mutters of laughter from other positions as Kopeki closed the deal with Raker. Kopeki's soulless army was now twenty strong.

The sun crested a stairstep ridge, lighting the river a blinding white and bathing the hills in gold. In the terraces above the river floodplain, an old man in the gray uniform of the police climbed toward Miami. The river breeze pinned the man's gray garb against his thin body. The old man cleared the last terrace and skittered through a patch of mist, finally coming upon Shane at the perimeter. Shane clutched his gun and called for the Afghan interpreter, Billy, who came running.

The old policeman had his gray wool hat pulled down low. His eyes were fearful when he said, "I bring news of the Egyptian."

Shane held out his palm. "Stop. I've gotta get the LT."

The old man looked over his shoulder, down to the villages fringing the river. "I'll be seen if I linger."

Shane said, "You're police. You should not be scared to patrol your home."

The old man said, "It's my own I fear. I've come with word. You seek the Egyptian. Yes?"

"Yes."

"You listen for him on the walkie-talkie?"

Of course, thought Shane, but there was no sense in telling the world. "Some do."

"You will not hear him. Listen for his captain, Aziz. Some nights Aziz sleeps in Balay." The man looked around again, casting nervous glances at the villages.

Shane lowered his helmet brim against the sun's glare. He began to pitch another question when the old man's face twisted up. It looked like he would cry out, but there were no words. As the old man fell to the ground, Shane heard the shot.

A second shot rang out from the eye of the sun. Left of Shane, there was the crack of lead hitting rock. Private Raker shrieked in pain, then tumbled down a granite slab, clutching his leg and screaming. Shane looked down at the old man, finding him frozen with death. Remembering himself, he ran for his wall and dove behind it. *Crack.* The sniper's third shot exploded a rock midway up the wall. The entire position teetered from the impact, but it held.

More shots zipped in. Shane felt light-headed. White fuzz clouded his vision. Shane was holding his breath. *Keep breathing,* he told himself. Another bullet snapped over his helmet. There was a puff of dust as another round skipped through the rocks. *Keep breathing.*

Shane's eyes darted around camp in search of his squad leader. He found Burch prairie-dogging from a rock pile. The sniper kept cracking off rounds. Burch raised his tiger-striped rifle and squinted into the scope. The sniper took another shot.

Burch yelled, "Trees on the ridge. Due south. Five hundred yards."

Newt machine guns drowned out Raker's screams. Bullets kicked up earth on the ridge; 7.62 rounds chopped a holly to pieces. Raker kept screaming. Off to the right, the platoon mascot was screeching and turning backflips and whipping, about to break the leash. Shane yelled to him, "Stay low, little buddy."

The platoon called for mortars. *Crump, crump, crump*—the shells hit the ridge. The sniper vanished. Shane never fired a shot.

"One WIA. Litter urgent. Send dustoff to Miami," was the call over the horn.

Shane helped stabilize Raker, holding the IV bag over his wounded buddy. "Be cool," he told Raker. "Be cool." He didn't know what else might help. Raker's wound was through and through, but femur fragments protruded from the exit hole. Beneath Raker, the rocks were shiny with blood.

It took forty minutes for the helicopter to arrive. The bird had a red cross on the side door, as if the enemy gave a shit. Shane grabbed a handle on the stretcher and charged through the dust. Raker moaned "Oh God" when they lifted him into the bird. Shane's hand touched the cabin's vibrating floor. He had the urge to jump in. He didn't. Another litter team picked up the dead old man and shoved him aboard. The chopper throttled and flew away.

The sound of the river came again. A dozen Newts formed an angry mob, standing on the hill in the golden light with Raker's blood on the rocks at their feet.

Shane stood in the center. "Raker sells his soul and then gets capped."

Austin, a big corporal in second squad, piped up, "This is bad juju."

His sidekick, Bloome, said, "Bad juju."

Others joined in: "No more games." "Deal's off."

The mob worked themselves into a frenzy. Shane said, "Let's get him," and they stormed through camp to find Kopeki.

Across the hilltop they found Kopeki at his hooch—a green poncho strung up in an A-frame between two dead hollies. The mob circled with hands on their guns. Kopeki reached into his hooch, coming up with a Nike shoebox under his arm. It was his vessel for purchased souls.

Shane stepped forward. "Kopeki, the deal's off. Give us back our souls."

Kopeki put his hands on his hips. "Sorry, I have a strict no-return policy."

"We'll give back the money."

"It's only paper to me. My army is almost complete. I will not dismantle it because of your superstitions."

"Cut the shit, dude, this is serious."

"Didn't you read the contract?"

Shane said, "We'll do this the hard way."

Kopeki set off running with the soul-filled shoebox under his arm. A dozen men gave chase. Kopeki sprinted through stunted trees and poncho hooches, yelling over his shoulder, "Get hold of yourselves!" The squad boys replied with angry promises. They split into two groups and sent three men for the right flank. Kopeki weaved through rocks the size of refrigerators, and by and by, the flanking element tackled him at the camp entrance. The boys let loose with their fists. Kopeki clung to the shoebox, curling his body around it while he rolled in the dirt. It didn't take long for the mob to pry the box from Kopeki's hands. Shane kicked him in the ribs for good measure. Then the mob formed a half circle and rifled through the box, each man taking his bill of sale as Kopeki sat up in the dirt with a bloody nose and his left cheek swelling.

Glaring at them, Kopeki said, "It doesn't matter, you idiots."

Once Shane found his own bill of sale, he sought out Burch to report the old policeman's dying words.

5

Baz village, People's Valley

Long ago, the Hindu Kush gave birth to warring tribes. Their villages dotted the slopes along the rivers. The people grew out of the rocks. As the centuries drifted by, they rooted into fractures and seams in the brittle schist.

The People were the most xenophobic tribe in the Kush valleys. Grand peaks nestled their homeland and crowned the watersheds for the mighty rivers. The tribes living along the mighty rivers were called the Lowlanders. The tribes inhabiting the most remote regions were known as the Pagans. Some said they still practiced the old ways, including witchcraft and sorcery.

Habibullah was a teenager of the People. Other tribal members knew him by the tear-shaped birthmark on his cheek. His upbringing was typical of tribal boys. At birth, his father, Zmarak, held him in the air while the boy still dripped womb fluids. A village elder fired an assault rifle next to Habibullah's head while another whispered in his ear, *"Allah akbar"*—God is great.

Mountains with clean lines and perfect symmetry looked down

on the boy. The peaks were from beyond time. They formed a great wall that blocked out competing beliefs and ideas. Habibullah's first steps were in the vertical terrain. The boy soon roamed the mountains barefoot.

He developed endurance herding goats and running messages for the elders through the holly-spangled hillsides. He carried his green blanket everywhere. It was a satchel, prayer mat, pillow, and shelter. Mountain life gave Habibullah mahogany skin that the summer heat could not burn. He was fleet-footed among the rocks, with strong thighs and remarkable lungs. He needed little water and food. The boy seemed to thrive on sunlight alone.

Zmarak told Habibullah, "This makes you different from the Lowlanders and those in the festering cities. They've destroyed the world to keep their soft bodies. They pin nature underfoot with iron and concrete and plastic."

Fog cloaked the hills the morning Habibullah's father brought his AK-47 to the meadow. Habibullah had grown as tall as his father's thigh, and that was old enough for a shooting lesson. Swatting the goats away, Zmarak strode through grass silky with dew and set targets under the old spruce at the meadow's edge.

Zmarak said, "Your grandfather used this tree when he taught me."

Habibullah lifted the rifle. He held stamped steel, wood trim, and a banana clip. He saw genius engineering, though he could not tongue the words. Habibullah sensed his father's eyes as he pulled the trigger for the first time. *A billy goat's kick. Ringing ears. Not so bad.* He held down the trigger. Wild bullets raced into the clouds while the bleating goats ran every which way. As the boy got taller, he craved the stiff punch of the rifle into his skinny shoulder. His aim was true, but his father taught him it was more important to show no fear.

Zmarak said, "My boy, you can lie prone and shoot men all day, but glory goes to the man who stands up straight in front of his enemy."

Habibullah never heard music. His tribe had war chants, and

during his shooting lessons, Zmarak sat knees up in the grass, eyes upon the Winter Spires, singing the People's battle hymn:

O son, one word I have for thee,
Fear no one and no one you flee,
Draw your sword and slay any man,
That lays poisoned eyes on our land.

When Habibullah had seen eight winters, Zmarak sold goats to fund his schooling at the Blue River Madrassa—a house for learning the Prophet Muhammad's teachings. Habibullah arrived in Safar and was there through the snows. The trees had just leafed out when a storm swept in and frosted the madrassa. Icicles reached down from the eves outside the classroom window. With steaming breath, Habibullah fingered tattered pages in his Koran and recited his verses. Habibullah was mouthing the sura named "The Cave" when Tariq, his eight-fingered cousin, arrived at the madrassa. Tariq had come from Habibullah's village.

Tariq had a message. "The mountains are our brothers, but they are fickle, so your father says. The Storm King sent snows that killed the early crop. Your father needs you back." The next day, Habibullah trekked back to his village. He took sure-footed steps with his hands clasped behind his back. Such was the hiking posture of the People.

Oral tradition filled the vacuum in Habibullah's life that spring. His father's stories were of fighting prowess. Zmarak had fought the Russians. Before the Russians, his people battled the British. Before that, the tribe raided the traders' caravans along the great rivers. And throughout the centuries, the tribes fought each other. His father's favorite stories were of feuds against fellow tribes. Habibullah's blood enemies were the Omari clan. Their feud began after the great fire. The spark was adultery.

Habibullah was gathering wood for this tenth winter when fighter jets rumbled over his valley with tails longer than any falling star. The noise was tremendous. His father told him Ameriki had invaded. One full moon passed before Habibullah saw the strange beings on foot. He thought them mad for dismounting their metal falcons. Habibullah was ready to fight. Zmarak gave him a lesson on the power of foreign invaders.

"The Ameriki are a temporary nuisance. Behold their fat bellies and addictions. Their men even have breasts. They're as delicate as the red flowers in the meadow. No staying power, you see? Come and go they will like snow on the Winter Spires. But this I know, the Ameriki will tip the balance between the tribes. We must watch for this and this alone. We will not take up jihad against the Ameriki, not at first. Let the invaders wear down the others. In the meantime, sell them soda and cigarettes."

As Habibullah grew the wisps of a beard, he spent much of his time shepherding in the high meadow. While the goats grazed, he collected firewood, placing sticks in his spruce-root backpack. Most nights, he returned home to the village of Baz, an enclave of mud huts freckled by tamarisk.

Around Baz, Habibullah and his father made their marks on the land. They cut steps in the mountains and made terraced fields. They laid stone stairs for sure footing on the village trail. They raised a swinging bridge to cross the People's River. Habibullah's family also harnessed planetary energy. Their mud house was built half underground, for the earth's temperature was constant just a few feet down. A singing stream ran below their village. They twice diverted its flow. Stone runnels fed gravity irrigation, which soaked their wheat fields. Sluice and waterwheel powered their millstone.

During his twelfth spring, Habibullah became terribly ill. Fever and chills shackled him to a cot for two moons. Vomit came after every meal. His mother caressed his tear-shaped birthmark and said the sickness came from fog over the high meadow. Habibullah's symptoms broke with the onset of summer, but he was always tired afterward.

Most days, a single piece of flatbread was his only sustenance. He ate one half on his way to pasture. That was the good half, fresh and hot. He ate the other in the afternoon when the bread was stiff and cold. Goat meat filled his belly twice a week. Sometimes he ate beans and corn. Just after Habibullah's thirteenth Ramadan, a mudslide destroyed his family's food store. Habibullah trapped lizards and rodents to survive a hard winter. His diet prevented him from growing big, in the Western sense. The boy was wiry, his features sharp, like all the People.

Inside Habibullah's home, three warped planks divided the goat barn from the family's sleeping quarters. His father said, "It's wise to keep the goats close, especially if the mountain lions are hungry when the leaves return." The goats had fleas, and so did Habibullah. He once scratched his crotch raw, and drops of blood fell upon his sandaled feet as he led goats to meadow. Habibullah kept his head shaved to ward off lice. His mother said lice came from the dirty Lowlanders.

In that twelfth year, summer came over the land and the meadow grasses stretched for the sky. Habibullah and his older brother, Mehtar, led goats to high pasture on the first day of Jumada al-Ula. A man from Balay village passed through the meadow. Mehtar called to the man, "Brother, our pasture is good. Join us."

The shepherds spoke of Islam, and what it meant to be a pious man. It was a casual debate at first, but Mehtar had a sharp mind, which earned him the favor of father and pedestal of chosen son. Mehtar's wit put the man from Balay in a corner. They began shouting. The man from Balay ripped the prayer beads from Mehtar's hand. The twine snapped. Beads rained onto the grass. The scuffle instantly turned into a fistfight. They flattened the grass where they rolled, strangling each other. The man from Balay was blue-faced when Habibullah broke them up.

AND THE WHOLE MOUNTAIN BURNED

The man from Balay said to his brother, "You've damned the Prophet. You'll pay for your sacrilege."

The next day, the man from Balay entered Baz with a black eye and a gang of mujahedeen. Their Taliban flag fluttered in the wind. They planted it in Habibullah's courtyard and leveled rifles on the family. They demanded Mehtar give himself up for his transgressions, but he'd already fled into the hills. After a day of searching and waiting, the fighters shot Habibullah's goats and vowed to behead Mehtar if he ever returned.

Just after dark, Mehtar slipped into the house and collected his scant belongings and rolled them into a blanket. He was tossing the contents of a drawer when Habibullah grabbed his hand. Habibullah had tears in his eyes.

Mehtar took him by the shoulders and said, "I'm sorry for bringing on the Taliban, and for giving our family a bad name among the People. I will escape their reach in Pakistan. I'll leave word with the stone dealer in Malakand. Ask after me there."

Habibullah begged Mehtar to stay. They could sit before the council of ruling elders, Habibullah reminded him. The elders would hear both sides and render justice.

Mehtar relented, but a few hours later he stole away. Habibullah watched his brother hurry toward the Blue River, with moonlight on his shoulders, bowed head, and belongings draped over a crooked stick.

After that day, Zmarak ordered Habibullah to stay away from the mujahedeen. Habibullah's world collapsed at once. In their stone courtyard, he argued with his father.

"What honor will I find as a shepherd? Glory goes to the guerrilla."

Twisting the end of his black beard, Zmarak said, "The Taliban stole our cause. They are beholden to an Egyptian. There is no longer honor in the fight."

Habibullah said, "I will bring honor back to it. I will fight as you showed me, without fear. I will clear Mehtar's name."

"Mehtar chose to flee," Zmarak said, "and so brings dishonor upon our house. Now his name is forever stained. The Taliban will not find him. He is too clever. I worry they will sacrifice you in Mehtar's place. You must stay away from them."

"You damn me to a life of sticks and stones."

"Yes, for now."

Habibullah obeyed his father's wish. And every day, he kept a close eye on the swinging bridge, awaiting his brother's return.

———

Habibullah would never forget the day Tabana, his mother, flicked her tongue at his father. The People did not tolerate defiant women. Zmarak choked her and dragged her into the courtyard. The repeated whip of a holly branch pierced the air. Tabana twisted and rolled, but never cried out. Habibullah saw a woman as strong as the stone she was lying upon.

Tabana worked the fields all through the light, planting and harvesting wheat. Her toil gave her a sun-wrinkled face. And when she stooped in the wheat, she chewed Naswar—a moist snuff—which stained her teeth black. Tabana was Muslim, but when her men fell sick, she still practiced the old ways. She mixed holly berries and a red flower to cure Habibullah's fog disease.

Marriage was the order during Habibullah's sixteenth feast of Eid Al-Fitr. Muska would be his wife. His father had arranged the union. It would strengthen their ties to the Gorbat clan. Habibullah gave no protest, for he'd seen Muska filling tin vases at the river one day. All the women were clucking back and forth along the bank, thinking themselves alone. Muska had her veil down, and she fluttered among the rocks with sparkling blue eyes. She was more beautiful to him than a hearth fire in a winter storm.

Habibullah's father viewed her another way. On the eve of the wedding, Zmarak said, "Women are meant for breeding. Your fellow boys are meant for pleasure."

After the wedding, a jealous boy said Muska's blue eyes came from a Russian soldier that had raped her mother. Habibullah knocked the boy out with a stone.

———

A year later, his wife bore him a son. The council of elders came for the birth ceremony, dressed in their finest white. Habibullah held his son in the air. One elder fired a Kalashnikov next to the baby's head while another whispered in the baby's ear, "*Allah akbar.*"

The elders were all mujahedeen, meaning they'd fought against foreign invaders, a deed required for a council seat. The head elder was called the Khan. He was a devout Taliban and he wore all black, whatever the occasion. Some whispered that he seized his position by slitting his rival's throat with a dull blade in the night.

After the birth ceremony, the Khan and his retinue of white-clad followers sat with Habibullah and his father for chai.

The Khan was draped in matte black. He stroked his long beard, saying, "O' Zmarak, killer of tanks, rally your clan and join the jihad against the Ameriki. They are afoot and easy game. And better yet, your old corporals are now captains. Loombara himself leads the southern militia."

Habibullah's father spoke for the clan. "Be patient with the Ameriki. If we bring chai and smiles, they will grow bored and leave. If we fight, they will bring more soldiers. So it was—your very words when the snows melted."

The Khan raised his bushy eyebrows and said, "At the time of our council, we did not know their intention. We thought the American camp was part of a spring offensive. Months have passed. Every day, they dig deeper. This is no offensive. Behold the scouts of a hungry empire. The Ameriki want to colonize the People's land, steal our mountains, give our children blue eyes. The Lowlanders will see us as weak. We must come together and fight. The Egyptian promises more bullets and rockets than we could ever fire."

With ridicule, Habibullah's father said, "The mighty Egyptian," and turned his face from the Khan. For a time, the two sat in hard silence. Then Habibullah's father said, "I must consult the clan."

The Khan said, "As you like."

Habibullah knew his father would never say what he really believed. He would never forgive the Taliban for banishing Mehtar, the chosen son.

6

Camp Holiday
Day 67

After two weeks at Miami, the Newts returned to Camp Holiday. Their best intelligence on the Egyptian was from the old policeman. He'd died bringing it, so Shane guessed it was worth following. The officers with clean uniforms felt the same. Now the Newts were staged at Holiday, ready to act on their lead. When they heard radio traffic from the Egyptian's captain, Aziz, they'd launch on Balay village. The intent was to roll up the network around the Egyptian, thus closing on their ultimate prey.

That morning the sky overhead was a blue dome endless in depth. Shane stood on Camp Holiday's perimeter, ready to leave the wire for a shooting drill. As he waited for Burch, Shane studied the valley through his scope. On the east side a foot trail gashed across a hill, running from the river to the high villages. A group of six Afghan men were descending the trail, one in all black, the others in white. They looked real done up, like they'd just come from a ceremony.

"Moving out," said Burch.

Shane racked a bullet into the chamber and passed through the Holiday perimeter. George the monkey ran ahead of the squad, frisking and leaping from rock to rock. They hiked a quarter mile to a crashed MiG fighter plane from the Soviet war. When they arrived, Sergeant Burch strolled up to the tailfin and spray-painted it with red dots. Shane hitched George to a tree with parachute cord and was soon blasting away at the dots. Burch paced the line and coached breathing and smooth trigger squeeze. Shane practiced firing from a knee. He was never supposed to fire while standing.

Burch had told him, "If you're standing up in a mountain gunfight, you ain't hitting shit."

Shane went prone and made the sun shine through the red dots. Burch stood over him.

"Not bad, Shane. Not bad at all." Burch examined the shot groups through his four-power ACOG and frowned at the results. "You're still a cherry bitch."

"Thanks, Sar'nt." Shane spat tobacco and wiped his mouth with the back of his hand. "Before long, this cherry bitch might tune up his squad leader."

The others heard the challenge. They responded with *oohs*.

Burch stroked his black scarf. "Tell you what. Let's have us a shootout. Me and you. Loser owes the winner a carton of cigarettes. And I'm not talking about Pines from Pakistan. No Lung Dogs. I'm talking American cigs."

"Roger, Sar'nt." Shane was cool on the outside, but squirming on the inside. Burch was the reigning champion of their company's annual shooting competition; he'd held the title four years in a row.

Burch said, "I'll even go first. Here's the deal—stress shoot. You do twenty-five burpees and then shoot four targets with two rounds each. All shooting is from the knee. You have one minute to complete the round."

The onlookers whispered bets. Shane dropped his assault pack next to George by the tree and thumped his magazine in his palm to seat the rounds.

Shane asked George, "What do you think?"

George smiled with his sharp little teeth and big black eyes.

Shane said, "This one's for you," and strode for the firing line.

Burch went first. He cranked out burpees and dropped to a knee. His tiger-striped M4 was melded to his arms. The buttstock was nestled perfectly in the crease of Burch's shoulder. His nose touched the charging handle as always. Burch could have been on the front cover of *Guns and Ammo*. Bullets drummed the aircraft alloy in rhythm—seven for eight, the last shot hitting two inches wide.

Shane knocked out his burpees in thirty seconds flat, cocked his helmet back, and settled onto a knee. He pulled his rifle into his shoulder. His sight picture swayed as he fought for his wind. Burch's eyes dug into his back. *Don't anticipate the shot*, Shane told himself.

Ping ping. He paused and let his aim settle. He was sitting on one foot and it throbbed something terrible from the burpees. *Ping ping*. Four more rounds dotted the tail and he stood.

Looking through his scope, Burch puffed his cheeks as he pushed out a breath. "Eight for eight, you little fuck." Burch slapped Shane on the butt. "You just took the championship from your own squad leader. That's flirting with insubordination. Great shooting. Now push."

Shane fired off seventy pushups without resting.

Laughing, Burch returned to the squad.

Shane got up at one hundred and glanced over at the platoon mascot. George had chewed himself free from the hitch. He was rummaging through Shane's assault pack. Before Shane could intervene, the monkey pulled out his night vision goggles, a vital piece of equipment the enemy did not have. The monkey scurried up a tree with his toy, taunting Shane to give chase. Shane called for help. The squad boys responded. They split into three teams and pursued, diving and flinging stones, but came up short as the monkey leapt from tree to rock and back to tree again. Then the monkey climbed for a high branch.

Shane said "Enough" and shimmied up the tree. His buddy had gone turncoat. Shit was going to get real. Shane balanced onto the branch. George ran for the end and spun round holding the goggles in the air.

Burch demanded, "Get down, Shane."

Shane dropped to the ground and crept away. Burch casually took aim with his M4 and blasted the monkey over and over, but the thieving creature wouldn't die. The monkey just squealed as bullets ripped through him. Burch emptied the rest of his mag. With the last shot, the monkey fell from the tree in a hail of branches and leaves. Then the monkey lay there, looking desperate and betrayed, waiting for Burch to end it.

Burch flashed a savage grin. At point-blank, he fired six more shots in perfect rhythm. Monkey blood splashed across Burch's uniform. With the back of his hand, Burch wiped a streak of blood from his face. He examined the red on his hand, smelled it. For a moment it looked as if he'd taste it. He didn't. At his feet, the dead monkey kept a firm grip on the goggles.

Burch turned to Shane, "That's a lot of blood from a little body."

With misty eyes, Shane said, "You didn't have to do him like that."

Burch said, "Sumbitch was an enemy spy."

Shane choked down a sob.

Burch said, "I'm thinking we need a new mascot."

Flies and crows followed the squad as they returned to Holiday in the afternoon. Shane took a position in Observation Post 2, a squat little box half underground, with a grenade launcher. Soon Burch joined Shane in the bunker. They swatted flies. One kept flying into

Shane's ear, right down the canal. The sound was that of a fighter plane.

Burch said, "Turn on the secret squirrel device."

Shane set a walkie-talkie in the bunker's firing slit and tuned to the enemy frequency. Using a black cable, Shane connected the walkie-talkie to the direction-finding device. Then Shane and Burch fixed scopes on Balay.

In the shimmering distance, the village was a cluster of tan huts that seemed to be a biological extension of the hills. The village was three miles south of Holiday, and reported to be crawling with mujahedeen, or "muj," as the Newts often referred to the enemy. Shane liked "muj," because it had a slanderous sound to it, like "gook."

From Balay village came the warbling call for prayer. Amplified by a mosque loudspeaker, the call carried through the valley, rousing the faithful.

Shane said to Burch, "They don't miss a beat when it comes to prayin'."

"No they don't."

"What's the word for their religion? Wabby, something or other."

Burch wiped his brow with his black scarf. "It's a severe form of Islam, never mind the word. It calls for absolute awe at their god, repression of bodily urges, and a ban on all vices; vice being defined as most daily American behavior. No dancing, no drinking, no music, no fun. They enforce law in medieval fashion. For instance, 'round here, if a wife cheats on her husband, they'll ruin her fun parts."

Shane said, "Jesus, this place is a drag. I wish we could fight in a place where the natives weren't so uptight. We should start a war in Brazil."

Burch said, "I hear you. The People are a bunch of party poopers. Their religion denies their urges, you know, their animal instincts. But those urges need release. The outlet for all their repressed energy is fighting. That's how they get their rocks off. In a way, their religion amplifies their warrior culture. It works like rap music for gangbangers. It's kind of beautiful."

———————

About 1530, a man named Aziz came over the radio.

Burch chuckled. "No shit. Old man was right." Burch turned to Shane. "It's the Egyptian's captain. What's his azimuth?"

Shane checked the screen on the direction finder and pointed due south to Balay.

Burch said, "Go suit up."

At 1600, Shane took his position at the front of the squad, right behind Burch, who turned and spoke to the squad. "Remember boys, we're trying to capture Aziz. Only kill if we have to. If Aziz knows something, it will be time-sensitive. Word will get out quick if we bag him."

They stepped off at 1605, followed by the entire platoon, all marching south to cordon and search Balay.

A thunderhead capped the peaks in the distance. Ten thousand feet below, the Newts advanced through a creek channel in the valley floor, where water laid bare a hundred million years of strata. Stately pines canopied the creek. Shane marched through shadows while the upper slopes basked in the late sun.

Leading the patrol, Burch took calculated steps. He was grooming Shane to be the platoon's point man—a high honor to bestow on a private.

Shane kept a close eye on his mentor. The first thing Burch modeled was "eyes ahead," not down at the ground. That was a tall order, because good footing was scarce. Spring floods had littered the creek channel with slick rock and logjams. Rising sheer from the water, the river slopes offered few options in route. Burch moved nice and steady, insisting, "Slow is smooth and smooth is fast." That was the key to it.

They rounded a bend. Burch disappeared in branches. He held

still as a tombstone: watching, listening, and smelling. Thirty seconds like that convinced him it was safe to move on. Burch angled left where the shadows were thickest and threaded the trees. He rotated his head while on the move.

"The key to seeing things in faint light," he said, "is keeping one's head on a swivel." He called it squirrel eyes. He explained, "If an object catches your attention in low-light conditions, it's best to not stare at it. You can see much better detail looking at it indirectly."

Shane figured Burch was yanking his chain.

Pointing to his eye, Burch said, "I'm serious. It's like cones and rods and stuff like that."

Burch knelt, picked up rocks, and felt each one. Then he palmed the sole of his boot and whispered to Shane, "Feel the footing." The round stones were smooth, almost polished. Little bits of moss and lichen stained others dull green. Those were the slippery ones. The angular stones hadn't been in the creek for long. They still had a sandpaper finish, so they were sound footing.

Burch rose and drew calm, deep breaths. His chest expanded and fell under his armor. A long *creak* came from above. Burch cocked an ear to it. His mouth was half open so his breathing wouldn't interfere with his hearing. "Wind in the pines," he judged, going forward once more.

A mile onward, a downed tree blocked their path. The trunk was four feet wide with spear-sized splinters for branches. Shane ran to help his squad leader over the trunk. Burch shooed him away and probed for a route around the obstacle instead. It took only thirty seconds to find a passage where floodwater had ripped the root ball from the bank. Burch sidled through the gap. The platoon filed in behind him. That was Burch's third lesson to Shane—go around the obstacles, not through them.

Burch explained, "The machine gun teams will get wrecked if we go climbing around like kids on a jungle gym."

Burch modeled technique for another mile, then waved at Shane. "Take point." Shane's heart walloped against his breastplate.

He was going to lead the platoon through the creek channel. His jitters rattled his gun. Shane hooked his fingers into a can of tobacco and jammed a wad into his lip. *That'll take the edge off,* thought Shane. He rubbed his rattlesnake headband for luck.

Shane dashed ahead, eager to please his squad leader. He kept his head on a swivel. His breaths were measured. Walking straight was his problem. For the first quarter mile, he molested every brush pile in sight. The trees tightened and the trench grew deeper. Shane climbed the bank and meandered. An undercut shelf gave way. He dropped with it and crashed to his knees. He rose and pushed forward undaunted. A thorny branch grabbed hold of the camo netting in his helmet and insisted he wait a minute. Down he went again.

Burch trailed twenty feet back. He didn't interfere.

They came to a fork. Shane veered left over a gravel bar. A few dozen trunks, black with water and rot, bridged the creek. They lay like sutures holding together the banks. Shane climbed onto one and raced across. He got one foot on the far bank. Below him, a branch gave way. Shane fell headfirst. A rush of pain shot through his spine. It was momentarily horrendous, and he curled into a ball, knowing he might catch a fist for it. Burch strode up on long legs, grabbed Shane by the fighting vest and lifted him to his feet.

Burch asked, "You hurt?"

"Negative."

Burch said, "You're seeing nothing more than your next step. Slow down, and you'll see your next twenty." Burch moved his hand in a snaking motion. "You've got to flow with it." Then Burch tidied the camo netting on Shane's helmet.

The squad boys in back launched insults at Shane: "Cherry bitch." "Dumbass." "Gonna get us killed."

Burch twisted toward the column of kneeling men, and hissed, "Shut the fuck up." Then to Shane, "Move out."

Shane understood now. He whispered, "Flow," and set off again through the alluvium. He picked left, scooted right, scaled a root ball and balanced across another pine. A careful slalom brought him to another bough across the path. This one rose to head level. Shane turned to his squad leader.

Burch said, "Probe around. Only tanks and planes move in straight lines."

Shane skirted the trunk and found a passage where the roots had separated from the bank, just as Burch had done. Five more tree trunks blocked the way to Gorbat. With each one, Shane got better at slowing down and seeing the way.

Balay appeared as the red star dipped behind the west wall. The village matted a steep ridge. The huts were stout, with bombproof walls two feet thick and turquoise trim around the windows. A tangle of ladders, winding paths, and stone steps linked the huts. On the creek's far side was the village of Gorbat, perched on a near-vertical ridge, just a few hundred yards opposite Balay.

Shane picked a line of ascent over pine snags and windthrow. It took a hundred panted steps to get free of the creek. They closed on the village: 250 yards...200...150...

One shot caromed through the hills. A dozen enemy muzzle flashes appeared at the same time. RPGs boomed from a brow over the village. PKMs crackled in full-auto while large-caliber weapons went *clop clop clop* in semi.

Shane's first thought was that his fabled enemy had terrible aim. He hoofed it on wobbly legs and crashed behind a tree trunk and lifted his barrel. It quivered with his adrenaline. *Steady now.* Shane elbowed the downed trunk. Enemy tracers streamed from house windows. He picked a window and took a bead, waiting for the muzzle flash to reappear.

Burch slammed Shane's barrel into the trunk. "Pipe down, boy."

Shane was bewildered. "I have a shot."

Burch said, "They ain't shooting at you." He pointed across the creek to Gorbat. The muj were firing into the other village. Gunfire was pouring from both villages.

Come to think of it, Shane hadn't heard the *snap*s and *ping*s of accurate fire.

The shooting came into focus: two villages in a throwdown. Hunched behind the tree trunk, Shane kept his scope on Balay. One fighter attracted his attention. The muj ran to the wall of a house and climbed a ladder to its flat roof. He moseyed across the roof with tracers zinging every which way. The muj then fired a Soviet machine gun from the hip, standing straight up for the entire world to see. The muzzle flash showed his howling face as he sprayed a full belt of lead into Balay. He leapt off the roof and made a graceful landing on his feet behind the house.

Shane sat with his mouth open.

Burch had seen it, too. He whispered to Shane, "From the hip, dude. That was some Hollywood shit. The sumbitch even stuck the landing."

The fight continued in the moonlight. Kneeling behind the trunk, Shane switched to his thermal optic. In Balay he saw three figures slip from a house. They ran downslope and veered into the river cut, heading straight for the Newts. The men disappeared here and there between the rocks, trees, and rills, but came closer nonetheless. The three men were now fifty yards out. Shane steadied his gun. Next to him Burch leaned over the trunk, drew a breath through his nose, and took a bead. The men were on the bank, two moving in front, one behind. Each had a rifle. They were about to walk right into the Newts.

Burch whispered, "We take down the ones in front. You shoot left. I shoot right. No head shots, aim center mass."

Shane said, "What about the third?"

Burch said, "I'll handle it."

Burch touched his nose to his charging handle. Shane flipped his selector from burst to semiauto. The men were bounding between the rocks just ten yards away. Burch's laser steadied on one man's heart; Shane's laser not so much. Either way, Shane figured he had a margin for error at such close range. *Pow.* Burch fired. Shane fired at a split second later. When the two men fell, their guns clacked on the rocks. The man moving behind them froze for a moment. He raised his gun to fire and scanned, unsure of his target. *Pow.* Burch winged him with a shot in the arm and he fell in place. Together, Shane and Burch approached the man. They found him rolling in pain, his legs half in the creek. Burch kicked his gun away, flipped him on his stomach and broke out the flex-cuffs.

Burch said, "Got us a prisoner. Best be on our way."

Orange explosions mirrored off the creek as Shane followed it back to Holiday. He marched with a sizable tear in the crotch of his pants and the wind fanning his taint. It felt good. Behind him, Burch kept the cuffed prisoner on a leash made of Army green-line rope. At midnight Shane slipped past the concertina wire at Holiday, took control of the prisoner, and escorted him to the interrogation bunker. Then Shane went for his GP medium tent. Inside, the Newts were shedding their gear. The gun teams dropped their 240s on bipod legs and shucked ammo belts, producing a metallic jingle. The Newts were animated after eight hours of silence. They spoke of tits and asses. Over in the corner, Kopeki was offering to buy souls. He would pay $50 to any takers. There were no takers.

Shane ripped open the Velcro on his bulletproof vest. That damn thing was a torture device. He threw it down and ripped off his blouse and plucked his wet shirt to let loose the heat. Even his blouse was soaked, and it occurred to Shane that he'd made a terrible mistake. He reached into the pocket on the blouse sleeve and fingered the photo of Candy. It was damp. He pulled it out in horror. Sweat had ruined the photo. Candy was smiling at him, her face partly smeared, like a half-truth of that other life.

"Gotta put that in a baggie if you're gonna hump it," said Cassidy, who occupied the cot next to Shane. Cassidy carried the SAW in the squad, a belt-fed fully automatic weapon that he was now cleaning.

Shane said, "Too late."

"Can I see?"

Shane held out the photo. Cassidy set aside the barrel of his SAW and took the photo. As he studied it, Shane realized Cassidy's fingers were greasy with gun oil.

Shane said, "It's definitely ruined now."

Cassidy said, "Sorry, bro. There's a mail bird coming before dawn. You best write a letter and ask her for another picture."

"I will. Thanks."

Handing back the photo, Cassidy said, "I remember her."

"Yeah?"

Cassidy said, "From the platoon barbeque."

Shane said, "Right. She came to the send-off, too."

"The send-off…what a mess."

"I know, all them women bawling."

Shane dropped onto his own cot and cracked open his gun and squeezed oil onto the bolt. "And the kids. Glad I don't got kids."

Cassidy nodded.

"Funny thing about us leaving," said Shane, "it was the young wives that cried. Not the old wives."

Cassidy said, "It's like the sergeants told their wives not to cry. That's discipline."

"My girl Candy, she didn't cry. She kept it together. There's something to that."

"I guess."

———

The boys went down one at a time on their cots, wrapping themselves in poncho liners and sleeping bags as cold crept into the tent late at night in the mountains. Shane stayed awake, cleaning his gun by headlamp light. Near the tent entrance, he could see the beam of Burch's headlamp. Shane thought of something to say, then picked up his rifle, wire brush, and rag and made for Burch's cot, where he asked, "Mind if I sit, Sar'nt?"

Burch nodded to an ammo crate.

Shane sat and cleaned his gun for a few moments before asking, "Sar'nt, what do you suppose the muj were duking it out over?"

"Hard to say for sure," said Burch. "These tribes love a good gunfight. Sometimes it's just for sport. That much I've gathered. Other times, gunfights settle disputes."

Shane said, "Tracking. How about the muj on the roof? What the hell was he thinking?"

Burch Q-tipped his bolt for a time. He said, "That was something."

Shane guessed, "He showing off?"

Burch said, "Mostly. These muj distinguish themselves through the way they fight. It's all about the daring they display."

Shane said, "Like style points."

"That's right. Gunfights aren't about body count. And I suppose that's in our favor."

Shane thought on that as he pulled the spring from his buttstock, lathered it in oil, and jammed it back in the buttstock. He said, "We just need to get the drop on these fuckers one time. They'll calm down after that."

Burch replied, "You got this whole thing figured out then, don't you?"

"No...I'm just saying that—"

Burch cut in. "You're ready to take them head-on? I'm thinking not. Don't you see? You're just ore, something to be broken down so the valuable matter can be extracted. I'm here to process you. I'll strip away that which has no value. You'll thank me, you'll weep and thank me, you will. Just wait. And then you'll be ready for them. You'll be ready to go head-on, in close. Maybe you'll get to kill one with your hands."

By 0130, all the boys had stopped jawing. Most were snoring

69

in their sleeping bags. Shane and Burch were sitting on opposite ends of the same cot, their legs astride the canvas, throwing hands of cards between them. The LT breached the tent and rushed up to Burch. As an officer, the LT had the privilege of interrogating prisoners, and it appeared he'd been busy with this, for the LT had blood on his vest, lots of blood.

Eagerly, the LT announced, "Guess who our prisoner is?"

Burch said, "The captain."

"That's right, Aziz himself."

Pointing at the blood on the LT's vest, Burch said, "You get hit, sir?"

The LT looked down at himself. "No, it's from Aziz, that shot you gave him in the arm."

"I only winged him to sit him down."

"I know, but it keeps bleeding. He's in terrible pain."

"From an arm wound?"

The LT smirked. "He's in terrible pain."

Burch chuckled. "Oh."

The LT said, "Our man says the People are in a feud. The Egyptian is backing the east side. He's gone up to Ghar for an ammo re-up. Aziz just pointed out the house where he is. This is big. The whole division will hear about the Newts."

Burch said, "Ghar is one helluva climb. Best we go at night."

The LT said, "Negative. We've only got until tomorrow evening. Maybe not even that long if they realize we've captured Aziz."

Burch said, "Sounds hairy. Any chance we get first platoon in on this, too? They've done nothing but circle-jerk the last two days."

The LT fired back, "And let those shitbags get their names on it? Negative, Sergeant."

"LT, you chasing headlines?"

"I'm executing our mission."

"Right."

The LT said, "We move out at 0400." Checking his watch, the LT warned, "You two better hit the rack." Then he marched out.

Shane looked across the cot at Burch, who pushed out a long, frustrated breath.

Shane asked, "Sarn't, how'd you know not to kill Aziz? How'd you know to take him prisoner?"

Burch said, "The guys that move in front are cannon fodder. He was moving in back. I figured he might be important."

Shane said, "So I'm cannon fodder?"

Burch laughed.

7

East side of the People's Valley
Day 68

The afternoon sun wicked Shane's fluids, baked his helmet, and cooked his brain. The squad boys said it was so hot the sand fleas got tired and quit the battlefield. Newt platoon was climbing to Ghar, a village shrouded by tectonic folds, about six miles southeast of Holiday. Their orders: attack the safe house, labeled "building 5" on their tactical maps, and kill or capture the Egyptian. Shane reckoned no one took the "capture" part seriously.

They were ten hours into the climb, staggering one behind the other in a file that snaked a half mile. Shane carried a ruck that sagged with two quarts of water, two rations, a thermal optic, a C4 explosive charge for breaching doors, and an extra combat load of ammo. It felt like a bag of bricks. Sweaty socks enflamed the blisters on his feet. He paused here and there between the hollies, which cast small islands of shade. The Newts kept bunching up in those little bits of shade, finding refuge for their sunstruck minds, but making easy targets all the while.

Sergeant Vasquez's heavy steps scuffed the rocks. The platoon sergeant stomped by Shane, heading for two privates hunched together under a holly. Kicking one in the rib cage, Vasquez hissed, "Spread out, you little vaginas. And if anyone's thinking about quitting, go right ahead, we'll leave you here." Vasquez boiled war down to a single maxim. He said it now to the two privates cowering beneath him in the shade on the ridge below Ghar:

"If you want to dance with the cobra, you've got to have hate in your heart."

Shane wasn't too keen on what he meant, but it sounded cool and cruel.

Up and up they went, weaving around gendarmes and stone cathedrals. A flock of crows circled in the thermals over Shane. The Muj Air Force. The birds had learned to follow the Newts, looking for food scraps and trash to spear their beaks into. Shane guessed the birds didn't mind a dead body or two to go with the trash. The problem was that the crows gave away the locations of patrols. Even when the Newts were disguised in trees, the crows circled above, showing their exact position. Shane had a thermal optic and night vision to find the mujahedeen. The enemy matched his advanced weapons with dirty black birds.

Another hour on marching brought them into a granite amphitheater. A jagged rib lay ahead and to the right.

Burch held up a fist to signal *halt*. He pointed to the rib, then turned to Shane, "Come with me."

At a stoop, they went forward, Shane behind Burch. They crossed through gooseberry and hawthorn, found a deer run, and followed it. Shane heard the light rustle of branches and the blood as it coursed through his head. They crawled the last ten feet to the crest of the rib and peered over.

Ghar village sat in the middle of the amphitheater, bordered by two ravines. No obvious boundary separated the work of man and native rock. Shane figured the huts had grown from the mountain itself. Atop the village was the Egyptian's compound, a brown smudge on naked rock.

Shane glassed the compound, judging it a thousand yards off and as many feet above. The outer wall blocked the interior from view. All was still—no smoke or guards or animals near the building.

Burch was on his elbows, one eye pressed into his optic, when he said, "You can lead us in. Keep right, follow the creek, and shoot the gap, there, and we'll be at the rally point in thirty mikes."

Shane heard himself say, "Party time." Inside he was scared shitless.

"Shane," said Burch, "I'm gonna tell you something that you can't tell anyone else."

"I ain't no rat, Sar'nt."

"It's not like that. Listen." Burch took his time before saying, "You're my best soldier. You remind me of...well, never mind. You're high speed, bro."

The statement possessed Shane right down to his bone marrow. "I won't let you down, Sar'nt."

Burch looked to the sky and frowned at the crows circling overhead. They wore a purple sheen in the afternoon sun.

Burch said, "I need you sharp. I've got a feeling about this one. Your first big fight is coming. The first one counts. It's a major psychological event that smashes into the brain like a neural cannonball. Dendrites will grow from the cannonball over time, programming your outlook in the grandest sense. That's why the first big fight needs to be a win. A loss will create an intense negative experience, which will destroy your fighting spirit."

Shane had no idea what *dendrite* meant, but he reckoned Burch was right. "Roger, Sar'nt."

Together, they backed away from the crest of the rib. After reaching the platoon, they shouldered their packs. Shane consulted his compass and set out under Burch's watchful eye. Guided by an azimuth of eighty degrees, Shane crept along, aiming for the creek. He heard falling water before he saw the channel between the pines. Then he climbed alongside the creek, minding the undercut banks.

Five hundred feet brought him to a grotto where the creek poured over a shelf. A turquoise pool lapped under the waterfall. Sunlight danced across the water, lighting the recesses of the pool, showing it ten feet deep. A glittering fish circled. It occurred to Shane this would make one hell of a swimming hole. He stuck his empty canteen in the pool. The rim bubbled as water rushed in. An iodine tab was the finishing touch.

Green tracers suddenly peppered the water at Shane's feet. Hammering fire came from two positions in an L-shaped ambush.

Goddamn crows gave us away, thought Shane.

In front of him a broad trunk swallowed a string of bullets. Fighting down panic, Shane followed Burch. They splashed across the cold creek, flanked left through a slash of trees, and assaulted uphill. Crashing through the foliage, Shane heaved for breath. Branches gashed his face. Capillaries burst in his lungs. RPG contrails threaded the trees. Shane was in his first big fight, and that first one mattered. He hoped his dendrites were okay.

Pine needles rolled under Shane's boot. He slipped to a knee just in time for a bullet to rip the camo net off his Kevlar. Shane leapt to his feet and tailed Burch again without a second thought. They closed the distance in gunfight smoke. The muj broke contact all at once. Shane and Burch paused while the rest of the Newts caught up. Two more squads arrived, panting and shredded by the understory. The three machine gun teams, with their twenty-four-pound guns, tripods, and eight hundred rounds of ammunition, were last to catch up.

The LT came forward and said to Burch, "Forget the building. Keep on these guys."

Burch was the platoon tracker, so he slammed ahead, cutting the enemy ambush line before reporting, "Looks to be about fifteen of 'em." He zeroed in on shoes with concentric rings on the sole. He pointed down and told Shane, "This fucker here is wearing black high-tops, Muj Air Jordans. You can see he was moving back and forth on their ambush line, putting guys into position. He's got a funny gait. Either he's carrying a heavy load slung to one side or he's got a limp. I'm thinking it's a limp. Who you suppose has a limp and puts guys into position?"

"The Egyptian," answered Shane.

Burch said, "They'll split if we start gaining on 'em. Whatever happens, we follow the Muj Air Jordans. We keep his tracks between us and the sun. That's the best way to see 'em."

Shane nodded.

Burch blasted up the mountainside locked onto the tracks. A mile brought them to soft soil in a meadow. Burch pointed at toe divots and waved at Shane to take a look. He explained, "Shane, you can tell a lot by the depth of the toe divots. These ones are deep, and they've been that way since we started. These guys are jogging."

Shane crooked his arm around a tree for a rest. He wondered how anyone could run up the slope. He was about to collapse under his gear.

Burch probed in a cloverleaf pattern, then reported, "They're still together." He set off again, now aiming for a saddle on the valley's east ridge. They soon crossed paths with the same creek where the ambush had begun. This time it was little more than a trickle. Burch fingered the sign along the water and said, "No indecision in these tracks. No milling around or navigational errors. These muj are running straight and true. This is their backyard."

A bit further and they gained the sweeping east ridge. Conifers ran the spine. The enemy tracks hooked south toward cloud forest and, farther on, Storm King proper. Burch kept on them for a mile or so. The forest grew black. Logs and tangled undergrowth hid the ground. The tracks disappeared in duff and deadfall.

The enemy was gone.

The only life Shane found was a snaggle-toothed marmot sunning itself on the nose of a crashed Chinook helicopter. The furry critter was the size of a beaver and had only one front tooth—perhaps it lost the other while snacking on the bullet shells scattered in the trees. When the marmot saw the patrol, it swaggered to a boulder and reared up on its hind legs. Now standing in a lone shaft of sun, the marmot showed off a golden belly as it stared at them with eyes like a pond at night. Then the marmot whistled. It was a shrill, piercing sound. Once, twice, three times.

Shane guessed the marmot was announcing: *The muj have won the foot race.*

Burch threw a rock at the marmot. "It's the Egyptian."

Shane looked at Burch with his mouth open.

Burch said, "The muj can turn into animals. I'm gonna cuff this shape-shifter and bring him in for questioning. Or better yet, we feed him Cheetos." He was deadly serious. "You ever see a marmot on Cheetos?"

Shane sensed a trap and didn't answer.

Burch went on, "Shit, Cheetos turn them li'l critters into fiends. It's like giving whiskey to the Indians. High fructose corn syrup, yellow number five, and enough preservatives to mummify a body. Cheetos, that's how we're gonna beat these muj."

The marmot scurried to the helicopter and dove through broken glass at the nose.

Darkness was rearing fast up in the east. Burch relayed orders to the squad, "Chase is over. We'll set an ambush on this ridge tonight in case they come back. Everyone stays awake."

They did, but no one came. In the morning the Newts started down the mountain for Camp Holiday. Shane found himself beset by exhaustion, overcome and listless, as if inflicted with a ruinous disease.

8

B y sundown, Newt platoon had descended five thousand feet from the crashed helicopter, heading back toward Holiday. Shane stood on a buttress above the dashing torrent called the People's River, which slashed through the mountains, creating a trench in the bedrock. It was a major obstacle to all movement in the valley. They had to cross the river to make it back to Holiday. They found a foot log spanning the two craggy banks, twenty-five feet above the water.

As he waited to cross, Shane closed his eyes. There were star clusters and scribbles of images from the gunfight. The prickly heat on his back was in full blossom. Shane opened his eyes again. There was a figure in the brush—a deer, maybe. He blinked hard. The fog lifted. His focus slowly returned. It was only a rock in the brush. "You're in bad shape," he whispered.

Shane held his wind as the other squads braved the foot log under an indigo sky. In short order twelve men crossed, looking like specters in the mist of the hungry rapid below. Then it was

Sergeant Harris's turn. Harris was a team leader in first squad. A vet of two combat tours, Harris handled himself well, always insisting his boys be "quiet professionals." Now Harris tiptoed onto the log, biting his lower lip, his face pinched in concentration. He'd shuffled to the halfway point when the hills flickered with gunfire.

The snarling river drowned the noise of the ambush. Harris sidled for the far bank ever faster. He teetered. He circled his arms to right himself, careened sideways, and fell. As he plunged, he made no cry or scream. His eyes only wanted to know *Why me?* Then he splashed into a rapid.

Shane fired off three frags. He scanned the river, too. Harris never resurfaced. Ten minutes after the ambush started, it was quiet again.

Shane tried not to make a show of what happened. If the enemy knew Harris was missing, they'd start their own search, hoping to capture a live soldier so they could kill him on YouTube. Even if Harris was dead, the enemy might find his thermal optic, rifle, and night vision. This gave everyone urgency, but gloom hung over the search, for Harris was wrapped in fifty pounds of gear when he fell in the rapidly flowing river.

Burch relayed orders to the squad, "We search the east side until we find Harris or hit the mouth of the river. Second platoon is en route. They'll cover the west side."

Pulling his scarf up to his eyes, Burch told Shane, "Stay close. Do what I do." Shane nodded. Burch set off, walking point. They traversed a slope to gain the bend where the mad river slowed. It was the most likely spot to find Harris. The shortcut saved the Newts at least twenty minutes, giving them time to search before the dying light went out. But there was no sign of Harris, and within minutes, a black curtain rose in the east. Night was soon upon them, the moon already overhead. The water in front of Shane looked to be a ribbon of quicksilver among sharp rocks. They had to cross a side stream. Burch said they'd build a rope bridge.

Shane volunteered to make the swim and set the rope.

Burch told Shane, "Negative. I don't need one of my boys drowning."

Shane was disappointed. It was a heroic opportunity.

Burch pushed a coil of rope into Shane's hands. "You can be the nearside knot man."

Burch stripped down to boots and pants, slung his tiger-striped M4, and secured Army greenline around his waist with a square knot. He slipped into the water and stroked with the current. After clawing up the far bank, he anchored the rope to a pine. On the near side, Shane tightened the rope, wrapped a trunk, and tied an overhand with a quick release. The rope bridge was set. Shane clipped in and forded—straining under his gear, using his pull-up muscles to make way. It took a minute to cross. Shane's teeth chattered on the north bank. He danced in place for warmth and waited for the others. Five minutes and they were all across.

They set out.

At first, Newt platoon's movement was well choreographed. Shane and his squad trundled along the bank. They probed the eddies with branches and dragged their feet in the calm pools behind boulders. Another squad kept watch. The remaining Newts scouted the crags and rock chimneys that strangled the river.

The search dragged on and on. When the moon disappeared behind high peaks, the night went tar black. Shane stumbled and rolled and groped at trees for balance. His feet slid around in wet socks. His pants chafed his thighs. His back throbbed against his armor plates. Darkness, fatigue, and terra had teamed up to smash the platoon's locomotion.

Up ahead two men from second squad entered tall reeds beside the river. They were in there for a while, perhaps turned around or stuck or having found something. As Shane drew closer, one man, Corporal Austin, emerged on the far side of the reeds. The other man, Bloome, did not.

Then there was a sound in the reeds, a slow cry, "Austin."

It was Bloome.

"Austin."

Bloome's voice grew louder, the fear naked in it. "Austin."

Shane smashed into the reeds, elbowing through, careful with his feet in the sucking mud. Shane stopped and listened for Bloome, who was still calling for his corporal. Shane yelled to him, "Turn on your laser, shine it uphill." Bloome did and Shane had gone thigh deep into slow water when he saw Bloome pulling himself from mud and matted reeds. There in the dark was a man turned to a boy, lost in a river that ate soldiers. Shane pulled Bloome out by a strap on his vest.

Bloome said, "This whole thing is fucked," and set out again.

On they went, the platoon often stopping to regroup, to gather their own lost men. About midnight, Shane saw his squad mate, Private Cassidy, acting strange: Cassidy was clubbing a holly tree with his SAW. Then Cassidy pushed his fingers into the trunk of the holly. Cassidy seemed to be pushing buttons. Cassidy shifted on his feet and shook the stunted trunk. He banged on the bark, clubbed it once more with his SAW and reached down for a knot, saying, "Piece-of-shit machine."

Shane approached Cassidy and hissed through his teeth, "What's this Mickey Mouse shit?"

Cassidy said, "I'm buying a cappuccino. This one here, it's no good. Let's find another one."

Shane said, "Cappuccinos are for snobby old hags. And you sure as fuck ain't getting one from a tree. You're hallucinating, bud." Shane grumbled and relieved Cassidy of two drums of SAW ammo, hoping to lighten the burden on his squad mate.

───────────

Captain Tracy, the company commander at Holiday, came over the Newt radio freq at 0100 with new orders for the platoon:

"We have an aircraft on station. They've picked up suspicious activity north of your position. Stand by for a new mission." The aircraft had been diverted from a Special Forces raid along the Blue River. The plane was now scanning the People's River for signs of Harris.

The LT answered for the platoon, "Go ahead."

Captain Tracy said, "One kilometer north of you, there's a side valley. Follow it east five hundred meters to a village. The center house has twelve people in the courtyard. Two guards on the roof. They may have our man. That house is your target. Your platoon will cordon and search the village and find Harris. Turn the target house inside out. Expect a fight. We'll keep air support on station for your infil. You have control of the Holiday mortars."

The LT answered, "Affirm. I'll report once we reach assault positions."

Back of LT, Shane switched on his red headlamp and squinted at his topo. The village in question was named Baz. The contour lines on the map showed Baz was surrounded by steep terrain.

Burch ordered Shane, "Take point." He paused, lipped a twist of tobacco, and added, "Let's go fuck up their program."

Shane trotted to the front of the column. The aircraft circling the valley powered up an infrared beam to show the location of Baz. Shane took note of it. He struggled through the river trench with the platoon in tow and came to the mouth of a side valley, then asked for another IR shine from the aircraft.

This was it. They had to dogleg right, but a labyrinth of cliffs and terraces guarded the high ground beyond. The climb to Baz looked to be impossible. Shane forged ahead. Burch had taught him to see the little things, like a route through tough ground or something out of place in a village. Shane believed he'd be as sharp as a bayonet if he kept listening. *Slow is smooth and smooth is fast*, he repeated to himself. Shane waded into cornstalks and meandered for a time, more swimming than walking. An unseen ledge sent him rolling. He landed on a goat trail stitching the terraces.

The tread was ever so slight. He climbed the trail and signaled the others to follow.

Burch came from behind and slapped Shane on the butt. "High speed, Shane, high fucking speed."

Shane said, "Too easy, Sar'nt."

Shane led the Newts out of the rock junkyard, and they trudged along the trail, making better pace. The slopes eased and the sky came into view, jammed with winking stars. Shane twice stumbled looking at them. Three hundred yards from the village, he halted so the platoon could posture. A sketch in the dirt was all it took to make an assault scheme. One squad peeled off and made a flanking climb to the high ground over the houses. They would watch for anyone fleeing. Two Newt machine guns stood on rock outcrops to cover the infil. The assault squads moved in line straight for the houses, ready to kick doors and find Harris. After spotlighting the target house with infrared, the aircraft returned to its mission on the Blue River. The Newts would hit Baz with no eyes above.

Shane toed into the village. A donkey woke up, just above the hovels, braying out to someone or maybe to itself, *hee haw, hee haw, hee haw*. Shane wasn't sure if that honking donkey was carrying on as usual or waking up all the People. Either way it seemed an alarm, and it revved him up as he stepped into a corridor. He adjusted the focus on his night vision and steadied his mind for a flurry of action.

Shane led the squads through a stinking alleyway. He grabbed a twisted ladder where the path forked and climbed over the house wall, all the while conscious of Burch right behind him. Shane kept hearing Burch's words from before—"You're my best soldier."

This assault would cement his reputation with Burch. All he had to do was act on what Burch had said: *The key to clearing houses is violence of action. Go in fast and hard. Don't give the enemy time to get his courage up.*

Shane slid across the courtyard of the target house. He leaned against the wall near the door, hard-baked mud grating his shoulder. Shane examined the hinges through his night vision goggles, which needed ambient light to work best. The moon was now absent, so the goggles painted green fuzz over the world. As Shane eyed the breach, that damned donkey carried on. Shane was about to be the one-man, the most dangerous job for soldiers clearing buildings. His main concern was looking tough for Burch.

From the corner of his eye, Shane glimpsed a glowing orange figure sprinting across the roof. With the infrared floodlight on his M4, Shane scanned thatched timbers. Nothing there. Nerves and weariness, he told himself. The squad was behind him now. Shane craned for Burch, whose lank figure stood out in the dark. Burch was five feet back, black scarf over his face, looking like he was about to rob the place.

Burch gave the thumbs-up.

Shane rubbed his rattlesnake headband for luck before he pivoted and mule-kicked the door. He rushed into a dark room with his heart thumping against his armor. The others filed in behind him. Lasers swept for targets as the team pied the room in an oft-repeated drill. All clear, save the spider dancing across a corner web. Two small doors hung on other walls leading to more rooms. Hand signals from Burch. Shane's team stacked on one door while bravo team moved to the second. Shane took deep breaths to slow the hammer in his chest. *Stand up and fight me*, he thought. He kicked a plank door and canted through to avoid a gear snag. The second room was empty, too.

Without waiting for the others, Shane rampaged into a third door, enjoying the destruction. Wood cracked in half against his shoulder and four steps had him in the middle of the room. He was alone in the light of a single candle. Terror filled him at once. A horned demon was coiled in the corner behind a chair. The demon flashed from one spot to another. It ran straight at Shane.

Firing on burst, Shane went blind in yellow explosions of light. Moments later, he saw the demon crumpled at his feet; except now the demon took dying breaths like a man. The man did the kickin' chicken for a few moments and then he was still. *You're hallucinating*, Shane told himself.

Burch squeezed into the room. Burch saw the man at Shane's feet and pushed his suppressor into the man's eye socket and blew out the back of his skull. Blood splattered as if the man's head was a water balloon. Burch grabbed Shane by the shoulder and pointed him to another door.

Burch said, "You good?"

Shane licked his lips. "Extra good."

"Keep moving. Violence of action."

Shane stormed into the last room with blood pulsing in his temples. A lantern illuminated the face of a teenage boy with a tear-shaped birthmark on his cheek. The teenager shielded an infant and an old woman with black teeth. Their faces showed they expected to be shot.

Shane saw the old woman's eyes flicker bright orange, just for a second. The hairs on his neck stood up—glowing eyes. It was a witch, but Shane was wiped out, and couldn't be sure. *She's just an old woman with black teeth and a slate cloak, that's all*, Shane told himself. He was still scared of what he might see next.

Burch waved his rifle and yelled in the Afghan tongue, "Stand with your hands up." The teenager with the birthmark didn't budge. He doggedly shielded the infant and old woman. Burch leveled his barrel. The teen stood his ground.

Burch charged toward the teenager. Making a fist, Burch cocked for a left hook, but suddenly pulled off. For a few seconds, he was frozen. Then Burch patted the teenager on the shoulder, saying, "Jesus Christ…*Sadboy*. Long time no see." He pulled his scarf down. "It's me, Burch."

Shane didn't know what the hell Burch was talking about. He figured his squad leader was hallucinating, too.

The teenager's nostrils flared. He spit in Burch's face.

Shane swooped in, grabbed the teenager's neck, and pressed him against the wall. After searching the teen and his baby, Shane took them to the courtyard and returned to help Burch. When Shane reentered, he saw the last in the room was the old woman, crouching under her slate cloak. Burch pulled her up by the shoulder. The old woman struck out like a viper, snarling those black teeth. She bit Burch. A trickle of blood ran from his forearm. Burch could have shot her for that, but he avoided making any further mess. He buttstocked her teeth and booted her neck instead.

The old woman's quickness wasn't right to Shane—she was lion fast. And the crazy bitch had just chomped his squad leader's arm. With a boot on her neck, Burch pushed his barrel into the old woman's forehead. She submitted. The red mark of the barrel was still on her head when Burch led her outside and slung her down in the dirt. Her cloak fluttered over her and settled.

"Somebody muzzle that bitch," said Burch.

Shane and Burch left the women and children wailing in the courtyard. Dust particles floated in their headlamp beams as they navigated back inside the house. The dead man was right where they left him. Shane approached with his gun up. The dead man had one ghoulish eye open. The other eye was a black hole. Little, squishy bits of brain were scattered in an arc behind the body. A pool of blood was drying on the dirt floor. Shane searched the body and found nothing of consequence. Blood stained Shane's knees and boots when he stood up.

Burch glanced at the door. It was just the two of them when he said, "He came at you, right?"

Shane thought about what he'd seen. Everything was blurry. He couldn't be certain. The only thing Shane was sure of was that he wanted the respect of his squad leader.

Burch moved in closer. His chin almost touched Shane's helmet. "He came at you, right?"

Shane said, "I think so."

Burch raised his voice. "He was a threat. It doesn't matter what happened, that's between you and that guy. I'm not gonna have the

LT or Cap'n messing with you. This is my squad. I'm the alpha. He was coming at you."

Shane said, "He came at me."

Burch said, "Don't worry. You did the right thing. And even if you didn't, you're a good kid, I'm gonna look out for you."

The squads finished clearing the other houses. They brought two fighting-age men and a gaggle of women and children to the court-yard of the target house.

Shane was ordered to guard them. He studied the prisoners as they huddled under his rifle. Three little girls wore frayed green dresses. They might grow up to be pretty, but Shane couldn't be sure because the young women wore burkas. The old women, maybe their grandmas, sat next to the girls. The old women had wrinkled faces and faded gowns. Shane figured the old women got to wear gowns instead of burkas because they were so ugly. The old bags couldn't make a man frisky, no matter how sex starved he was.

Two men sat next to the women. The men looked annoyed. Shane reckoned they'd been through this drill before. Little boys squatted next to the men. The boys scratched themselves vigor-ously for fleas. They made no attempt to hide their fear and con-fusion. They had no idea why the Americans were picking a fight. *They'll figure it out before long*, thought Shane.

Shane paced the line of prisoners and stood over the teenager with the tear-shaped birthmark. At first, the teenager rocked back and forth with the infant boy in his arms and whispered sad things. When the teenager saw the blood on Shane's boots and knees, his face went cherry. The teenager was now glaring at the American before him.

As Shane stared right back, he kept hearing Burch's line: *Fuck up their program.*

———

The LT questioned the prisoners and soon came to the teenager. Billy, the platoon's Afghan interpreter, spoke for the officer. Billy had a cross eye, or a lazy eye, or maybe it was both. Shane wasn't sure.

With the one eye wandering as it wished, Billy questioned the teen. "Name."

The teen held up his chin with pride. "Habibullah."

"Is this your home?"

Habibullah said, "Yes. My father was killed in the house." Habibullah pointed to the old woman with black teeth, who was holding the infant. "My mother is also your prisoner. And that is my son."

"Who came to your village tonight?"

Without hesitation, Habibullah said, "Our friend from Gorbat brought news that you were searching for a soldier in the water. Some thought we should flee into the hills. I said we should stay in the village until dawn. If we run uphill in the night, you Ameriki will mistake us for fighters. So we stayed, and still, you came in the night with a sword."

The LT made no apologies. He said, "You can come to our camp for payment over your father."

After completing his interrogations, the LT called into HQ. "No sign of Harris."

The Newts prepared to leave Baz.

Shane kept watch on the villagers in the courtyard. In spite of his urge to look away, he stared at Habibullah and his infant son. Guilt twitched inside Shane. He wondered what he'd do if someone came to his Mississippi trailer in the night and shot down his own dad. Shane was sure he'd fight back and die on the spot. Habibullah didn't fight back, though. He just watched with fury as the platoon slid into the dark beyond the village.

Sunlight touched the river. The Newts resumed their search for Harris, scouring the banks once more. They reconnected with the main channel and made it a mile downstream when a boy appeared in the rocks. The boy was filthy, his cheeks dirt smeared. His eyes were dim. One look in those eyes and Shane knew the boy was half-witted. A dim kid, Shane decided. The dim kid ran up and pocketed his slingshot and tugged on Shane's pant leg, speaking more with grunts than words. The dim kid pointed ahead to a side channel in the river, then grabbed Shane's hand.

Shane followed. After a hundred yards, they came to Harris's body lodged against a rock. Harris's face was blue. His bloated corpse was on the verge of popping. Thermal, rifle, and night vision were still with him. The dim kid hadn't stolen a thing. Neither had the river. Shane took out his poncho liner blanket and knelt beside the dim kid.

Shane said, "You done real good, little buddy," as he handed the kid his poncho liner.

With both hands, the dim kid squeezed the poncho liner into his chest. He ran off, laughing half-witted laughs.

Shane and Burch dragged the body from the river. As they pushed the limp frame onto the bank, a vacant luster invaded Burch's eyes. Burch stutter-stepped, then teetered and fell backward with a splash. He made no effort to get to his feet. Shane lifted his squad leader by the arm.

Shane asked, "You all right, Sar'nt?"

Burch said, "Just a little dizzy."

They gained the top of the bank, wrapped Harris in a poncho, and traversed to a jeep road. The Newts took turns carrying the body on the slog back to Camp Holiday.

At 1700, Captain Tracy interviewed Shane in camp headquarters about the raid in Baz. Formal questioning was standard procedure when a soldier killed an unarmed civilian. Shane wasn't in a hurry to talk about it. The act was gnawing at him as if he'd swallowed a live crow. Troubled as he was, Shane stuck to the line Burch gave him: The man came forward and he felt threatened.

Burch vouched for Shane as well, but Burch was seized by illness on the walk back to camp, which forced him to speak from a cot. Three more interviews and the commander made his decision.

"Private Shane did the right thing. Clearing houses in the dark is a messy business."

Right after the verdict, Burch fell into sweaty delirium. The medics ushered Burch to the medical tent, where he screamed of fires and witches. For two days and nights, all could hear the commotion down in the medical tent. The medics examined Burch and ruled out dysentery and flu. They concluded it might be malaria. No one seemed to notice the old woman's bite mark on Burch's forearm.

Shane wanted to tell someone about the bite. He found Doc Juanito Soto, Newt platoon's Cuban-born medic, leaning against a holly tree and fidgeting with his cross. Doc Soto had watched over Burch during his delirium.

Shane figured it best not to start with the bite. He eased into conversation with Doc. "You think Burch will be all right?"

Crooked teeth flashed when Doc grinned. "Senior medic thinks Burch got malaria. I don't. Burch's symptoms were all over the place." The medic hooted and slapped his knee. "Last night, Burch was two seconds from having his head spin round in a full circle. He fuckin' spoke in tongues, but with the voice of a little girl. I knew it for sure—Burch got hit by the *Ojo*, you know, the evil eye. I was so scared I went and got Kopeki. I asked if he'd bought Burch's soul, but he hadn't. Anyways, Kopeki wanted in. Said we needed to perform an exorcism, and we did."

Doc put it like this: "I painted my face and called myself Santo Cholo," which meant Saint Hoodlum. "I put a cross made of two holly branches on Burch's chest. I popped purple smoke and waved it over him. It was beautiful, man, real trippy. Kopeki spun in circles like a whirling dervish. Dude worked himself into a frenzy, then hummed this badass chant and wet Burch with goat's blood. Kopeki spoke in tongues, too, but I'm pretty sure it was pig Latin. We held hands and I prayed: *Dios te salve, Maria. Llena eres de gracia: El Señor es contigo. Bendita tú eres entre todas las mujeres...*" Doc looked at the sky while he finished reciting the prayer. He drew a long breath. "Burch fell into a deep sleep. I think we fixed him."

That was how Doc Soto recalled the exorcism of Sergeant Burch. Doc said his only regret was he didn't film any of it, because he was sure it would go viral. That was Doc Soto. Shane had him pegged as full of shit since he joined the platoon. Now Doc was laying it on thick.

Next morning, when Burch rejoined his squad in the tent, he looked fresh and happy.

Shane ran up to him and asked, "You good, Sar'nt?"

Burch said, "Yep. Good ole Army medicine—pop some ibuprofen, take a knee, and drink water. Problem solved." Then Burch whistled to call the squad together. "Third turds, form up. We got a mission."

The other squads gathered, too, and soon the Newts had organized into four squad columns, sitting on cots and ammo crates, spitting tobacco on the plywood floor of the tent. The LT stood before them and folded his hands behind him. He wore a ball cap ornamented with an American flag.

The LT said, "We got close to the Egyptian in Ghar, real close." He held up two fingers about a millimeter apart, as if to show how close. "No one's done that for a long time. And I know it cost us Harris, a heavy price. The best thing we can do is stay aggressive. There will be no licking our wounds in camp."

He spread a topographic map on the ground in front of the Newts. "It's time to hit back. We have a source that says the Egyptian is running scared. He's going deep. Far, far away from us. He's heading south toward a village called Barge Matall. It will take him a while to get around Storm King. We're gonna take choppers, jump ahead of him, and lay a trap. When he comes, we'll be ready."

SUMMER

9

B lack Hawk helicopters thumped over the mountains. Shane sat next to Burch in the open door of the first bird, his legs dangling in the wind. Veridian forest and mine tailings zoomed by under his tan boots. The rotor blades rattled his guts. He'd forgotten his earplugs, and twenty minutes into the ride he stopped hearing the blades. All he could hear now was a dull ring. Shane felt like an action hero.

The helicopters were taking Newt platoon deep into the mountains, to Barge Matall, a village on the south flank of Storm King, just below alpine. The village was remote, even lost, separated from the main valley by the eighteen-thousand-foot thrust of Storm King and a mess of satellite peaks. Barge Matall would give the Newts "strike position," meaning from the village they'd be poised to quickly act on further intelligence on the Egyptian.

The helicopters deposited the Newts in terraced fields a mile below Barge Matall. Forty-one Newts and a two-man mortar team spilled out and barreled uphill under sixty-pound packs. They raced for the village, unsure how the villagers would react. Shane's quads and calves burned while he trotted behind Burch. The thin air singed his lungs. At first, his knees were ready to burst under his pack. But the fire of high-elevation movement was now familiar, and he found his rhythm: Inhale. Step up. Lock the knee. Exhale. Repeat. The ringing in his ears faded as he followed Burch up the mountain.

Spring lingered in the air. Under spruce, snow patches clung to the mountains. The terraces sat in the full sun, so they were dry, the dirt just turned with new seeds. The platoon serpentined through the ten-foot terraces, bunching up and spreading out as they tried to find the way. Hidden rock staircases connected the levels. Only the locals knew the route, passing the secret down over the centuries. The Newts kept climbing in accordion fashion. Up above, Shane saw villagers taking off for the forest.

The Newts came to a stone hut at the foot of Barge Matall. A sordid gang of natives had gathered on the roof. Each wore a red blanket draped over one shoulder. Tattoos of raptors and serpents inked their wrists. Wild hair fell down over their faces. Some looked scared, some curious.

The platoon's Afghan interpreter, Billy, asked an old man with a curved back, "Why do the villagers run away?"

"Rue-ski."

The interpreter laughed and said to Shane, "They think you are the Russians."

The villagers were a little behind on world news.

The interpreter asked the old man, "Where is the mosque?"

The old man scratched his head. Generally, the mosque was the center of village life and best place to find elders.

The old man said, "The mosque is a house for the Lowlanders."

The conversation went on. Shane's eyes wandered above the village. There was a verdant hillside of stunning beauty, spangled with ferns and wildflower meadows. Rhododendron groves exploded in white and pink hues all over the slope. Spruce were anchored to rock outcrops in impossible ways. Cascades of steel-colored melt-water sluiced down in small channels, bounding over shelves and cliffs. In the streams, rock islets lay speckled with grasses and wetland plants. Butterflies fluttered through the meadows while songbirds trilled in concert.

In the grasses and ferns, Shane saw rabbits—hundreds, maybe thousands, of rabbits. Shane had been in Afghanistan for months and had yet to see a rabbit. Now they were everywhere, on all levels of the hanging garden, clustered in the vegetation, hopping to and fro while snacking on emerald grass.

The fat rabbits had soft, clean fur and slender feet. They sported coats of black, white, gray, sage, and cinnamon. Some were spotted like dairy cows. Shane turned to his friend, Cassidy, to tell him about the bunny-covered slope. The gape on the SAW gunner's face said he had already seen them.

Time passed and village elders came down from the garden. They wore snow leopard hides, which alone distinguished them from the red-clad commoners. The elders met with the LT and said the soldiers were welcome. The leather-faced chief offered shelter to the Newts. There was only one rule.

The chief said, "Soldiers must not enter the garden. It is sacred ground."

The LT agreed. The Newts took a clay house in the village center and posted 100 percent security for those early hours in the lost village on the big mountain.

Day dragged to night. The squads claimed sleeping spaces in the house. There was argument over areas that did not smell. Burch managed to stake off a whole room with twine cots and a wood-stove for his squad. Now off guard duty, the eight men of the squad sat to eat while Burch grabbed his notepad and left for a meeting in the courtyard. It was just the boys there now in the room. Shane set his ruck on his cot and leaned back against the ruck with his legs straight out and opened his dinner ration. Cassidy sat down next to him.

While they ate, Cassidy stroked his SAW, which rested on bipod legs beside him.

With a mouthful of pound cake, Shane said, "You keep petting that steel like it's your dog."

Cassidy said, "Burch told me you gotta let it know how you feel."

Shane said, "Weird, man."

"Say, did your girl, uhh..." Cassidy snapped his fingers quickly. "Candy."

"Right, did she send another picture?"

Nodding, Shane fished into his sleeve pocket and pulled out a picture in a Ziploc.

"You're using a baggie now."

"Uh-huh." Shane studied the photo for a time, then handed it to Cassidy, warning him, "Keep it in the bag. I don't need your filthy dickbeaters all over it."

Cassidy examined Candy with a wrinkled brow. He whistled. "You're in love with those tits, ain't you? Damn. You buy her that diamond necklace?"

"No," said Shane. "First I seen it was this picture."

"She got rich parents?" asked Cassidy.

"No."

"Then I think you bought it, you just don't know it yet."

"That's fine," said Shane. "I like taking care of her."

Cassidy handed the photo back to Shane, who pocketed it, and walked to the woodstove. Soot from stove fires had blackened the room's walls. Shane kneeled and peered inside the stove.

From across the room, Cassidy called, "Shane. You think you could do me a favor?"

"Maybe. What?"

"My girl from high school, we ain't together no more. Maybe you could ask Candy to hook me up with a friend."

"Sure," answered Shane. "Next letter."

Shane stuffed kindling in the woodstove and brought forth a fire. He fed logs to the flames and adjusted the stack with his bayonet. Soon the fire grew and needed no more tending. Suddenly bored, Shane and Cassidy fired up a game of grabass. Shane tied his rattlesnake headband across his brow, took off his shirt, and poured nasal snuff onto a scrap of cardboard. It took him thirty seconds to dump out the entire tin. Shane scraped his bayonet, and the snuff became a six-inch line—enough nicotine to paralyze a normal adult.

Cassidy looked on, rubbing his hands together.

Shane said, "Here goes," and put his nose in the line, snorted hard, and took it all up in one big rip. It felt like a nail was driven into his face. Shane reared back and clawed his forehead and fell to the floor, where he rolled and thrashed—brown powder ringing one nostril—yelling, "I took it in the face. *In the face.*"

Cassidy almost giggled himself to death.

Vasquez, the platoon sergeant, stepped from the shadows and proclaimed, "Shane, that's some cowboy shit. I'm pleased with your spirit."

Vasquez was good at sneaking up on the privates. After all, the platoon sergeant had started as a private. Shane would have to keep his squirrel eyes on in the future. At the moment, his eyes were bloodred from the megadose of nicotine.

Shane wiped away tears and said, "Much obliged, Sar'nt."

Vasquez suddenly looked pissed. The big sergeant glared and said, "What's that shit wrapped around your head, Private?"

"This here is my warbonnet, Sar'nt. It's a diamondback rattler, one helluva snake."

"That headband is a shade too pink, can't be a rattler. You sure that's not a trouser snake wrapped around your head?"

Shane cocked his head, not getting it.

"Never mind," said Vasquez. "Stow that headband and get your fucking armor on. This ain't 'Nam, and you ain't no dope-smoking draftee. You volunteered to be here. And now you're a Newt. All good Newts have hate in their hearts, and they don't look like gypsies when they take the field."

Shane threw on his gear and tucked away the headband.

Vasquez lingered.

Shane asked, "Sar'nt V, did you see all those bunnies today? I didn't know the Stan had rabbits. Have you seen rabbits before?"

Vasquez spit. "Nope. Just camels and lizards in this damn rock pile."

He spoke from experience. This was his third combat tour. The Newts had a rumor mill, and one of their favorite topics was Vasquez. Shane didn't start rumors, but he liked hearing them. Shane had heard Vasquez left the military for a while, ready to do something less taxing. A six-month job search landed him a position driving a forklift at a hardware store.

Word round the campfire was that Vasquez drank gallons of bourbon to make the forklift go away. He told combat stories to anyone who would listen, even the pizza guy. One year passed. Vasquez came back to the infantry. He was twenty pounds heavier than when he left.

———

A blood moon soaked the village during their second night. The villagers—Pagans, it turned out—gathered under phantom trees, lit a fire, and danced around a couple dozen rabbits. Shane had a fine seat as he pulled guard above the platoon house.

In the flickering firelight, the leather-faced Pagan chief danced forward and flung off his leopard skin, waving his arms. The rabbits hopped around the licking flames, oblivious to the conjuring. Just above the ritual, a figure floated through the trees. Shane aimed his rifle and followed the figure. It gained the high ground and stepped from the shadows and took form. Even under camo pants, the platoon sergeant's massive legs couldn't be missed. Vasquez was trying to catch Shane nodding off. Shane had his chin whiskers shaved, bolt oiled, and gear in perfect order. Ritual or not, Shane wasn't going to let anyone sneak up on the platoon.

———

The days in Barge Matall swirled together. The villagers came to the Newts' house at dawn and dusk with goat chai, flatbread, and plates of rice and beans. Shane found the food delicious. The village was surrounded by crops of every kind, so it was no surprise to find fresh food. Sometimes the villagers brought goat meat. Shane had to grab the meat with a piece of flatbread because there wasn't a fork for a thousand miles. He wasn't too fond of goat. It had the consistency of chewed-up pemmican. He still choked it down, because the LT told the boys, "It's rude to turn up your noses when the locals offer food."

Shane thought the best part of the meals was the red sauce. Boy oh boy, did that red sauce flavor up the rice. Every time Shane ate the sauce, a wave of euphoria swept over him. All the Newts caught on. They called it magic sauce. They quarreled over who got first dibs and slapped each other's hands to get it.

After each meal, Shane would undo the top button on his camo pants. He'd lean back, giggling, loose, and happy as a fat cat. His comrades did the same, and everyone would lay around, sputtering nonsense and laughing at the goats trimming the grassy hillside. Burch and a few others tried to get the villagers to reveal the magic sauce recipe. The villagers kept their secret.

Saturday was a festive day for the Pagans. They brought a big meal to the platoon and sat to eat. Over crossed legs and silver plates, the villagers pointed at the Americans, asking about this and that piece of equipment. Sergeant Martinez, the first-squad leader, soon got their attention.

Martinez had a thick black mustache, and the sleeves on his camo top were rolled so that everyone could see the tattoos on his forearms. There were tats of two hands pressed together in prayer and an Aztec princess wearing feathers and a snake wrapped around the upper forearm below Martinez's elbow. The villagers were very impressed. Martinez was soon rolling his arms and pointing at the ink and telling how it all came to be. When he came to the snake, he said, "I used to have my gang tat here, but I covered it with this viper when I enlisted."

Billy the interpreter fumbled for the translation. The villagers nodded eagerly. No one had a clue.

About then, the LT scooted forward, saying, "Tattoos later. We've much to talk about." Shane listened as the LT told stories about September 11 and the battles with the Taliban. The LT asked the villagers about the Egyptian, and did he have a camp nearby. The villagers promised they knew nothing and asked more questions about the world. The LT sat there in splendid posture, racing them through decades of world news. The LT seemed delighted to have the sole privilege of enlightening them. Shane figured the LT was pretending to be Meriwether Lewis. It was a shame the officer had forgotten his trading beads and brass kettles.

The villagers told the Newts about their religion. The villagers came up from the center of the earth. Magma deposited them alongside the rocks and minerals when the peaks above the village were born. The great blue glacier gouged out the valleys and freed their ancestors from their stone lair. The spring snowmelt carried them down from alpine. Their ancestors settled on this slope, mesmerized by the beauty of the hanging garden. The villagers knelt before the sun and moon and spoke of fairies in the forest. They told the Newts about the bunnies in the garden. The bunnies were the spirits of their dead ancestors. Those who lived by their beliefs got to come back as bunnies and spend their time in the soft grass.

The chief Pagan whispered, "One bunny in the garden is special. He has a bright orange streak between his ears. It runs down his back."

Shane had seen the bunny as he passed around the garden on patrol. He gave the bunny a name that stuck—Mohawk. The villagers said Mohawk was a magic bunny that drew his lineage back to the first of their kind. Mohawk was used in rituals. When the moon was full, he cured all manner of disease.

During the Newts' second week in the village, a storm dusted the houses and hills with snow. After the storm, Shane didn't like the woods surrounding the village anymore. On a morning recon, Shane heard enemy radios crackling through the understory. He searched the brambles and found nothing. Another Newt heard whistling in a cave. The wind was howling through a deep cavern, but he stuck his head in and saw the cave was only a few feet deep. A new guy saw a fairy with long black hair at twilight. He swore on his mother the fairy had the most beautiful face. Shane didn't buy that story at all.

But then, one evening, Cassidy came back from patrol and said, "No shit, dude, I saw a stream glowing green in the moonlight."

Shane and Cassidy tried to come up with an explanation. The forest was dark, with giant evergreens, and no wind at night, which was unusual in the Kush. A mind could wander in such a place.

Shane told himself all these things could be explained by weather, animals, or tired eyes. But the village was just as creepy. It was so quiet after dark: no barking dogs, bleating donkeys, or cooking fires. The silence was splendid and unnerving. Shane was also spooked by the villagers' bizarre rituals and their love of the rabbits.

More than anything, Shane was sick of the young men from the village. They would hang around the platoon's house and talk to Shane. They'd lay their red blankets next to Shane and touch him and say he looked good. "Come to my house after dark. I'll wait for you in the barn," said one. Shane didn't want to admit that the Pagan men wanted to push his shit in.

Shane told Vasquez about the romantic advances from the village men. Vasquez spat and said, "I've seen queer Afghans before. They love the young soldiers, especially the ones with baby faces like you. They'll try to stretch out your balloon knot, so if they touch you again, shoot them in the face."

Burch got protective when he heard about the gay villagers wooing his favorite soldier. Burch jabbed his thumb into his chest and told Shane, "Tell them you're my bitch."

By the third week, Shane wanted out of Barge Matall. Even Burch was anxious. Burch was known to sleep like a rock, the way a man sleeps when he's spent and carries no guilt. But one night, Burch rolled in his sleeping bag, mumbling about a witch, and began moaning.

Shane thought of the woman in Baz, with those awful black teeth.

Suddenly, Burch shot up in his bag, thrashing and slapping himself. "Spiders, big black tarantulas," he said. Burch was certain they were real. "They were fast," he told Shane, "fast as lightning and furry as bears." He had the same dream three nights in a row. He was so convincing that Shane kept checking his own sleeping bag. Shane never found a spider, but he was certain this place was drenched in bad vibes.

Thankfully, the LT gathered the Newts one evening. Off in the west, the clouds were pink banners. The last rays of sun were on the LT's face when he said, "The Egyptian has stopped moving. He's in an old mining camp one valley west of here. We'll march tonight and attack the camp tomorrow." The LT paused and scanned the crowd. "Listen close, it's weapons hot on this target. Everyone is bad. We're steppin' at 2200. Don't make a show of it."

Shane glanced at Burch.

Burch said, "Weapons hot. This is gonna be fun."

When the Newts broke up, Shane slid off into the shadows. He ducked behind a hedgerow and ran up to the garden, where he grabbed five pounds of precious cargo and stashed it in his ruck. Then he was ready.

10

Above Barge Matall
Day 108

When Newt platoon left Barge Matall, the night sky was awash in clouds. A chandelier of stars beamed through a gap. Shane was point man for the movement. He climbed alongside the hanging garden, made haste to a pass near the blue glacier, and closed on a precipitous ridge they'd scouted the week before.

The ridge was made of white granite. Rectangular rocks popped out like piano keys. The Newts named the ridge "the keyboard," and now Shane stepped onto it. A hard wind blew and blew across the keyboard, whistling in Shane's ears and cracking his lips. *No big deal.* Shane scuttled the spine like he'd been there before. He was playing the keyboard, and Burch was watching.

They made good time as the moon slid through the clouds. The ridge gradually narrowed, and just before dawn it tapered to a knife edge fifty feet long. The rock fell away on both sides, and in the dark, the drop seemed to be a thousand miles. The platoon whipped out rope and climbing gear. Shane had navigated all night. He insisted on leading the way across the knife edge.

"This ridge is my bitch."

Burch said, "Okay, it's your show."

Shane tied the rope to his harness, slung his rifle, and clipped cams, stoppers, and nuts around his waist.

As Burch doled out the rope, he asked, "You sure you got this?"

Shane stared at the route. He didn't answer.

Burch said, "How 'bout I do it for you?"

Shane said, "Naw. Too easy, Sar'nt."

"Be sure you set an anchor and clip in. You're not on belay 'til then."

Shane shined his red headlamp and edged onto the knife. *Three points of contact*, he told himself, *knees parallel to the rock*. Precise footwork brought him to a ledge. He had to get an anchor in a crevice, but the white granite was so smooth—not a crack in sight. Shane balanced on, using smear technique, clinging to finger-sized holds. His knees got to shaking. It occurred to Shane that if he fell to his death, the others would only laugh. His arms trembled with surging lactic acid. The wind roared. Shane lost his balance.

He fell with his eyes on the stars.

Thump. Shane landed on a small shelf twenty feet down. His headlamp kept swirling in an endless fall. Up above, a couple dozen headlamps came on, scanning in panicky swaths. The Newts were scrambling for their fallen man.

Shane groaned, "Fuck me," as he crawled to his feet. Nothing was broken, but he was in a jam. A handhold protruded above his head. He couldn't reach it.

Shane repeated, "Fuck me."

He yelled for help. The wind carried his voice away. Shane leaned into the cliff. Cold rock stung his cheek. There was dull pain in the tips of his fingers. He took deep breaths and peeled off his armor and made a few sad little jumps at the handhold. He wasn't even close. Suddenly the rope came taut at his waist. There were three tugs. Shane responded with three tugs to let Burch know he was okay.

After a few minutes, a headlamp came from above. Shane put his tongue to his teeth and gave a shrill whistle. Up above, the headlamp reflected off the wall and showed Burch's face. He moved with grace on those long legs. His black scarf shielded his neck from the wind. Shane saw white wings on his squad leader. Burch grabbed Shane's arm and lifted him up to the handhold. Shane wanted to look tough, but he just couldn't hide the hurt from his fall.

He whimpered, "Thanks, Sar'nt."

Burch grinned, showing yellow teeth, and said, "I thought maybe you went down there to play your skin flute." He pointed to a crack in the granite Shane hadn't seen. "I'm gonna start charging you for my services." And then he dangled an extra headlamp.

Shane climbed a dihedral, placing two cams and a number 3 stopper, and set the fixed rope line for the rest of the platoon. The last Newt unclipped from the line under a kaleidoscope dawn. Shane opened his ruck to check on his precious cargo before moving out. The ridge widened again. The Newts moved a half mile to a pinnacle and took shelter in the lee of white boulders.

Shane's shirt was plastered to his back after a seven-hour hump. The high peaks of the Himalayas exploded over the horizon. High winds sent banner clouds off their summits. Shane peered into a valley below the keyboard. A few small trees lined a gully just downhill. A couple thousand feet lower, the forest began in earnest, and farther still, it was a thick blanket interrupted by two ponds shimmering in the morning sun. The valley was uninhabited and untrammeled, pure wilderness—a sight to behold.

Shane wetted a ration heater to brew coffee. The Newts pulled on cigarettes after a long night without. Shane threw in a dip and relaxed. The boogie man and those shit packers from Barge Matall were far behind. All was well now that he could see for miles in every direction.

Shane finished his coffee-filled water bottle. A figure appeared on the keyboard from the way they'd just come. *Maybe a goat*, he thought. It was a small black dot at first, lost in a nebula of mountain, cloud, and rock.

Another figure emerged behind it. The dots took form. They wore red blankets.

The Newt gunners clicked into tripods for range. Burch moved Shane into position, telling him, "Be ready to fire." The men skittered closer. Their blankets flapped in the wind, but they were lithe among the rocks. Without pause, the men bear-crawled across the knife edge where Shane fell.

At hailing distance, the men called, "Friends…friends…talk with us." Their voices were lost in the wind. They kept calling, "Talk with us."

Billy the interpreter yelled, "What is your business here?"

"We come from Barge Matall. We seek your help."

The LT and Vasquez greeted the men in the shadow of a granite pinnacle. The men sounded friendly from a distance, but up close they were troubled, their eyes hawkish. Shane recognized the adult sons of the Barge Matall elders. *Shit.* He saw the Pagan prince, the one who wanted to meet him in the barn.

The Pagan prince said to the LT, "The orange rabbit is missing. You must help us find it."

The LT shuffled on his feet and said, "We have a mission. We can't help you."

The Pagan prince said, "When did you last see the orange rabbit? Ask your men."

The LT said, "I'm sorry, we have orders. We cannot go back to the village."

The Pagan said, "The orange rabbit is missing. Fire and floods will descend upon us. Don't you see? You *must* help find him."

The LT said, "I'm not sure what we can do. Don't worry. He'll turn up."

The Pagan said, "You speak to me as if I were a child."

Billy pulled the Pagans into a side conversation. The Afghans spoke in clipped exchanges. The Pagan prince kept pointing at the Newts.

Billy turned and addressed the Newts. "They think you took the rabbit. This is not good for us. We should turn back."

Shane gulped. Gripping his rifle a little tighter, he looked at his leadership. The LT glanced at Sergeant Vasquez, as if seeking relief. The LT was book smart, and he had all the figures memorized. He'd quiz the Newts at random. He once asked Shane a whole slew of questions like *How big is the beaten zone of a 240 machine gun at eight hundred meters?* But angry Pagans and their rabbits... well, they didn't teach that at Fort Benning. Vasquez would have to handle this one. And he did. He picked up the radio hand mike and made a call. He nodded his head several times, looking very officious as he spoke to the man on the other end.

Funny thing, thought Shane, *Vasquez never pressed the button to transmit.*

Shane tongued the wad in his lip because it helped him think. He wondered how Vasquez would convince the Pagans that Mohawk was just a stupid rabbit. These Pagans loved their bunnies. Now they wanted to make trouble over the critters. Well, people this stupid were bound to get hurt.

Vasquez stepped forward and faced the Pagans. "We've called headquarters. The commander is sending others to help you. They'll arrive tomorrow in your village."

The Pagan prince said, "As you like," and walked away with eyes still on Vasquez. All the Pagans followed. Their angry whispers faded in the wind.

Vasquez said, "We keep moving."

The Newts resumed their ridge march, further distancing themselves from Barge Matall. After a windy morning, the platoon descended into a new valley toward the target. Around them, conifers bowed in the wind. Burch moved to the front under the needle canopy. He would hunt for sign.

Burch whispered to Shane, "Stay close."

He speared forward in the shady forest. Every so often, he cut left and right for sign. An hour into the drill, Burch found broken branches and matted vegetation. The hide was a good twenty feet across. But acorn droppings and split hooves showed nothing more than a deer bed-down. He kept on. A slow mile brought them to a muddy corridor through a thicket. Burch said to Shane, "This is a classic track-trap. Briars funnel everything into here. It's how you locate sign." Burch studied the mud and pointed to animal tracks. "Just ungulates moving through here."

Each time Burch stopped to inspect, he reported what he saw, what it meant, and what it didn't mean. About noon, Burch found a bubbly spring ringed by tracks. A goat trail ran downhill with hoof and sandal prints. Burch got on hands and knees to study the divots. He sniffed the ground. Suddenly Burch's body stiffened. He rolled in the dirt, grabbing his stomach and spoiling the tracks. Grunts of pain came up from deep inside him.

Shane said, "You okay, Sar'nt? What is it, bubble guts?"

Burch took a few labored breaths and uncoiled a little. "Don't know."

Shane said, "I'll get Doc."

"No. No. I just need a minute." Burch lay there on his side for a time. The sickness passed, and he came onto his feet, still holding his stomach.

Burch said, "I'm okay. Let's move."

They continued through early evening. With a look at his map, Shane judged the mining camp to be four miles north. Through a break in the forest, Shane watched the sun sink in the west. Shane willed the sun down faster. Under cover of night, they'd have an edge on the Egyptian.

Purple light came in shoots as the sun finally set. Shane was hopping over downed boughs. He could not help noticing that Burch kept scanning backward.

Burch's face was tight when he said, "Something about the way the Pagan said, 'As you like.' It didn't sit right. Listen, if them sumbitches come at us, aim at the muzzle flashes, and if you don't see muzzle flashes, aim around the bases of trees; that's where they'll be."

The shade went long, and then it was all shadows and tangled understory. They continued along, mere ants among old-growth spruce, the tree crowns waving in the evening wind. Here and there, cones fell and landed with a soft *plunk*.

At last light came the crackle of gunfire.

From upslope bullets swept in, eager for flesh. The enemy held three attack positions in an arc around the Newts.

Over his right shoulder, Shane saw a line of orange muzzle flashes. He aimed and engaged, first with bullets, then with a couple grenades. And when the twinkling muzzle flashes paused, he engaged the bases of trees. Shane kept telling himself to breathe, just keep breathing and fire between breaths. He was fighting his tendency to hold his breath, anticipating a bullet's impact.

Thump...thump...thump, the Newts' 60 mm mortar team sent shells in the air. Two shells landed behind the mujahedeen. The third exploded on a cluster of muzzle flashes. It was a direct hit. Shane could smell the gunfight now, gunpowder mixed with earth and sweat.

Amidst the guns and rockets, Shane saw an enemy PKM firing without pause. The continuous muzzle flash looked like fire from a baby dragon. It was best to shoot in bursts to allow for resets in aim. But this muj was full of bravado, and his green tracers zipped by Shane. Off to the right, Shane could just make out Burch. He was standing up straight, slinging lead at the baby dragon. Burch baited the gunner then ducked to reload. He was smiling a crazy smile as if enjoying the fight. Shane fired a couple more frags but couldn't make himself smile.

Burch's ploy gave the Newt machine gunners a chance to zero onto the baby dragon. As they pinned him, rounds bounced off stones and rocketed into the purple sky. The baby dragon kept up. Red and green tracers crisscrossed through the trees. The opposing machine gunners played a game of chicken, but the Newt gunners fired in controlled bursts and made adjustments. Brass piled up. Powder fogged the forest. The Newt gunners shredded the mossy log that hid their opponent.

Just then, Shane took aim, pointing his tube right above the log to account for slope angle and the trajectory of his grenade. He pulled the trigger. The grenade leapt out with a *bloop*. A fraction of a second later there was a boom, right on the log, and a hoop of fire. The gun fell silent. Muj retreated between the trees. Deep breaths slowed Shane's pounding heart. *I got one*, he thought. *I for sure got one.*

Burch came running, black scarf hiding his face, and scooped up Shane. They dashed uphill to the enemy positions. Six bounds later they slowed at the spot where the baby dragon had been.

With his rifle at the high ready, Shane stepped through bullet-riddled trees. He kicked the mossy log. The gunner was right behind it, draped over his gun, blood from his mouth dripping off the feed tray. Shane recognized the Pagan prince.

"Sar'nt. We got one."

As Shane waited for Burch, he stared at the fighter, feeling triumphant. Shane whispered to the body, "You thought I was a kid. You thought I'd meet you in the barn. Look at you now."

When Burch saw the body, he thought it well to lie down on his stomach. Burch spat on his hand and, using the utmost diligence, locked palms with the dead gunner. Then he arm-wrestled his limp opponent. He slapped the ground. Veins popped out of his hands. He twisted to bring more muscles into a thrust. Blood poured from the gunner's mouth as they jostled back and forth.

Burch grunted, "I'm coming over the top." He looked up and said in one quick breath, "Shane, get a picture."

Burch smiled and flexed his bicep with the dead muj. *Click. Click. Click.* Burch stood up, wiped blood on his thighs, and said, "That skinny little bastard is strong."

Shane laughed, because Burch was his squad leader and Shane

held him in high regard. But a nasty cramp ran through his stomach. What Burch did was plain evil. Worse off, it was bound to cause bad luck. Shane wasn't sure what was happening, but Burch hadn't been the same since that mission to Baz.

The squad came downhill in the dark. They reported killing the prince of Barge Matall.

The LT furrowed his brow. He said to Vasquez, "Goddamn goat rope."

Vasquez said, "What choice did we have?"

"You could have handled those guys better this morning."

"I'm not going for their bullshit," said Vasquez. "The Afghans spin up some yarn about us thieving a bunny and I'm supposed to cry them a river. I won't stand for it. We need to keep moving. The target is only three miles. They may have heard the fight."

The LT frowned and hurried off.

———————

At 0330, Newt platoon set blocking positions around the target, crawling through pine needles and cones on the forest floor with their guns cradled in their arms. The mining camp was a cluster of dilapidated stone huts. Around the huts, piles of tailings resembled twenty-foot-high anthills. Working in fire teams, the Newts cleared each hut. Then they hit the outbuildings. Sergeant Martinez led first squad into a lone mineshaft. Two minutes later, the men came out choking, wet to the knees. "The shaft is flooded," Sergeant Martinez reported, "and full of bad air."

The search of the camp revealed no live targets. There were footprints everywhere.

From the backside of a pile of tailings, Burch called softly for Shane.

When Shane came around the tailings, he found Burch shining a headlamp on the ground.

Burch pointed to footprints left by a pair of black high-tops.

"Guy with the limp again. There was a large group here. They must have bailed when they heard our gunfight."

At that moment, Shane realized he had made a big mistake. Dizziness overtook him. He rocked on his heels. He dared not look Burch in the eye but spun away, saying, "Maybe they're still about. Best we keep looking." Then he staggered off into the forest, pretending to follow tracks.

———————

Night gave way to steel in the east. The squads doggedly searched the area around the mine. Shane was rifling the contents of a mine cart, rucksack on his back, when one of the boys said, "Hey Shane, there's something moving in your ruck."

Shane froze.

A couple others overheard and fired questions. "What is it?" "Take it out." "Show us."

Burch heard too. "Shane. What're you packin'?"

"It's, it's... nothing."

Burch said, "Open your ruck."

"It's nothing, Sar'nt."

Burch said, "You can lie at the bar. You can lie to your lady. You can lie to your battle buddies. But you must never lie to me."

Shane set his pack down gently.

Burch reached in and grabbed a black bag and opened it. Burch pulled in a sharp breath. The others looked on, waiting to know. Burch took the black bag in one hand. With the other hand, Burch seized Shane's arm with a vise grip. "The jig's up. Let's go find Sergeant V."

Shane's legs were jelly as they approached the stone hut. Burch shoved him through the narrow doorway. Inside, they found Vasquez sitting on a block of wood.

Vasquez barely looked up from his map. "What's up, Burch?"

With clenched fists, Burch said, "Shane, tell him."

Shane cringed in silence.

Burch said, "*Tell him.*"

Vasquez cracked his knuckles as he stared at Shane.

Shane was scared of Vasquez. Motherfucker was so mean he'd take away your birthday. Vasquez could fly off the handle so fast. His favorite punishment for the Newts involved an aluminum baseball bat. Vasquez would order a misbehaving Newt, "Helmet on." Then he'd swing his aluminum bat at the helmet. He didn't try to hit home runs. No. He did it in quarter swings, over and over, until the Newt couldn't remember his own name.

Shane cowered and said, "I...I...I took the bunny. I took Mohawk from the garden."

Vasquez was stone.

Shane said, "I thought we needed a mascot. I didn't think they'd come shootin' over it."

He reckoned he was done for. He wouldn't answer to the cap'n. The platoon sergeant didn't take things up the chain. Vasquez would dish out his own justice, maybe with the aluminum baseball bat, or maybe something worse.

Vasquez stood up straight and held his chin high. Then came the verdict. "Yeah, I know. I know you took the bunny. Back in the village, I could see it moving in your pack."

Shane's mouth fell open.

Vasquez was polite. "Hand Mohawk over so we can make this right."

He seized the bunny and ducked through the door. Determined strides brought him to a waist-high rock. Vasquez clutched the bag's draw string and wheeled Mohawk over his head and brought the bunny down on the rock with all his weight. There was a sick thud and a sudden squeak.

With rage, Vasquez said, "*This bunny.*"

Again, he wheeled the bag overhead and slammed it down—another thud, no squeak this time. Vasquez sneered as he smashed Mohawk on the rock a third time. "This bunny," he fumed, and followed up with a fourth impact. The bludgeoned rabbit bled through the bag. Vasquez held it up with the proudest look on his face.

Then he turned to Shane.

Holding his breath, Shane braced himself for a blow. Vasquez stepped on Shane's boot, pushed his chin in Shane's face, and glowered. Vasquez held steady like the Sphinx. Shane's knees got to clacking.

Vasquez said, "Get back to work."

Shane and Burch bolted without hesitation.

A mile downhill, Shane came upon a fallen hut. He was lost in thought as he approached the door. It took vast stores of energy to hate the world the way Vasquez did. Shane figured all that hate burned up a body, made it rotten on the inside. Shane entered the hut with his gun up. He surprised a dozing goat herder. He bought a goat from the wide-eyed shepherd and brought it up to the platoon.

Seeing the goat, Vasquez said, "We'll bivouac here and get some sleep."

The Newts fortified the huts. One squad snuck into the woods to lay in ambush. At noon, Vasquez placed spruce logs in a woodstove and made fire. He whistled over the cracking flames and stirred a broth. He said he was whipping up a special goat stew. Soon after, the Newts sat cross-legged under a thatched roof and devoured the meal. The LT took a few bites and poked his food with a ration spoon.

The LT asked Vasquez, "You said this was goat?"

Vasquez said, "Affirm. I gave you heart, liver, and lung. Those parts are the best."

The LT shrugged and kept eating.

Shane knew the secret ingredient in the stew. When he was a kid outside Tupelo, his dad took him rabbit hunting once in a while. His dad taught him how to aim, how to skin and gut the rabbit, and the trick to cooking it just right. His father said, "Never kill an animal for fun." Shane remembered the taste of rabbit. Vasquez had put Mohawk in the stew.

They were eating magic bunny.

Shane glanced at Vasquez. The platoon sergeant winked.

The woodfire crackled long after the meal was over. Shane peeled off his wet socks and steamed them by the flame. Then Shane pulled his sleeping bag up to his eyes and emptied his thoughts and drifted to sleep. Shane had a dream like never before. He and Cassidy were all alone in the hanging garden above Barge Matall. They napped in the shade of a giant fern. Mohawk was close by, nibbling on emerald grass. The earth began to tremble and, moments later, it was heaving. The ground ripped and tilted. Cliffs shot up around the hanging garden. Shane beheld soaring walls of white granite. The quake died and the cliffs stopped shaking. A deep rumbling lingered for a bit, sending rocks plummeting from the cliffs.

The serene sounds of the garden returned—the bubbling creeks, the songbirds. Shane stepped through grass toward the polished wall where the soft edge of the garden had once been. A chasm guarded the granite. Shane looked down and saw the planet's entrails.

They were trapped in the garden. Cassidy saw the chasm and looked resigned for a time. Then a sublime look crossed his face. He said, "Time for some shut-eye." Shane and Cassidy lay down in the shade of the giant fern. The soft grass wet their backs. Mohawk was nearby, nibbling on an emerald tuft. A king cobra snatched Mohawk and slithered off.

11

Baz village, People's Valley

Habibullah woke on his twine cot. A breath of wind played with the yellow wheat outside his window. He draped a blanket over his shoulder and loafed about his home, though there was much work to be done. When he stepped into the den, he saw the cooking fire shining on his mother's face. She turned and touched the birthmark on his cheek, telling him, "Take the goats to high pasture." She handed him an orchid. "And give this to your father."

The goats ran from their pen one behind another, their hooves clattering on the rocks, their chin tufts waving in the wind. Habibullah climbed the trail after them. In the far distance, the clouds breaking across Storm King told him rain would soon come. Habibullah gained the first height above the village, where he stopped at his father's grave. It was marked by a tattered flag mounted on a wishbone branch. The flag showed that Zmarak was once mujahedeen. River cobbles atop the grave would keep away mountain lions. Two full moons had passed since the Americans killed his father.

Habibullah set the orchid on the cobbles. "Glory to the guerrilla."

He climbed on. The rises above Baz gave way to slopes mottled with grass, then a talus field, the seep where he drew water, and finally the high meadow long used by the family. Habibullah sat and slapped mosquitos. The goats bleated and snatched the meadow grass. He meditated on fleeing the valley to distance his family from Americans and war. He didn't know where they would go—the parched land down below was no good for crops or goats, save the flats flooded by the great rivers in the spring. But the flats were long claimed by Lowland tribes.

Habibullah thought of his older brother, Mehtar. No word had ever come back from him. Habibullah was sure his brother was alive. He vowed to seek the lost one across the great range. Habibullah could take his wife and son and make a new life with his brother, wherever he was. Sticks and stones were all they needed.

The sun wheeled across the sky. Shadows touched the river. That was his signal to corral the goats for home. A few hours of daylight remained, more than enough time to wander down and pen the goats. Habibullah could have grazed his flock until dusk, but staying up high as the day waned was risky. The mujahedeen usually attacked the Ameriki late in the day. The invaders would fight back with artillery. Anyone in the hills could be shelled; their intentions didn't matter.

———

Rain came that night. Inside Habibullah's room, drops pattered the floor from a leak. Twice he woke to change the bucket. The next morning, he discovered a terrace wall spilled by a mudslide. He gathered his implements and went to work, placing stones and slabbing wet clay to hold them in place. Habibullah rotated through the tools neatly arranged at his side. Practice had taught him the right stone in the right place would set forever. All the People knew that. The hard part was seeing how all the stones went together.

The rectangular rocks above the village were best for making mountains into fields. The stream cobbles just below were easiest to haul, but they were poor for building walls. Habibullah remembered his father's words on building rock walls: *Don't bother with the round rocks. Use the flat ones, and not too thin.* And when they had built the stone terrace Habibullah was now fixing, Zmarak had said, *Each stone has its place, my boy.*

As the afternoon wore on, the terrace wall took form again. Habibullah leveled the top and packed his tools in his green blanket. As he stood, there came the sound of automatic weapons above Baz. The mujahedeen were in the forest near his pasture, firing over the river at the Ameriki's camp. After a time, the Americans responded with shells. One by one, they arced over Baz. The explosions rumbled in Habibullah's stomach. He crouched in a nook to wait out the fighting.

Not long after the bombs stopped, Habibullah saw mujahedeen. They passed through once in a while, moving up or down the mountain to attack the American camp. Habibullah avoided the mujahedeen. He feared they'd see him and remember his older brother, just as his father had said.

The four mujahedeen laced the singing stream below his village. Habibullah guessed they would stick to the water, so he stayed in the wheat and eyed them from a crouch. The mujahedeen were just downhill when the lead fighter locked eyes with Habibullah. At once, the fighters veered left and came straight for him. Their rusty machine guns slowed their climb. Checkered scarves covered their faces. A limping fighter had his arms over two others. He jumped on one foot and crawled over rocks as they navigated the terraces. Blood stained the rocks where he stepped.

The lead fighter gained the final terrace and stood in front of Habibullah. The scarf over the fighter's mouth flapped with each hard breath. He asked, "Are you the boy of the medicine woman?"

Habibullah rose in the yellow wheat. He held his chin high. "I am."

The fighter said, "I am Loombara. I come from Gorbat. We seek your help." Loombara pointed to the injured fighter. "The Ameriki hit him with a bomb. Can the medicine woman heal him?"

Habibullah did not want to mix with the fighters, but a good man had to shelter visitors in need. Hospitality was tribal code.

"Yes. Follow me through the rocks."

Habibullah led the fighters through the terraces and up a jagged rock staircase. The others lifted the injured one up the steps. His groans were deep, mortal. Habibullah thought the fighter brave for bearing such a wound. Here was a man who might not see sundown. Habibullah climbed a twisted ladder and signaled the fighters to continue up the stairs. Moments later, they stooped through a pine door cracked in half by the Americans. Habibullah found his mother, Tabana, the one the fighters called the medicine woman. She was pulling flatbread from the hearth.

Tabana cocked her head around, just as an eagle would, and squinted at the masked men. Moments later, her suspicious face turned warm. Her shrill voice had no fear. "What are you, bandits? Take off your masks." With black teeth, she smiled at the head fighter. "Loombara, I know your eyes, and I know your mother."

These are not the men who seek my brother, thought Habibullah.

The fighters removed their scarves, revealing red beards dyed by henna paste. Tabana studied the wounded fighter before pointing to a cot. The mujahedeen took her cue. Tabana settled into her cloak and then reached for a purple plant. She kneaded the leaves and mixed in holly berries. She turned with her cloak wheeling, then waved at them and said, "Let me work."

Loombara told her, "Bless you, mother." With that, the fighters filed out of the house.

Loombara said, "We must hide our guns."

Habibullah looked at the weapons, which did not bear Taliban inscriptions. He pointed to a rock pile above the houses. "The rocks are safe. Never hide guns in the village, so my father said."

Loombara nodded approval, a faint smile on his cracked lips, as if he was proud of Habibullah.

The fighters wasted no time stashing their weapons. Meanwhile, Habibullah sat in his courtyard, hiding in the oval shade of a strung-up parachute. After a few minutes, Loombara found him there. Loombara collapsed against a wall and pushed out a long breath.

Habibullah stole a look at the fighter at his side. Loombara's beard had never seen scissors. It bloomed from his face, covered his neck, and landed on an olive drab fighting vest. The beard showed touches of gray at the roots; Loombara was too young for gray hair. Maybe it was the peril of fighting Ameriki, thought Habibullah.

He glanced at Loombara's black high-tops. Many commanders wore them, for the coveted sneakers were light in weight yet sturdy in the rocks. Habibullah had once seen them for sale at the Blue River bazaar. They cost two thousand rupees, a full season of work. Habibullah could not afford them. Such was the shepherd's life.

Habibullah had seen Loombara before, somewhere in Gorbat. He couldn't remember exactly. Habibullah's family went to the village during Ramadan to see the rest of their clan and visit the white mosque. They'd arrive in the evening, just as the prayer call sounded. Then Habibullah would join the file of men heading for the mosque. He remembered Loombara now—in the mosque, Loombara knelt in front, among men of clout. And when Loombara spoke, others had stopped and listened.

Loombara was staring at the holly-pocked hills above Baz when he said, "I told him not to run. I told him a fighter must shelter in stones until the bombs stop. Then his escape is an easy one." It seemed Loombara was rehearsing what to tell his commander.

Habibullah nodded to show he was listening.

Loombara said, "My friend showed fear when the first explosions came. He thought he could outrun the bombs."

A helicopter echoed in the distance. Loombara eyed the northern sky, where the day's heat had built a storm. He said, "And now we know." Habibullah waited for more, but the fighter fell silent. The winged beast cleared the heights above Baz. Loombara shuddered. He sprung to a knee, then froze, and settled down. Helicopters would not fire on villages unless fired upon.

The helicopter prowled over Baz. Waves of wind fluttered the parachute over Habibullah's courtyard. The helicopter circled twice, ascended the mountainside, and fanned the uplands where Loombara had been.

Habibullah followed the helicopter with his eyes and asked, "Are the helicopters worse than the bombs?"

Loombara said, "O' my boy. One must always listen for their sound. A broken man is a burden when the helicopters loom. Yet we cannot leave one another, even under the pursuit of pounding helicopters. This I know: The helicopter makes the mujahedeen shiver. But I know this, too: The helicopters only come when soldiers are dead. In this way, the helicopters tell us we've done well."

As Loombara spoke, his right thumb shuffled prayer beads in his cupped palm. The click was constant, soothing, the sound of faith. Loombara looked down and noticed his idling hand.

"The others told me we should not come here, to Baz, to seek your mother's medicine. They called her a witch." Loombara eyed the prayer beads again. "I know your mother. Her medicine is good. It touched me when I was a boy. And her husband is with Allah now, so her medicine is stronger."

Habibullah looked up at the mention of his father. He said, "We buried him in the grove, next to the others from Baz. It has always been that way."

Loombara said, "I shall visit his grave. Not now—maybe when the rains come before the snow." He looked at the house's cracked door. "I know what the Ameriki did here. They were looking for the soldier who fell in the river."

Habibullah said, "Yes, they came in the night, as they do when they are angry."

Loombara said, "Indeed, we own the day. They lurk in the moonlight."

"And they find only shadows in the hills, so they come to sleeping villages to make war."

Loombara said, "Do not grieve, my boy. Zmarak died at the Ameriki's hands. He is a martyr, and so finds paradise, a fertile land of fragrant plants and ripe fruit where rivers run high and fields blossom in golden splendor. Better still, Allah has given your father a beautiful face and many fine wives to keep. You should be so lucky."

Habibullah said, "This I know."

Loombara said, "Zmarak was a good man, very brave. Before you were born, he killed many communists. He showed me how to pierce the soft stomach of their tanks. The dead tank by the Blue River is Zmarak's trophy from those times. He must have told you."

Habibullah said, "No. I've heard whispers—whispers he was the killer of tanks, but his stories were of feuds against Lowland tribes. He took me to fight them. He taught me to show no fear."

Loombara said, "O'. A thousand brave acts against the Lowland clans fall short of one brave act against the invaders. They bring metal falcons and soldiers who see in the dark." Loombara shuffled his prayer beads once more. "What will you do now, my boy?"

Habibullah said, "I'll go to the Blue River and ask about my brother in Pakistan."

Loombara shook his head. He leaned into Habibullah's face and said, "You cannot go to the Lowland tribes. They bicker among themselves and pant like dogs for American scraps. Send your boy and wife down, but not to the Lowlanders. We have men in Asadabad who can take them to the Indus. It's safe there."

Habibullah said, "This takes trust to send away one's family to men never seen. The mujahedeen made trouble for us before. The men from Balay came for my brother. He fled by the moonlight. Many winters have passed. Still we have not heard from him."

Loombara said, "My boy, the mujahedeen from Balay swear allegiance to the Taliban. My gun bears my name, not the black flag. We are the People's mujahedeen. We fight a common enemy with them, nothing more."

Habibullah answered, "A shepherd does not see the different shades among the fighters. Not until this day." He sat in silence. The clicking prayer beads kept time. Habibullah rubbed his temples and thought on the fighter's offer. In the distance was the buzzing helicopter.

He finally said, "Your word is good. I will accompany my wife and son for the journey."

Loombara said, "This I swear: Our people will care for them. So join them on the trip to Asadabad. Then return to your home."

Habibullah asked, "Why not stay with them all the way? Such is a man's duty, to protect his family."

Loombara smiled. "Join us, my boy. *That* is a man's duty. You can be a lion on a mountaintop with us." He stared at the hilltop above the village. "The infidels will seek you with poisoned eyes, and shake in their boots when they find your silhouette against the sun."

Habibullah said, "A lion. How beautiful."

Loombara put his hand on Habibullah's shoulder. "Many boys from Gorbat have come of age. A lion will lead them. His name is Habibullah."

12

Camp Holiday
Day 113

In a bunker on the Holiday perimeter, Shane used the back of his hand to sweep hot brass off the sandbags. Then Shane watched the Apache fan the uplands over Baz. The Newts had just come back from Barge Matall that morning. *A fine place to come back to*, thought Shane. The Egyptian had gone to ground after the near miss at the mining camp, and his trail was cold, so the Newts had been assigned camp duty while the intel shop developed new leads. After a month in Barge Matall, Shane found comfort in camp. It was home, as sad as that was.

About 1600, the Apache pilot over Baz called "Red on fuel" and nosed for the valley entrance. Shane turned his eyes west. Just in front of him, a strand of razor wire delineated their precarious foothold in the People's Valley. Beyond the wire, a horseshoe hill fell into shadow. Pinks and reds painted the western sky, heralding the coming dark. Somewhere up the valley, an electric storm was underway. Its thunder rolled through the hills like artillery, except the rumble of a storm wasn't as crisp as the howitzers' echo.

Two serrated ridges turned black as shadows swept the land. Clotted memories of the Baz raid took hold of Shane, for those ridges seemed to be the witch's awful black teeth. The steel storm clouds were her cloak. *This is a little boy's fear*, Shane told himself, *nothing more*. He flushed the image from his mind and refocused on the horseshoe hill.

A 107 rocket whooshed in and exploded on the prow. Gunfire came on its heels. The day's second attack was from the horseshoe hill. Its rocks and gullies sparkled with muzzle flashes. A round splintered the timber over Shane. He crouched, gathered his mettle, and rose. With both thumbs, he depressed the trigger on a .50-cal and blazed away. There was much firing at machine-gun distances, but no enemy attempt to take ground. The mujahedeen got sloppy, or maybe greedy. They stayed on the attack longer than usual, which gave time for an artillery response.

Howitzer shells whirled into the valley like so many iron meteors. Ear-busting detonations followed—*Whump Whump Whump*. One shell smashed an enemy position. Their fire ceased. Howitzer shells kept falling. *Whump Whump Whump.* The attack sputtered. The Newts were ordered to clear the horseshoe hill. All fell quiet while the squads gathered at Shane's bunker.

Shane found Private Cassidy, who still carried the SAW, though he'd been campaigning for a machine gunner position.

As they waited together, Shane asked, "When they gonna give you a real gun?"

"Any day now."

"You gotta hit something first."

"The 240 spits 950 rounds per minute," said Cassidy. "What I need aim for? I got a strong back. That's what counts."

The platoon launched a sortie, moving in a wedge. It took fifteen minutes to cross the open and reach the foot of the hill. Forming buddy teams, the Newts fanned over the bomb-pocked slopes.

Shane and Cassidy wandered toward a gully that looked to be a good exfil route. They shrub-bashed for a good while and found the gully but no bodies in it.

Shane and Cassidy made quick time back to the foot of the horseshoe hill and waited. For a while, copper light held on to the horizon, and then it was dark. The boys slowly returned in twos. Altogether they'd covered a good square kilometer, but no one found any bodies. Sergeant Burch counted heads, and they all moved toward Holiday.

A fast march put the patrol back at the wire, where they bunched up, waiting to pass one small gap. Kneeling there, Shane heard two Newts whispering behind him. One hushed the other. Shane cocked an ear backward just in time to hear them say:

"It could be garnets."

"No. They're rubies. Now shut the fuck up about it."

It was Austin and Bloome. These two were battle buddies, meaning they were supposed to stick together and look out for each other. Shane remembered the night in the river when Bloome became separated from Austin in the reeds. Thinking on this, Shane decided everyone needed someone to look up to, but some made better choices than others.

———

The word *ruby* bubbled inside Shane for days. He got to thinking— the artillery shells had exposed gems, and now Austin and Bloome had a trove on the horseshoe hill. Indeed, mines pocked the whole province. Shane remembered the mine where Mohawk died, or rather, where Mohawk was murdered.

It was now early afternoon. The sun was furious, downright evil. Camp Holiday stood still. The valley did, too. Everyone was hiding from the heat. Below the prow, Shane found Austin and Bloome lounging against a log, enjoying the cone of shade cast by the prow. Austin was leaning back with his fingers laced behind his head.

Bloome doodled with a stick in the dirt. His sketch of giant tits was almost done.

Shane pointed at the tits, saying, "Bloome, are those your mom's?"

Bloome spat and kept drawing.

Shane came right out with it: "I heard ya'll found something on the hill the other day."

Austin said, "And what would that be?"

Shane said, "Stones."

"Plenty of them around."

"Rubies."

Austin twitched and covered it with a smile. "That'd be nice."

Shane said, "I want in."

"What are you talking about?"

"Cut me in. I'll help you."

"You been smoking that Hindu Kush ganja, huh, Shane?"

Shane glanced at Bloome, who kept his eyes on the tits in the dirt.

Balling his fists, Austin rose and took three quick steps toward Shane.

Shane said, "Maybe later," and retreated.

Bloome called after him, "Shane, we're taking bets."

Shane asked, "On what?"

Bloome said, "We're gonna see how long we can trick Billy into wearing an eye patch."

"What's the minimum?"

"Fifty bucks."

"I'll think about it."

———————

The sun retreated behind the valley wall. Shane moseyed to the Holiday chow tent for dinner. Plastic containers steamed with beans, greens, and meats. Shane ladled and slopped food high on his plate. Plywood tables were strewn about. Shane set his plate on one and pulled up an ammo crate as a seat. He gobbled his food under the cover of the dusty old canvas. Billy, the platoon's Afghan interpreter, came into the tent, grabbed a plate, and sat alone to eat.

Billy was from Kabul, the Afghan capital. He said he had been an electrician before the war. He joined the American side because he hated the Taliban, and because interpreters were paid better than electricians. Shane couldn't remember Billy's Afghan name. Billy never used it. He seemed to like the name Billy a whole lot more.

Shane picked up his plate, crossed the tent, and stood in front of Billy. "Mind if I join you?"

Billy looked up smiling. "Doood. Take a seat."

Shane set his plate down. "It's 'dude.'"

"Dood."

"Closer."

"I've been practicing."

Shane forked his chow and didn't look at Billy directly. Billy's left eye was crossed and a little lazy, never cooperating with the right. Shane never could bring himself to look at Billy square. Some of the Newts made fun of Billy's cross-eye. Corporal Austin in particular never missed a chance to ask Billy, "How many fingers am I holding up?"

Billy was just a few weeks from the end of his tour. For four months, he'd set the bar for terps. An impressed LT gave Billy a coin stamped with the Newt's unit insignia. Billy had fashioned the coin into a necklace. It now dangled from his neck as he ate.

Billy said, "I must tell you about Afghan negotiations, so you can be ready once I'm gone."

Shane said, "Go right ahead."

Billy wiped his scarf over his mouth and sat up straight, looking very pleased to be teaching an American. He said, "An Afghan will always start a negotiation with an offer that is high and wild. You must not get offended. You must be ready with a counteroffer that is also wild. And you must always, always negotiate, whatever it is.

A man who doesn't negotiate is a *bacha*, you know, a chai boy, a bitch."

Shane said, "'Chai boy.' I like that."

Billy stopped and looked across the tent at Corporal Austin. "Austin calls me chai boy. I do not like it."

Shane said, "Best not to stare."

Billy said, "Austin is all show. He scores a lucky shot one day and everyone thinks he's a real warrior. I know what he is."

Shane said, "Best keep quiet."

Billy said, "He'd just as soon shoot me as he would the mujahedeen."

Shane said, "If he wanted to, he'd have done it by now." He drew a long breath. "Listen Billy, be careful. I think some—" He stopped when he saw Austin stand and come their way.

Austin strode up, swinging his arms. There was tobacco in his smile. He winked at Shane and tapped the interpreter on the shoulder. "Billy, is that a picture of Usher on your shirt?"

Billy looked down at his screen-printed shirt. "Yes."

Austin said, "Usher is cool, if you're a chick." He laughed at his own joke. "I hear your tour is just about through."

Billy kept eating. He didn't make eye contact with Austin. "Yes, short time left."

Austin said, "You gotta be careful, don't want to get killed at the end."

Billy set his mouth crooked.

Austin said, "I haven't been real nice to you Billy, but we give each other a hard time here in Newt platoon. That's just the way it is." He looked at Shane again and smirked. "Billy, we want to send you off right for all the good work you've put in. Here's the thing, I was talking with Doc. Our brigade surgeon can fix your eye. There's a new medical procedure."

Billy kept his head down and asked, "Oh?"

Austin said, "We're helping terps get American citizenship, I'm sure you've heard. We can help with medical procedures, too, especially since you've been here in the People's Valley. Hasn't the LT told you about this?"

Billy raised his chin. "No."

Austin said, "It's a new laser procedure. Ain't that right, Shane?"

Shane froze for a moment. He nodded, allowing the sick joke to continue.

Austin eyed Billy again, "LT's probably too busy to give you the inside track, but Doc will. Go see him." Austin spun and left.

———

In the afternoon, Shane walked to camp headquarters, where the temp gauge showed 102. Shane ran his finger down the guard roster searching for two men. Austin and Bloome had a four-hour guard shift in Bunker 2, the position overlooking the horseshoe hill. Shane raced uphill to the bunker. At the back entrance, Shane kneeled and listened. The north wind whistled through the box. No voices inside. That was odd. Austin was never one for silence.

He announced himself, "Shane coming in," and ducked through the opening. A moment later, his eyes adjusted to the dark box. Bloome was sitting by himself, wearing a T-shirt under his body armor. His blond chin whiskers were the longest one could hope to get away with.

Bloome said, "You lost?"

Shane said, "My laptop shit the bed. I'm killing time. Say, what's the joke on Billy?"

With a sly grin, Bloome leaned back against the timber wall. "We tell Billy there's a new surgery to fix his eye and send him to Doc. Doc schedules the surgery for next week, and orders Billy to wear the eye patch as part of his preop. We got bets on how long Billy wears the patch. Pretty simple. Lots of fun. Bets closed last night. Sorry."

Shane said, "I suppose Billy had it coming." He looked around the bunker. "Where's Austin?"

"He went to take a crap."

Shane said, "I'll wait. I got something Austin needs to know."

"You can tell me."

"I'll wait."

Bloome tongued the inside of his cheek. "Suit yourself."

Ten minutes passed. The hot wind picked up. A faint clanking came with a gust. It sounded like metal on rock. Shane couldn't tell the exact direction.

He said, "Your boyfriend's been gone awhile."

Bloome glared at him.

Shane scanned the bunker. Each position had the same supplies. Five ammo crates were stacked in the corner. A radio and a speaker box were fastened to the wall. A bag for a thermal optic lay by the .50-caliber machine gun.

Shane asked, "Where's the pick and shovel?"

Bloome stared at the horseshoe hill. "Don't know."

Shane said, "I do. You need to cut me in, or I'll sit here for as long as it takes. I'll see that bastard coming back from your ruby stash. Then it's every man for hisself."

Bloome kept his eyes forward.

Five minutes later, Sergeant Burch ducked into the bunker with his black scarf round his neck. His face was flush from climbing the hill.

"Hey pups. Looky here." Burch revealed two logs of Copenhagen, a sought-after prize at their Spartan camp. "Got it off a dude in first platoon who just came back from leave. Well, he didn't know he gave it to me. Now I'm giving it to you. Make it last." Burch handed them each a log.

Shane ran his fingernail across the side of a can, opened it and jammed a mouse-sized wad in his lip.

Burch shook his head and looked toward the hills. He said, "Trail goes cold and we're stuck in camp like pogues. Jesus, I've watched *The Lion King* fourteen times. That cat Scar is such a dick."

He paused and lipped a pinch of tobacco. "More bad news:

The battalion commander is visiting tomorrow. You two stay away from the colonel. He'll show up in that helicopter of his and want to talk to *the men*. He'll come find you in a bunker, just like this, sit next to you, point his rifle at the hills, and look through his scope that ain't never seen a live target. He'll make real nice to get you to drop your guard, asking about whether you get enough food and time to call home. You answer him honest and I'll be sunk. So keep your distance. If he gets ahold of you, say everything is just right, all a soldier could ask for. You'd rather be here than home."

Burch paused and tugged his scarf. "Shane, what's the drill for battalion commander visits?"

Shane said, "Make myself scarce, Sar'nt."

Burch said, "Good boy. You got that, Bloome?"

"Roger, Sergeant."

Burch inspected the bunker's .50-caliber machine gun. First he flipped up the feed tray cover and gazed at the bullets with bliss. Then he keyed the head space and timing, and caressed the long barrel.

He was beaming at the gun when he said, "Boys, God hisself created the .50-cal. The Army changes guns more than my old lady changes hairstyles, but not the .50. The design is perfect. The .50 hasn't changed once, not once, since its inception. Only the Creator is capable of such beauty. Some boys call it finicky. That's a bunch of nonsense. It fires straight and true for the man who has hate in his heart. The muj, hell, they consider it an honor to be killed by the .50."

Burch rummaged through the bunker, looking for signs of laziness. "Shane, you on guard?"

"Negative, Sar'nt."

"Why you here?"

"Looking for Austin."

"Where's he?"

"Taking a dump. Been gone awhile."

"Never mind that. Shane, you come with me. I need bodies for a work detail at the prow."

Shane fired a long, hard look at Bloome.

Bloome gave him the bird and said, "Bye, sweetheart."

Shane spat in reply, picked up his rifle, and followed Burch down the hill.

———

In the evening, Shane headed for chow with his helmet swinging in his hand. Searing wind sent leaves and bits of trash skipping through camp. As Shane approached the chow tent, he saw Billy pull back the flap and stand in the doorway for a moment, silhouetted by a camping lantern inside. Billy stepped out to leave. A black patch sat over Billy's eye. He bumped into Shane and said, "Oh sorry. It's hard to see."

Shane said, "Where'd you get that eye patch, Billy?"

Billy pulled the patch and it snapped back on his face. "It's for the procedure. Doc said the muscles in my eye aren't attached right. A laser will fix it. The paperwork is already done. It's my reward for my service here."

Shane spat from the side of his mouth.

Billy went on, "The procedure only takes a half hour. I'll go back to Kabul a new man. It will be a joyous homecoming, just as I imagined." Billy thumbed his coin-necklace stamped with the Newt insignia. "I'll tell everyone about the good-hearted Americans."

Shane said, "I wouldn't go that far."

"Shane, is something wrong?"

Shane was quiet for a time. "It's…it's…I hope the surgery goes well. You deserve it."

"Doc told me it's a breeze. Don't worry."

Shane let him go off into the dark.

The next day, it was ninety degrees by midmorning. Shane lined up behind six others to dunk a towel in a bucket of ice water. Gasping, he wrapped the cold towel around his neck. Then he reported for sentry duty at the camp gate.

Shifts went like this: Two men held each position, rotating in off-set intervals to avoid vulnerability when changing guard. One man relieved another, and twenty minutes later, the second man was re-lieved. The roster in the bunker said Austin would be Shane's shift partner. After the shift, Shane would have twenty minutes before Austin was off. It was the best chance he'd get.

Austin stooped into the bunker right on time.

Shane greeted him, "The party's just getting started." Dusting a scope lens, Shane explained, "Radio chatter's been nonstop. The muj are feeling sporty today. I think they're gonna get their courage up during our shift."

They passed the time glassing the hills. The river terraces bloomed with corn and wheat. The rills that braided the middle slopes were dry. High above, dust curled off a windy ridge, and far-ther still, clouds hid the tips of the peaks. A storm-beaten summit appeared in a rift. For a few moments, the summit horn glowed in brilliant light. It was lost once more in clouds. Shane willed the clouds to come his way.

Austin said, "I heard we're about to start doing stupid shit."

Shane said, "Like what?"

"LT wants to arrest the Egyptian's wife."

"She might talk," said Shane. "What else have we got?"

"All I'm saying is, that ain't a real op. The other platoons are gonna laugh."

It occurred to Shane that they would. He didn't like the thought. Seeking a new subject, he said, "You should tell Billy about the joke."

Austin said, "I don't gotta tell him shit. And you'll keep your mouth shut."

Shane shook his head.

Austin said, "I've seen you palling around with that damn terp, all buddy buddy. Whose side are you on anyway?"

"It's mean. That's all. There's no need for it."

"Change your tampon, Shane. You're being a little bitch."

———————

When Shane's replacement ducked into the bunker at 1400, Shane left without a word. He strolled until the bunker was out of view. Then he galloped, crunching the gravel. When he reached Austin's tent he pulled in a few breaths and peeled back the flap. All the boys had gone on patrol after the attack. The tent was empty. There were neat rows of squeaky cots and salty clothes hanging stiff on the wall. The plywood floor creaked as Shane walked across. He studied Austin's cot for a few moments and then rummaged through Austin's gear. The hygiene kit was empty, so was the duffel bag. Shane checked the folded woobie and an empty carton of Camels. A pelican case held a set of brass knuckles and a bottle of Vicodin pills prescribed to one Gregory Miller. Shane had no idea who that was.

Shane picked up the guitar under Austin's cot and sat on the amplifier. Austin had brought the guitar and amp back from his midtour leave. He prized the instruments and played off-key most evenings. It was an achievement to get big items into camp. The corporal must have cut a deal with a Chinook crew chief. Strumming the guitar, Shane pondered hiding places for the rubies. Chances were that Austin hid them somewhere in camp, maybe in the rocks at the prow or under a tree. That made the places to look about infinite.

Shane picked up the light vest that Austin wore for guard duty. A chalky white powder covered the vest. It wasn't normal moondust. That was odd. Shane tore open the Velcro patches, rifling each nook and cranny on the vest. A bandana was wadded at the bottom of an ammo pouch. When Shane opened the bandana, something fell out and landed on the plywood with a *tink*. God damn. It was a bloodred ruby the size of a nickel. Shane snatched it up. The gem rolled around in his callused palm. Then he took out a can of tobacco, pulled off the top, and dropped the ruby in the can.

Shane set the guitar and the amp back under the cot and shot out of the tent. He ran for the prow. Once there, he squatted behind a holly and glanced about to ensure he was alone. He pinched the gem in the tobacco can, pulled it out, and held it to the sun. The gem split the light into a dozen rays, creating an infinite shine. In the red prisms at the core, Shane saw the house he would buy. It sat among live oaks on a hilltop. The house had big white columns. An air conditioner the size of a car cooled the house. Shane was going to crank that air conditioner at night and go deep in his blankets. The rubies would make it all real.

Shane tucked the ruby back in the can of tobacco. With trembling legs, he started down for lunch.

13

Camp Holiday
Day 118

A thick fog hovered over the People's River. Shane lined up for patrol at the camp gate, a large panel of sheet metal guided by a rail. There were stickers on the gate, mostly of rock bands, some doom metal. Shane eyed the stickers, amazed the others had thought to bring them. Just then, the mustached leader of first squad, Sergeant Martinez, walked to the gate, reached into his cargo pocket, and produced a sticker of the rap group Cypress Hill. Martinez peeled the backing from the sticker and slapped it on the metal gate. *Gong.*

Pointing to the other stickers, Martinez said, "Fuck all that." Then he joined the squad leaders in a huddle.

Today, the Newts were going south to Zangay village, home of the Khan, the head elder in the valley. The Khan's daughter was married to the Egyptian, and the Newts had a hot tip.

The LT gave the mission brief to the squad leaders beside the Holiday gate. "The Khan's daughter is at home for a visit. The

139

Egyptian might be there. If not, we'll arrest the daughter and hold her for a while to stir things up. She's about twenty. Shouldn't be too many women on the target to pick from. This raid is capture only. Not kill."

Shane looked to Burch and mouthed a question: *The wife?*

Burch shrugged his shoulders.

Fog over the river meant a humid day ahead. Shane sipped hot water from his canteen while the machine-gun teams readied their loads. Two men slid the gate open. A flock of crows waited outside to follow the Newts and collect the bounty. Spitting tobacco, Shane yelled "Sonsabitches!" and threw rocks at the scavengers. The unimpressed birds cawed and stood their ground, showing the violet sheen on their black uniforms.

Just beyond the crows was an Afghan boy dressed in rags. Seeing the boy, Shane reached down into his memories. There it was: the dim kid who'd found Harris's body. The dim kid picked through the trash pit outside the gate, pocketing things no one else would touch. *Being retarded is a tough break in a country where everyone barely survives*, thought Shane. The boy plucked an empty water bottle from the pit, examined it, and jetted for the river.

Shane whistled at him.

The dim kid stopped and turned.

Shane waved him over.

The dim kid stood there for a few moments. Then he approached, looking hesitant. Recognition came into his eyes. He smiled at Shane and spouted meaningless words with glee.

Shane unzipped his assault pack and dug out a ration of beef stew. It was Shane's favorite. He pushed the ration into the dim kid's hands. "This'll hold you over." The dim kid tugged on Shane's pant leg, smiling and making silly noises. Shane said, "Go on," and nudged the kid on his way.

He returned to the line of Newts inside the gate and sat against a sandbagged wall. The others from the squad leaned along the wall beside him, saving their legs and ducking the early sun. Billy the Terp came running down from the tents with the black eye patch on.

Corporal Austin said to Billy, "Shiver me timbers. Where's the buried treasure?"

Billy hurried on and fell in next to the LT.

The LT said, "Nice patch, Billy. Did you get poked in the eye?"

Billy said, "It's for the procedure."

The LT said, "Right." Then he was on the radio, cussing at the weapons squad for holding up their departure.

The delinquent squad fell in line after a few minutes. Shane yanked his charging handle and set off, afoot and so encumbered. The Newts kicked up moondust as they streamed from camp, creating the impression of a great army on the move, but they were far from that. They were just one platoon, dogged by a flock of nasty crows. They passed a rock formation crowned with spires like the broken masts of a ghost ship. Shane rounded a bend. He heard the enemy through his walkie-talkie. The muj reported the platoon's dust cloud, but it didn't sound like an attack was at hand.

The Newts halted in a row of terraces that staircased up from the river. Ducking into a crevice, Shane scanned the hills. Billy wandered by, picking red flowers that grew among the weeps in the terrace walls. Billy was singing a pop song. Shane didn't know the song's name, but he knew the chorus, and Billy was butchering it.

Corporal Austin heard it, too. He said, "Billy, you aren't singing it right. Now shut the fuck up."

The patrol opened ranks to fifteen-yard intervals and moved again. Another mile brought them into Zangay. They stepped into close quarters with no fanfare. Children fled through alleys where trickles of water had cut rills in the dirt. Slamming doors sounded across the hamlet. A rooster strutted into the village thoroughfare like it was the mayor. It clucked at Shane and then ran, half-flapping, and disappeared in an alley. Even the poultry was muj in Zangay.

They split and surrounded the Khan's compound. Stolen razor wire was fixed atop the outer wall. Wrought iron bars covered his windows. Shane climbed a ladder to a rooftop to watch for anyone squirting out the back door. The LT banged on the compound door. They waited. The LT yelled, "We'll blow this gate." Moments later, the door creaked open. Two squads of Newts poured inside and split and stormed through the rooms.

Shane looked left off the rooftop. Below him was an alleyway. Austin and Bloome were there, each on a knee, pulling security. They were less than ten yards from Shane.

After a time, Austin sat down with his back against the alley wall and wiped his brow. He said, "Tired of this heat and these bullshit missions."

Bloome said, "I don't care. All I can think about is them stones."

Austin said to Bloome, "The rock is getting real hard. The pick isn't working anymore. We'll need explosives to keep going."

Bloome said, "Burch knows demo."

Austin said, "Word's gonna get out if we start blowing stuff up. Then the LT's gonna come sniffing around. Next thing you know, he'll be givin' our stash to the fuckin' Afghans."

"So there's no more?"

"There might be, but we can't get 'em unless we go full miner out there. I'm done."

"What if we call for artillery on TRP Four again?"

"We'd need to have a direct hit," said Austin. "That ain't how artillery works."

Shane's heart thumped at the mention of TRP Four. Everyone knew the location of Target Reference Points for artillery. Shane now had the location of the rubies. Laughing to himself, he dipped out of sight.

Ten minutes passed before the LT emerged from the Khan's compound. Behind him came a woman in an aqua-colored burka.

A squad came out behind her, rifles half upon her, corralling her without force. From inside the compound came deep wailing. The Khan emerged, red-faced and decked in all black. He cussed the Newts with vigor.

The LT yelled the Khan back into the house, then marshaled the sergeants in the alley below Shane. He said, "Change the route back to Holiday. Follow the river trail. Use the trees to shield our movement." The LT pointed to the woman in the aqua-colored burka. "She moves in back with 3-7. I want a fire team on security detail. Don't cuff her. Just keep her on a short leash."

Third squad led out down the river trail, followed by first. Shane stood in the alley awaiting his turn. The narrow trail snaked ahead through crags and terraces, forcing the Newts one behind the other. So they marched with fifteen-yard gaps between men, to prevent multiple casualties from a blast or burst of fire. With these gaps, it took almost ten minutes from the time the first man stepped off until Shane did the same. The platoon was stretched across a half mile.

The walkie-talkie on Shane's vest crackled to life. There was an exchange of coded messages on the enemy frequency, followed by, "Don't hit my daughter."

Shane moved with his head on a swivel. Up ahead, the LT was busy on the horn, demanding air assets. From the sound of it, none were coming. Billy trailed the LT, once again picking flowers from the terrace walls and stashing them in the cargo pocket of his woodland cammies. Lost in his flower picking, Billy soon wandered out of formation.

A bullet ripped through Shane's sleeve. The round was supersonic, so it beat the sound of the ambush. Shane dove behind a pile of gray rubble. He popped up, sprayed the hillside and assessed his position. A walled house was one hundred yards ahead. Between the house and Shane was a long stretch of open ground. Billy was caught in the middle of it, all alone. There were puffs of dust around him. Billy wiggled behind a skinny tree. An enemy gunner dialed him in. Leaves rained down on Billy. Bullets shattered rocks. Twin RPKs converged on Billy, who covered his head with his hands.

Shane rose again, thumped a frag at the gunners, and ducked. Deep breaths kept him even. He tubed another grenade. A bullet snapped. A stone fragment speared into Shane's chin. Hot blood ran down his neck and followed his shirt collar. He was pinned down, but his cover would hold. Out in the open, Billy kept squirming behind that skinny tree. The trunk was maybe the width of a man's thigh. Billy jostled to one side and the other, and contorted to keep behind it. It was only a matter of time.

Shane made up his mind. He fired off three grenades and then ran, one hand pumping his rifle, and pushed out his heels and slid to a stop beside Billy. When the terp looked up, his coin-necklace glinted in the sun. Billy had splinters in his face. The patch over his eye was dusty when he looked at Shane in disbelief. Seizing Billy's collar, Shane ran for the walled house. His gear rattled and flapped against his chest, feeling like short punches. They'd gotten twenty-five yards when Billy tripped and slid downhill. Shane fired in three-round bursts while Billy got back to his feet. A train of 7.62 rounds zipped past. Shane grabbed Billy once more, and they ran for the house wall. Lead collided with everything. Rock shards stung Shane's face and hands. They dove behind the wall and landed on each other in a tangle.

Shane rose and helped Billy up. A group of Newts were slinging lead from the far end of the house. All was safe for now.

Billy said, "This eye patch makes it very hard to run."

Shane ripped the patch off Billy's head and threw it in the dirt.

Billy dropped to his knees and picked it up. "Shane, what is wrong with you? You've ruined my surgery."

"There ain't no fucking surgery. Jesus Christ, man. Why you gotta be so stupid?"

"It's real. I saw Doc do the paperwork. There will be a laser and I will be well."

"You make it so easy." With that, Shane resumed fighting.

The shooting went on for a long time. A couple dozen mortar rounds put a stop to it. The taste of high explosives drifted through the bottomlands. Shane leaned against the wall and glanced at Billy. Tears cut through the dirt on Billy's cheeks. Behind Billy appeared the guard detail on the Khan's daughter. They marched with solemn faces in a ring around the mute burka. When they came to a ledge, Corporal Austin shoved the woman from behind. She fell with a little grunt. Her burka settled in the dust. She calmly rolled onto her bottom and sat as if used to looking at men from the dirt. She said nothing.

Austin told her, "If your hubby starts shooting again, you'll catch a stray bullet, I'm sure of it."

A black lens climbed up the eastern sky. Darkness enveloped the lowlands as the Newts set out for camp once more. They marched in a staggered column, scanning the folds and shadows around them with IR spotlights. The scent of cordite drifted away. Jagged silhouettes framed the night sky. The air was clean. No pollution. When they crossed the concertina wire, Shane could see the stardust in the Milky Way. Just on the other side of the wire, the cap'n stood waiting. He locked the LT at attention. *Damn*, thought Shane, *no one did that garrison shit out in the field, even the cap'n.*

The cap'n pointed at the Khan's daughter and hissed, "I didn't authorize this shit. You were supposed to question the Khan."

The LT said, "Waste of time. Time to try something new."

"Let her go." The cap'n thrust a finger in the LT's face. "You start messing with the women and we'll have every tribe for five hundred miles taking shots at us."

The LT was quiet for a moment, his jaw tight. "Roger that."

The cap'n said, "Stupid," and stomped off.

A week passed. In the predawn dark, Shane woke from dreams of bloodred rubies and prepared himself for a run at TRP Four. When he reached the observation post, he found Kopeki nodding in and out of sleep. Shane settled in beside the M2 and watched alpenglow take hold of the distant peaks. Soon after, gray light marched down into the lower reaches and brought form to the horseshoe hill.

Pointing to the hill, Shane said, "Left my radio out there."

Kopeki asked, "Where?"

"TRP Four. I've gotta get it or I'll be sunk with Burch. Cover for me?"

"Yeah."

Rising to leave, Shane said, "Do me a favor—don't call for artillery on TRP Four."

"Hurry up."

At best, Shane figured he had fifteen minutes. He ran with his gear jangling against him and didn't stop until he reached the cratered slope that marked TRP Four. Standing there, he scanned the crevices and slabs. Where the ground slanted away, Shane found a pick and shovel beside a black rock that looked like book pages. Shells had ripped the book pages in half and there were fragments of red lying in the rubble. This was Austin's stash. Shane looked back. He was out of sight from Holiday.

Shane lifted the pickaxe and traced his hand over the black rock. He saw a whitish band that looked different from the rest. The band ran diagonal across the black rock and plunged into the earth itself. There were white scuffs in the rock that Shane believed to be Austin's pick marks. With all his strength, Shane swung the pick at the contact point where the white band disappeared below ground. The steel-hard rock rattled the pick in his hands. He swung again and rubbed the pain from his wrist. He kept swinging, the hard rock sending jolts through his body. Little by little, the rock came away in dust and thin pages. Shane bloodied his knuckles as he swung with abandon.

The rock was very hard, just as Austin had said. It was no use going on. Shane gave up for lack of explosives. When he set down the pick, there was a sparkle in the dust at his feet. Shane knelt. The sparkle was only visible when he leaned just right. *Was it?*

Shane scooped up a ruby. It was water clear and crimson in hue. The gem rolled in his bloody hand and seemed to catch fire in the morning sun. Shane screamed inside his throat. He looked at the coloring sky and the gem and his bloody hands. A beeping brought him back to the present. It was his watch alarm, telling him fifteen minutes had passed. He placed the pickaxe exactly as he'd found it and wiped away his footprints with the leaves on a branch and left. He stopped before crossing the wire and took one last look at the gem and stashed it in a can of tobacco. He'd never felt better in his life.

———————

Next morning Shane woke in his sour sleeping bag. He wiped the sweat from his brow and guzzled a whole canteen. At 0600, he slung his rifle and headed for breakfast. The smell of grease drifted from the chow tent, leading Shane in. Over in the corner, Billy was eating alone. At least he wasn't wearing that eye patch anymore.

Shane loaded his plate with tater tots, kicked a Red Bull can off an ammo crate, and sat with Billy. "Last day?" he asked.

"Yes. The bird is coming at lunch."

"We'll miss you, Billy. You done real good here."

"Thank you. I will miss the Newts." Billy thumbed the coin-necklace around his neck. "It's too bad about the surgery."

"Don't let Austin leave you riled. You made it out of here. Today, you're better off than me."

"I'm not done with Austin."

Shane said, "The platoon's stepping out for patrol at 1100. I got a guard shift at OP-1 this morning, so I'll be around. Once you've packed, I'll take any DVDs you don't want."

Shane spent the morning in OP-1. He remained on guard at 1100, so he missed the platoon's mission for the day. He figured it was for the best, since the mission was chickenshit. The Newts were taking the cap'n to Zangay to meet with the Khan. Word had it the cap'n would apologize for the arrest of the Khan's daughter.

Shane counted the Newts as they passed by one at a time, marching south. The Newts got smaller and smaller in the distance. A half mile south, they disappeared behind a rise. Only their dust cloud remained. The breeze soon whisked that away. Shane listened to the LT's radio reports until his guard shift ended at 1145.

Shane hunched through the bunker door, exited, and stood with his hands pressed into his lower back. Up above, he saw someone moving by his tent. One had to be on guard for booty hunters and buddy fuckers. Shane wasn't about to let one of the other platoons ratfuck his comrades' gear. He crunched across the camp gravel to intervene. The figure disappeared into Shane's tent. Shane ran. When Shane came to the tent, he slowed and crept toward three bullet holes in the canvas wall.

Peering through one hole, Shane saw Billy standing at the foot of Corporal Austin's cot. Billy said "Don't puss out" to himself, a phrase he learned from the Newts. He reached into his camo pants and pulled out a rusty screwdriver. The old electrician picked up Austin's guitar, unscrewed the input jack, and knifed the guts. Tilting the amp, Billy removed a panel and aimed his flashlight inside. Shane guessed he was going to cut the internal wiring. Billy set down his flashlight and reached into the box. He pulled out a black bag used for night vision goggles and shook the bag. The sound was that of rocks. Billy raised his eyebrows quizzically, ripped open the bag, and dumped the contents in his hand.

Billy sat there with his mouth wide open, gazing at a pile of rubies. In the far distance was the thump of a helicopter that would soon land at Holiday.

Shane sprinted for the tent door and burst through. The floor creaked under Shane's boots as he closed on Billy, who now realized he was caught.

Billy's one good eye settled on Shane's rifle. "Can I have them, Shane?"

The sound of the chopper was now a roar. Shane turned and saw a Black Hawk approaching Holiday. Dust rose off the landing pad. Battle flags over headquarters snapped in the haze.

Billy said, "Please, Shane. This is my country."

Shane drummed his fingers on his rifle. "Give them to me."

Tears welled up in Billy's eyes as he held out the black bag.

Shane reached out, took the bag, and held it at his side. He glanced at the chopper. The boys were running stooped toward the bird. A crewman was kicking ammo crates out the cabin.

Shane said, "You said I should start negotiations high and wild."

Billy focused his one good eye on Shane.

Shane said, "I'm messing with you, Billy. Take 'em and get your eye fixed." He tossed the bag into Billy's lap.

Billy smiled. "I will, Shane. I will."

Shane frowned as he thought of the white-columned house he'd never have.

Billy rose, peeled off his backpack, and shoved the black bag to the bottom. Then Billy ran for the tent entrance and pulled back the flap. Sunlight poured in. Just downhill, boys due for leave were hopping on the Black Hawk.

Billy stopped and marched back to Shane, then fished out the black bag.

"Shane, hold out your hand."

Shane couldn't help but stand there looking dumb.

Billy looked at the chopper. It was a blur in the swirling dust. "Shane, open your hand. Now."

Shane did. Flaming rubies dropped into his palm, not the whole bag, but a good handful.

Shane said, "Much obliged, Billy. I'll catch you later."

"Probably not."

Billy put the rubies in his backpack once more. Then he set his coin-necklace on the amp to let Austin know who the rubies belonged to. Billy ran for the chopper, climbed aboard, and dropped into a netted seat. He flashed a peace sign at Shane. The chopper took off and rattled away.

Shane glanced at the rubies in his hand. What to do?

14

Camp Holiday
Day 126

In August the high grasses turned to straw. Even the ninja leaves wilted in the heat. The trail on the Egyptian was still cold, but there was reason for feeling good. Shane was alive, and still had all his body parts. The paperwork came in for his promotion to corporal. The Newts gathered for the ceremony on the Holiday HLZ. Burch would pin on Shane's new rank.

Shane pulled off his shirt, because Burch insisted on doing the promotion as "bloody brass." Meaning, Burch removed the backing from the pin-on chevron and stuck the two metal points into Shane's bare chest. Using the heel of his fist, Burch punched in the points. When it was over, Shane's blood was smeared on his new rank. That seemed appropriate. Then Shane noticed his own ribs. He could count every one.

Corporal Shane—it felt good to say, but it quickly wore off. His responsibilities were the same, and there was a long way to go in the tour, too far to go. It seemed the valley was his home, and as the days passed, he was melded with it. Here was all the world and all of time, right here, between ridges arrayed like craving teeth.

Today, while he ate a hot dog for lunch, there was a vision projected onto the back of his eyes like a silent movie: He was climbing a hill, and his friends were getting clipped, one at a time. The funny thing was the raw silence. No shots. No explosions, screams, or struggling. One by one, the boys fell stone dead all around him. Shane kept moving up, and then he was at the top, under a crimson sky. He was alone, staring at the next hill he had to climb. Doom sat on his shoulders when he snapped out of the vision, for in the end, the last one on the hill might not even be him. He might fall in silence like the rest. Some found comfort in the idea of a quick death. Shane didn't. He was rattled by the possibility of having no chance to fight, or of simply hanging on a few moments longer and having those last thoughts, however insignificant. One second you had a whole lot going for you, the next it was all black. There was no comfort in that.

———————

Shane was gnawing a toothpick in the chow tent when the LT called the Newts to camp headquarters for a mission. Shane hustled across camp, then stood among the others, spitting and scratching himself in the plywood hut they called HQ.

The LT said, "We're going three klicks south. Our mission: Seize and hold the white house. The enemy has been quiet as of late. We need to provoke them, stir up radio traffic. We'll look for patterns on the enemy net. S2 wants to confirm whether the Egyptian is still in the valley."

All we have to do is sit there and draw fire, thought Shane. That was easy enough.

At noon Shane shouldered his ruck and topped off his canteens. He began the march with Newts at his front and rear, and the sun hard at work on his neck. After a quiet walk, the white house appeared. It commanded the high ground over Gorbat. White stucco shielded the exterior. Intricate woodwork laced big windows on the second story. The house was palatial compared to everything else in the People's Valley. The house also bore the scars of fighting. A mortar had smashed the north facade, revealing the building's stone bones.

Shane kicked a wood door and climbed to the second level with Cassidy on his tail. The "All clear" call emanated from the rooms. No one was home. Shane and Cassidy set up in a room with a walnut dresser in the corner—a goddamn walnut dresser. Back home, Shane kept his clothes in Tupperware shelving from Walmart. After rifling the dresser, he came up with a wad of rupees.

Shane licked his finger, counted the bills, then said to Cassidy, "I'm keeping this."

Taking a position at the window, Shane scanned his sector. He kept looking back at that walnut dresser. This house was far nicer than the Mississippi trailer from his childhood. He tried not to dwell on it, but the idea of luxury in the Kush really messed up his well-ordered world.

Private Cassidy sat on a twine cot nearby, shifting in his body armor. He hung well back from a second window opening, smoking like a freight train and stubbing butts on the dresser. Through the scope on his SAW, Cassidy surveilled the hills above the river.

They did not speak to each other, and soon, Shane found his mind drifting, replaying old battles and winning them all. Shane heard the voices of Austin and Bloome from one window over. They spoke with venom. Shane cocked his ear.

Bloome asked, "You think it was Billy?"

Austin said, "Of course. He left his necklace."

Bloome said, "Now what?"

Austin said, "Goddamn terp. I'll find him in Kabul and kill him in the street with my bare hands."

"Find him? He ain't exactly in the phone book."

"I'll find him."

"Doubt it."

Shane muffled his laughter with his palm. He was glad to have sent his rubies to Candy on the last mail bird, for there was no longer evidence of his involvement. Better still, Shane was now a corporal, and so beyond Austin's bullying. And after all, thought Shane, what recourse did the thief have when outdone by another thief? He thought no more of their revenge.

As the sun cooked the pleated land outside, Shane wet the windowsill with tobacco juice. Dipping and spitting was rhythmic and relaxing. It helped him think, and now it made him remember the letter from Candy. Shane rummaged in his pack and fished out the handwritten letter she'd sent two weeks before. Candy was good about sending pictures, but wasn't one for writing, so Shane planned to keep reading the letter until she sent another.

Shane opened it and read to himself:

Hey Danny Boy. I'm so empty without you. I barely drink anymore. I just get so sad when I do. Oh. I got the rubies. I took them to a jeweler on 14th. The rubies are totally real. Honest to God. The jeweler said 100 carats, maybe 60 grand in all, and I think he was lowballing me. Can you believe it? I put them in a safe deposit box. We'll save them for a house with white columns. I'll send you the deets soon. I'm being more careful with your pay, I promise. I've got one last purse and riding boots picked out for my birthday, but that's totally it, really. I'm totally gonna stop, or at least cut back, or do lay-away, or sell other stuff on Craigslist every time I buy something.

Candy also remembered his request. He had asked her to think about ladies who might be a good match for Cassidy. The letter had three names. They were all strippers.

Shane worked his tongue at a plug and grinned at his battle buddy.

Cassidy asked, "What are you smiling about?"

Shane said, "I've got some candidates for you, real good ones, top shelf."

Cassidy said, "Any chicks I know?"

Shane said, "Some of the crew that Candy brought to the platoon barbeque."

Cassidy said, "Let's hear 'em."

"You remember Porsha, right, how about her?"

"A goddamned pregnant stripper. That'll be the day."

"She's probably had it by now."

"And I'm supposed to be daddy?"

Shane asked, "What about Kiki?"

"C'mon, man. She's got droopy boobs."

Shane said, "You remember Delicious, right? How about her?"

"Naw, that girl's a head case. She told me she has to fuck her pain away. And I heard she tried to kill herself by driving her car into the lake."

Shane threw up his hands. "Beggars can't be choosers. Besides, if it doesn't work out with Delicious, take her back to the lake."

Cassidy grimaced. "Sorry, man. It's just hard to think about what comes after all this."

Shane said, "You sound whupt. Thought you wanted to be a gunner and spray some motherfuckers."

Cassidy said, "I know, I know. But it's like I'm living in dog years out here. I guess I wasn't expecting this shit."

"What where you expecting?"

Cassidy said, "I just thought it would be more…fun." He lifted his chin. "I appreciate you and Candy playing matchmaker for me. I guess the truth is: I'm saving myself for your mom. Boy oh boy, do I love me some trailer pussy."

A storm gathered in the distance. Lightning soon danced over the high peaks. Shane stared out the window, bored to tears. On a trail below the house, an Afghan boy appeared. He wore tattered clothes. Shane recognized the dim kid from the river.

The dim kid was alone, playing with a water bottle from the Holiday trash pit. The kid had tied a string around the bottle and was walking it like a pet. He climbed a terrace and spun his bottle in vigorous circles and dragged it over steps and ledges. So engulfed in his solo game, he didn't notice six village boys emerge from a house and circle him. The little boys taunted the dim kid, and then, without provocation, one boy ripped the bottle from the kid's hand. A moment later, the gang threw rocks at the dim kid. Nearby, an old man was tending his donkey. He stopped to watch.

At first Shane was mesmerized by the abuse. The dim kid was weak, and the valley had a way of handling the weak. Rocks kept flying. The village boys escalated their attack, launching fist-sized stones with all their might. They scored multiple hits on the dim kid, who tried to block the projectiles, but was too slow to protect himself. The village boys threw and threw their rocks from every direction. One rock hit the dim kid's face. He fell to the ground. Blood pumped from his eye socket.

With sandaled feet, the boys kicked the dim kid's stomach. They giggled as the kid bawled and writhed and rolled in desperation. Shane's innards twisted in anguish. He cringed with each thumping kick. The lynching proved too vicious.

Shane banged on the windowpane and scolded, "*Hey, hey.* Stop it. Stop it you little dirt-eatin' bastards."

The gang of boys paid no mind. Shane put on his warbonnet and barreled down the stairs. He was going to break up the lynching, and maybe punch a boy or two in the mouth. As Shane approached, the old man with the donkey took notice. He was an idle spectator until he saw the American run for the fight. That's when the old man leapt into action. He hustled straight for the boys. Shane did the same. The old man veered in front of him, blocked his path, and waved Shane away. He spouted warnings and curses in his guttural Pashto tongue. Shane didn't understand a word, but the Afghan's body language was clear. He was saying, *Stay out of this.*

Shane leaned against the doorframe of the house. With a bull's strength, the old man grabbed the boys by their waists and flung them off. Two boys kept on the assault, lost in their bloodlust. The old man stung them with a switch. It whipped and split the brown skin on their necks. They ran off, yelping. The dust settled. The old man looked content as he returned to his donkey. In the dirt, the dim kid lay bleeding. No one took notice but Shane.

A few minutes passed. Shane made up his mind to check on the dim kid. Just as Shane stepped from the door, the kid picked his head up, looking dizzy. He swayed as he came to his feet. The kid held his bloody eye with one hand. With the other, he picked up his pet water bottle, now crushed from the fight. The kid moped away sobbing, blood running through the fingers over his eye.

Shane couldn't help himself. He ran and stopped the kid, then unzipped his emergency medical pouch. Shane knelt in front of the casualty and ripped open a roll of gauze. It was a bad idea, and Shane knew it. His bleeder kit was reserved for treating his own wounds.

Cassidy yelled from the window, "Shane, don't use your kit on Humpty Dumpty! What if you get hit?"

He had a point, but Shane couldn't leave the kid in such a state. He gave Cassidy the finger. He palmed the kid's eye to stop the bleeding. All the while, he whispered, "Easy, boy, easy." The frightened kid calmed down after a bit, and gave a bright smile as Shane flushed the wound and folded gauze. Shane placed his field dressing over the injured eye and handed the kid a new water bottle to play with. The kid wandered off.

Shane whistled as he climbed the house steps two at a time, plenty high on himself. He found Cassidy shaking his head.

Cassidy said, "Watch out, everyone. Saint Shane is gonna put this fuckhole of a country back together again."

Shane spit tobacco juice in front of Cassidy.

Cassidy said, "I don't know if you deserve to wear that war-bonnet no more. You think you're an Injun with that thing, but I'll tell you what, Injuns took scalps. They didn't hand out Band-Aids."

Shane spit tobacco juice into Cassidy's lap.

15

Camp Holiday
Day 126

Sergeant Burch was the only Newt absent from the white house mission. Burch was due for midtour leave, so he stayed at Holiday. The chopper would come for him at last light. Burch had time to kill. He walked to the prow, set a radio at his side, and cranked the volume to monitor the action on the Newt frequency. Then he put his feet on a sandbag and opened a WWII memoir.

He read about soldiers bound for the war in Europe. They crossed the Atlantic on sturdy ships colored gunmetal gray. The voyage took weeks. A long land journey followed. Thousands moved together by rail, truck, and foot to the battlefields. They learned survival tricks each step of the way. The soldiers also readied themselves for what they might see, how they would act, and what they could lose.

Burch reckoned things had changed a bit since then. When the Newts flew to Afghanistan, they got on commercial planes with pretty flight attendants. The medics passed out tranquilizers, and the Newts fell into dreamless sleep. They landed at Bagram Air-field fifteen hours later, groggy and jet-lagged. From Bagram, they boarded helicopters for the People's Valley. The flight was two hours. Total time from peace to war: twenty hours.

Right after dusk, the long-awaited helicopter flew over Holiday. The others scheduled for leave jumped to their feet and shouted about the things they would do. Burch remained silent, standing apart from the rest. The bird landed. Burch climbed into a seat and glanced at his trembling hands. He was frightened, though not sure why.

Just like his trip into the war, his trip back to the States was swift. One day he toiled in a far-flung mountain valley. It seemed he'd always been there. Next day he was home in the North Dakota plains.

On his first afternoon back home, Burch loaded his wife, Eliza-beth, and nine-year-old son into their old Z71 crew cab and drove toward town for a movie. Burch zoomed down a one-lane county road going 75 in a 40 mph zone, thinking, *Rules? Fuck the rules.*

Elizabeth screamed, "Slow down. What's wrong with you?"

Burch huffed and eased off the accelerator. A black truck was on their tailgate a minute later. It was so close Burch could see the bugs on the grill. Blind turns in the road kept the pickup from passing. The driver would surely keep at it until Burch pulled over.

Burch stomped the brake and T-boned his truck across the road. Behind him, the pickup screeched to a halt. Burch eased the door open and moseyed toward the black truck.

Elizabeth yelled, "Babe, please, not in front of our son."

A fat man with a trucker hat got out of the pickup with a crowbar.

Burch held up his palms and said "We're cool, we're cool" be-fore punching the fat man's throat. The trucker hat flew as the man dropped. Two turkey vultures watched from a fencepost. Burch wrapped callused hands round the man's neck and slammed his head onto fresh asphalt. The vultures shrieked with delight. The fat man's eyes bulged from their sockets as the back of his head went soft.

Burch launched the man's car keys into the waist-high grass on the roadside and whistled on the walk back to his truck. He took the wheel with blood on his jeans and locked eyes with his crying son in the rearview.

Burch asked the boy, "You still want to watch *The Incredible Hulk*?"

Elizabeth didn't speak to Burch the rest of the day. At seven in the evening, they sat for dinner in the kitchen. The oak table squeaked under Burch's elbows. Elizabeth set a pork chop in front of him. Burch cut neat squares and took a few bites without looking up.

"Where's the boy?" asked Burch.

"He's in his room. I told him to stay there."

Burch forked another bite and looked up at last. "What's this about?"

Elizabeth said, "I keep seeing that fat man's bulging eyes." She drew a breath. "You're still in the war, I'm sure of it."

"I'm right here."

"You know what I mean. I need you calm while you're here. I'll think of some things for us to do, things like we used to do. Don't worry about planning nothing. I'll take care of it. Enjoy yourself these next two weeks."

The next morning, Burch woke before the sun and crept down to the living room to his recliner. Potato chip crumps were scattered across the seat. Sweeping them away, Burch said, "That boy's a goddamn slob." He sunk into his recliner and reveled at the silence. He'd just started to decipher his thoughts when Elizabeth came into the living room. She asked if he wanted to fish the reservoir by Williston. She'd drive. He said no. The next morning, she came in and asked if he wanted to go buy hunting gear at the Cabela's in Dickinson. "No." The morning after, she asked if he wanted to drive the loop road in Theodore Roosevelt National Park and see the buffalo. "No."

The next time she came in, Burch was ramrod straight in his recliner. His fingers clawed the old leather. He was staring at the TV screen, but it wasn't on.

Burch said to the TV, "You followed me here."

Elizabeth dropped her purse. Burch jumped in his chair. He shot a look at her. She wore a blue sundress and petunias in her hair. Sweat peppered her brow. Elizabeth shifted on her feet for a moment. She picked up her purse and pivoted to leave. In the doorway she stopped and whispered to herself.

Burch turned back to the blank TV screen.

She came and touched his hand. "Hey babe, let's get some fresh air. How about I drive you to the Lil Missouri?"

Burch didn't answer.

She was tender with her voice. "Honey, let's go to the river."

Burch said, "I'm busy."

"Honey, please, let's go to the river."

"Why?"

"It's our spot."

Burch exhaled. "Fine."

As Elizabeth drove for the river, Burch rubbed the bite mark on his forearm. Only a faint red oval remained. Elizabeth pressed a CD into the radio and hummed along with Mary J. Blige. Burch thumb-punched the dial. Off went the radio. Elizabeth mustered a half smile that was almost a wince.

"Tell me a story," she said.

Burch glanced out the window.

"Honey?"

"I ain't got no stories you wanna hear," was his reply.

"What about that boy Shane you like so much? What about him?"

Burch said, "He's coming along." The humming tires filled in the rest.

The road narrowed and they followed it down to the Little Missouri River. When they were in high school, Burch used to drive her to this same cottonwood grove along the Little Missouri. The quiet spot was hidden under tall, tan bluffs. No one else knew of it.

Elizabeth parked by the water and unrolled a wool blanket on a sunny patch of grass. She caressed the blanket next to her and said, "Remember this blanket? Come lay with me."

Burch didn't take notice.

She said, "The boy ran for two touchdowns in his last game—a left sweep both times, no one touched him. He's that fast, just like Pops."

She droned on. Burch never sat down. The tall bluffs above the river held his eyes. Deep gullies ran between the bluffs. Ash trees threw shadows in the folds.

Elizabeth asked, "Babe, are you okay?"

Burch shook his head. "This is a bad spot."

"It's our spot."

Burch kept his eyes on the bluffs. The river bubbled along.

"It's a bad spot. You shouldn't have brought me here."

She spun away. "Okay, babe, let's go."

———————

Leave was draining. After two long weeks, Burch hid weakness as he said good-bye. Elizabeth made him promise to call once settling in.

Burch said, "Fine, but stop being so fucking clingy."

Two days later, Sergeant Burch returned to the People's Valley. As he flew over the west wall in a Black Hawk, he spied the battered camp clinging to the hillside by the river. He rolled his shoulders and sat up straight as a lodgepole. Burch sensed energy off the mountains, and he could see it, too, like a heat shimmer. An image welled up in his mind. There he was, wading into a dark pond. On the pond's shore were stalagmites in glistening columns. He saw himself naked and white against the black water. He'd gone chest deep when the bubbles started. A dozen fumeroles rose from the depths and belched sulfurous gas in unison. The tail of something monstrous slapped the water and the wave rolled and shoved him down and he was stroking for the surface when he snapped out of it.

16

Landing zone, Camp Holiday
Day 140

Corporal Shane stood on the edge of the helicopter pad awaiting Burch. The chopper flared over Holiday. Shane squinted through the dust. Burch hopped off the bird. With a broad smile, Shane jogged forward and shook his hand. Burch shouted something against the rotor noise. Shane kept on smiling and nodding his head in agreement. He had no idea what Burch said, but hell, Shane guessed he agreed. Then he trailed his squad leader into their tent.

Shane said, "Glad you're back, Sar'nt. We've been running the valley like assholes."

Burch dropped his ruck on his cot and pushed fresh batteries into his night vision goggles. Then he stood with his thumbs hooked in his belt. "Anyone been hit?"

Shane said, "Couple new guys in first squad, Powers and whats-his-nuts... Temple."

"No matter. They were buddy fuckers."

"Buddy fuckers always get their due. Say, you coming with us this afternoon?"

"Where we going?"

"Balay. Shit just got hot. The Egyptian was hiding out in Pakistan. He came back when he heard we bagged his wife. Some said we beat her up. Now the Egyptian's called a war council in Balay. We're gonna break it up, see if he got any slower from vacation."

In the afternoon the Newts were gathered at the Holiday gate. Shane thumbed his bolt release and eased back the charging handle to ensure the bullet was seated.

Burch said, "Move out."

The patrol set off down the trail for Balay. In front of them corn terraces fell down in ten-foot steps all the way to the river. A cool snake of wind followed the water and sang through the stalks. After twenty minutes, the patrol left the trail, skirted a hillside, and passed through a ribbon of forest. Shane slid behind a trunk. Shutting one eye, he peered through his optic at the approach. Beveled slopes and water-sculpted land lay ahead. Balay was in the distance—a few flat roofs in a mess of crags. He set off again. The trees faded into rocks and sparse cover. The walkie-talkie on his shoulder came to life with enemy traffic. Shane quickened his pace while the muj exchanged coded messages.

The enemy commander said, "Tariq. Do you have the donkeys?"—code for *PKMs*.

"O'. The boys are with me on the hill."

The enemy commander said, "Very good. We're in the place. Do you see the children?"—code for *Americans*.

"O'. Should we wait for the others to find the rock?"

His commander ordered, "No, do not delay."

"The plan was to wait, and let the others find the rock."

"The People are watching. Loombara is watching."

"Haste brings casualties."

"This is not yours to decide."

A long radio silence followed. "As you like."

Enemy bullets ripped into the platoon from a ridgeline two hundred yards above. Shane dove for cover and emptied a magazine in three-round bursts. He jammed a frag in the tube and squeezed it off and saw a tree fall in the explosion. Burch snarled orders. Everyone had a pull as the Newts established fire superiority, which meant spray and pray for a while.

The muj were closer than usual, but their aim was wild and they were clustered together. A nearby hill was unoccupied. It would have given the muj enfilading fire. They had missed a perfect position. To Shane, the attack was amateurish. The enemy B-team was on duty.

Amidst whizzing rounds, Burch pulled his black scarf up to his eyes. "Shane, cover me."

Shane fired off a couple more frags, thinking Burch was heading for better cover. Burch dove into cornstalks fifty yards distant. Moments later, he appeared at the foot of a draw. He picked through the rocks, up and up, until he hit the ridge. Then he scrambled unseen across the spine.

The closest Newt machine gun was twenty yards from Shane. He ran for it and dove over a rock wall, knocking off the top stone. Kopeki was there firing, his birth control goggles steamed from the heat. Kopeki leaned left and right, gun in his shoulder, while his 7.62 rounds swept the entire ridge.

Shane said, "Adjust fire. Burch is on the ridge."

Kopeki said, "What?"

"Burch is up there. Adjust fire north."

"What the fuck?"

Shane cleared the rock wall again, ran headlong, and dove into the corn terrace. He saw a swath of broken stalks left by Burch. Shane streaked through the corn. He hit the draw and climbed, scrabbling for roots, rocks slipping away underfoot. When he came to the ridge, he hunched and scanned. Burch was stalking just below the crest. The Newts had adjusted fire to the north. Shane sprinted, hurdling rocks, and dove behind a pine just short of

Burch. It would do no good to surprise him. Shane yelled to get his attention. Burch didn't hear or didn't care.

Shane crawled forward, but not fast enough to catch up. He called out again, "Sar'nt. Sar'nt." Burch dropped to his belly and elbowed to a rock. A PKM barked from the other side. Burch sprang over the rock and fired from the hip. The PKM went silent. Then Burch thought himself a panther. He jumped off a twenty-foot cliff toward another muj. His legs buckled and he rolled downhill, clawing the dirt to stop. He got up to run and fell. He got up again, dragging one leg, and fell once more.

Still, Burch crawled forward, groaning, like a zombie crippled by an ax. He ripped a pin and lobbed a frag over a rock steeple. The explosion blew one muj into a boulder. The mangled fighter crawled off, but the blood trail gave him away behind a holly. Burch dove onto the fighter, bit his bearded face, and ripped off his cheek. The two wrestled into death rolls, making all manner of primal sounds. They exchanged short punches. More death rolls. Burch struck with a headbutt. The fighter's nose exploded in blood. Shane raised his rifle to take a shot. The bullet might hit Burch. The bayonet flashed in the sun when Shane drew it from the sheath. Shane crept forward, hoping to get a clean stab into Burch's opponent.

The fighter pushed a hand with two missing fingers into Burch's face, drilling his thumb into Burch's eye. Burch reared back, howling in pain, and bit down on his opponent's thumb. *Chomp. Chomp. Snap.* The thumb came away. Blood spurted and frothed like champagne. Once more, the fighter clawed at Burch's eyes. With his Kevlar dome, Burch headbutted the fighter over and over. Blood splattered. The fighter's head turned to pulp.

Burch never spit out the thumb. Shane stood there, bewildered, until he was shoved from behind. It was the LT, running for Burch. The Newts had finally caught up. The LT yanked Burch off the carcass. Burch turned around with a fist ready for the LT. Cartilage and plasma lathered Burch's face. He rose, hopped on one leg and fell down, wincing.

Just then, the enemy commander gave orders through the walkie-talkie, "They got Tariq and two others. Move from the place, *now*."

With complete calm, Burch whispered into his walkie-talkie, "Sadboy, this is your old pal Burch—you're next."

The LT smacked the radio from Burch's hand. "Pull your shit together, Sergeant. We don't say anything to the muj."

Burch said, "Naw, LT, it's cool. We go way back."

The radio lay on a pile of holly leaves, hissing with static. It beeped. The enemy commander came across, "Burch. You are a pooh-see. Pooh-see."

Standing again, Burch cackled and clapped his hands in applause. "I taught him that." He reached down for the radio.

The LT shoved Burch, who hopped twice on his good foot and landed on his face. Using both arms, Burch scooped a pile of holly leaves and threw them in the air. They showered over him. Burch laughed and laughed.

The LT stood over Burch. "Stand down, Sergeant." He turned to the Newts and said, "Prep the litter. We're going back to Holiday."

Burch asked, "What about Balay?"

The LT said, "I'm sure they've already bailed. And what would we do with you?"

"Leave me," said Burch. "I'm good on my own."

The LT said, "You'll do no more talking." Then to the litter bearers, "Let's move."

Shane grabbed the front right pole of the stretcher. Three others joined in. By the time they descended the ridge, Burch's ankle had swelled three times over. The last obstacle was a terrace wall. They lifted Burch over. As the sweaty litter bearers grunted, Burch launched into song:

"Take me out to the ball game. Take me out to the crowd. Buy me some peanuts and…"

Burch sang it the entire way back. Well, not the entire way. He switched to "Swing Low, Sweet Chariot" a half mile from camp.

As the Newts crossed the wire, the walkie-talkie beeped again, "Ameriki. Ameriki. I saw what you did to Tariq. My name is *Habibullah* and I am the messenger of Allah. My valley is your grave."

Shane clicked off his walkie-talkie.

Burch was confined to camp so his ankle could heal.

FALL

17

Camp Holiday
Day 163

T he heat eased in late September. The days shortened little by little. Shane woke on a crisp morning and cleaned his rifle with a salty sleeve ripped from a T-shirt. It was not long before he snapped the rifle pieces back together and checked the chamber, then slung the rifle over one shoulder. He exited the tent and splayed on a rock to deepen his tan. Cirrus flitted across the cobalt sky. The rock was still cool from the night, and it contrasted nicely with the sun's heat on his stomach and chest. Shane was just browning when the LT marched up.

The LT said, "Shane, my RTO's heading home with broken vertebrae. I need someone sharp to hump an extra radio, just until we get a replacement. You'll be trained at HQ."

"Yessir."

The RTO ran satellite and FM communications for the platoon, meaning he carried ten pounds of batteries, a collapsible satellite antennae, and a shoebox-sized radio. Shane wasn't pumped about humping the extra weight, but at least he'd be plugged into everything going on. Without a radio, he was reliant on Burch. After what he had seen on the ridge above Balay, Shane wanted distance from Burch.

Seven days in a row, Shane reported to camp headquarters for training. HQ was a plywood hooch buried in sandbags. Laminated battle maps adorned the inside walls. Blue computer screens cast pale light on the maps. In the corner, a diagram showed the enemy's command structure in the region, complete with photos of muj captains and lieutenants. The Egyptian was at the top.

Inside HQ, Shane saw the machinations of the officers. At present they were focused on their best source of human intelligence, an Afghan they called Smoky. Back in the spring, Smoky split from the mujahedeen ranks after being passed over for lieutenant. The American officers had given Smoky a satellite phone, which he had used to pass the intel on Barge Matall.

The latest call from Smoky was troubling. Smoky said the Newts' detainment of the Egyptian's wife had gotten the People riled. Rumor had it the Newts had raped her three times. The Egyptian wanted revenge. He would array his forces and attack Holiday once the muj had stockpiled enough mortars and rockets for a proper fireworks show. The staging area for fighters, 107 rockets, and two new mortar tubes was Tiger Village.

Hearing all this, the cap'n ordered a cordon and search of Tiger Village. Tiger was the American name for a hamlet at the back of the valley, a place no one had ever been. Beyond Tiger, the land broke into soaring peaks that no one lived in or fought for.

———

Shane was already at camp headquarters when the LT called in the Newts for the mission brief. The boys trickled down from the tents in threes and fours and formed a half circle around the LT, who wore his ball cap with the American flag on the front.

The LT said, "Boys, we've talked about Tiger Village before. This is the epicenter of the enemy. The Egyptian is down there, gathering men and weapons to overrun our lovely little home. We'll punch first. We're going down there with every swinging dick we've got. We'll cordon and search and destroy any resistance."

He pointed to a wall map with icons and arrows showing the order of battle, and went on: "The plan for Tiger Village is simple. We'll infil at night and take blocking positions on the high ground above the village. The Afghan army will come in behind us and clear the village from north to south. The muj won't fight in the village. Chances are they'll run straight into us. Whatever happens, the hills will give us plenty of work. Our source says the Egyptian has a base camp above the village, somewhere on top of Tiger Mountain. He's got two new mortar tubes at the camp. Let's be clear—if the Egyptian gets those tubes zeroed on Holiday, we're gonna be in a world of shit. And last thing, Chinooks will sling in jeeps for this op. We'll have plenty of firepower if things go sideways."

Second platoon had already volunteered to drive the jeeps. *The wine-cooler killers*, thought Shane. But he was just fine with that. The Newts were better on foot.

From the crowd, Sergeant Martinez, the mustached leader of first squad, asked, "Who's 3-7 for this op?" He wanted to know who'd fill in at platoon sergeant.

The LT said, "I'm not sure yet. We'll need someone with sand."

Shane's trepidation grew as the mission drew closer. The prudent choice was to wait and hit Tiger Village when Newt platoon was at full strength. A litany of combat and terrain injuries had the Newts limping along with thirty men. They were well below the original count of forty-three. Nine-man squads now had five or six. It meant less sleep, more gear to hump, and, worse, less firepower in gunfights.

Casualties in the sergeant ranks had hit the Newts like a sledge-hammer swung into an old fence. NCO replacements were hard to come by, because fine sergeants were years in the making, and Army production facilities couldn't keep up with battlefield demand.

The biggest hole in Newt platoon was the platoon sergeant. Vasquez had been injured by an enemy bullet in early September. His vest stopped the round, but the bullet cracked a rib. So he was on the mend and not going out. The next ranking sergeant was Burch. A bum ankle kept him laid up at Holiday. Most supposed it was for the better. Burch needed time to sort himself out. So Martinez, the tattooed, mustached first squad leader, seemed the natural choice.

One red evening at Holiday, Shane and the boys gathered at a burned holly above their tents. It was their usual meeting spot for rumor milling and grabassing. They speculated on who would be platoon sergeant for the Tiger Village mission. Sergeant Martinez was there with his shirt off and tattoos so numerous the skin couldn't be seen. Martinez had a full head of jet black hair that he kept slicked back with pomade jelly.

Some of the boys were saying to Martinez, "You're up, Sergeant" and "You're the man." Others said, "I heard they're moving 2-7 into the platoon" and "Naw, Top is gonna take over."

Martinez dismissed all that, and instead insisted on telling a story to everyone gathered at the holly. Shane had already heard it. In fact, just about everyone had heard it twice. The story began with Martinez taking a dump.

"Bro, Bro…no shit, there I was, pushing out a ferret, one hand wrapped around a holly so I didn't have to squat. The muj started rockin' their PKMs. Bullets all around. I didn't have time to wipe. I didn't even have time to pull up my cammies. I waddled to an AT4, pants around my ankles. I squeezed one off and got a direct hit. That makes me the first grunt in history to fire a bazooka with my wang blowing in the wind."

Out of the dark, a headlamp approached the burned holly. It was the LT. All the boys went quiet and shuffled nervously. It wasn't every day an officer showed up at their hangout.

Martinez said, "Hey sir, you lost?"

The LT said, "Martinez, you're the platoon sergeant for Tiger Village."

Martinez, "For real?"

The LT said, "Can you hack it?"

Martinez said, "Fuckin' A."

The LT said, "This is varsity shit, don't fuck it up," and walked off.

Martinez turned back to the boys. Grinning from ear to ear, he said, "Stand aside, li'l bitches. The pain train is coming through."

———————

After a week of planning, the Newts gathered under a crescent moon for the trek to Tiger Village. Shane had done himself up real scary. His face was painted with black and green stripes. Crow feathers protruded from his helmet. He'd tied his warbonnet around the outside of his Kevlar. The snake scales glistened in the moonlight. He was guilty of two significant uniform violations, but fuck, what were they going to do about it—make him go to Tiger Village?

Shane had gotten the nod to walk point for the platoon's movement into the deepest, darkest corner of the valley. He'd do it without Burch's watchful eye. Shane crossed through the wire, shaking with exhilaration and dread. Early in the tour, this task would have gotten him killed, but now he believed himself up to it.

He marched south at an even pace, his mind on the route details, seeing each leg and all the decision points in sequence. The rest of Newt platoon followed him. Taking the jeep road south, Shane crept through a handful of sleeping villages. Martinez bounced through the column, cracking jokes, offering encouragement, and nipping at stragglers.

Shane chuckled as Martinez ran around with a herding dog's energy. The sergeant was easy to spot in the dark, because he never shook that Crip limp from growing up in LA. In the end, Martinez would cover twice the march distance. The young sergeant seemed to be reveling in the challenge. Maybe his zeal would rub off on everyone.

As point man, Shane was the tip of a long spear. Four more platoons, two U.S. and two Afghan, marched behind the Newts. A caravan of jeeps bearing supplies and heavy guns trailed the five platoons. Shane marched for eight hours, three times leaving the road and going overland to shorten the foot march. Stopping at the predetermined rally point, he studied a long rib. He picked a line of ascent and climbed, kicking steps into loose gravel. He topped out. A hundred yards south, windows shined with fading moonlight. Roofs ran flat across dark slopes. They'd reached the objective. The Newts formed three groups in silence and set out for blocking positions to trap the enemy in the village.

At 0530 came the predawn light, when everything is gray and has no form. The Afghan soldiers were supposed to initiate the search right then, but they got lost in the formless ether. Sitting in blocking position one, Shane watched the Afghans march in circles. It was a tragic parade with Helen Keller as grand marshal. Martinez must have seen the parade, because he sailed down from blocking position two and put the Afghans on the right approach.

The search began as the sun touched the flat roofs of the village. The Afghan soldiers cleared houses for a couple hours, but found no resistance. Shane saw no one fleeing. The company scouts were down in the river channel, set deep in the valley bedrock. They reported a sighting as the Afghan army cleared a nook in the village: About twelve armed fighters with scarves over their faces ran through the crevices along the river. The black-clad fighters fled into trees straddling a draw. The scouts got off a few shots, but didn't hit anyone.

Scanning the green ribbon, Shane reported to the LT, "Too much dead space. Can't see shit. They're gone."

The LT radioed the scout platoon leader: "Great work. You guys are all over it."

The Afghan army cleared the village and surrounding barns for two days. They found no guns, muj, or resistance. The elders said they had never seen fighters near the village. They had no idea who the Egyptian was. They didn't let foreigners into the valley.

Typical, thought Shane.

———

The grand finale was scheduled for the third day. Newt platoon was ordered to clear Tiger Mountain and locate the Egyptian's camp. Shane and his group vacated blocking position one and picked their way down to the village. It was midafternoon when Shane pushed open the metal door of a compound with the LT at his side. Afghan soldiers were in the courtyard of the compound, lounging, smoking, and laughing it up. A few were chewing the fat with village elders. It looked to be a family reunion.

Standing in the courtyard, Shane raised his binos and adjusted focus on Tiger Mountain. The slopes of the monolith rose four thousand feet to a tabletop covered in dense timber. Palisade rocks jutted between the trees. Lower down, on the mountain's east slope, was a rope-equipped slide made of timber. It must have been two thousand feet in length. There were pulleys at each landing.

Pointing at the slide, Shane said, "LT, look, it's a muj waterslide. I heard they run a waterpark here in the summer. Down go the women, *whish*, nipples showing through wet burkas." Shane shook his head. "Shit, wish we were invited."

The LT said, "It's a log flume."

Shane said, "It's a waterslide."

Things could get messy on Tiger Mountain, so the LT spoke with the Afghan commander in the courtyard, trying to recruit an

Afghan platoon to join the Newts. The commander, a potbellied fellow named Nabi, resisted with enthusiasm. The mission would require serious exertion and good tactical discipline: no fires, no chai, no bullshit. Nabi wasn't keen on any of that.

The LT called Nabi a chai boy and that seemed to settle the matter. Nabi agreed to join the Newts and bring thirty-five Afghan soldiers.

In the sapphire light after sundown, they started the four-thousand-foot climb up Tiger Mountain. Shane led the movement, keeping the log flume to his left. The lower grades of the mountain were scree fields—vast areas of small, loose rocks—which formed as freeze-thaw cleaved the country rock and erosion grated the rest. With each step up, the scree gave way and settled, erasing half the progress. One step forward, a half step back—so went a scree march. And some steps triggered tongue-shaped slides that a man could ride downslope.

Shane slogged up the gravel treadmill, stiff in the knees, his rucksack pulling him back. It took an hour to climb the first seven hundred feet. He was skirting a rock outcrop when, below him, one of the Newts lost his balance. There was a metallic clink of man and rifle spilling into rocks, followed by a grinding racket as the man zoomed downhill. The same sound came minutes later. Then, a third man fell. Hours ticked by, just like that, the boys falling, sliding and fumbling in the dark.

Finally, the grade leveled and the Newts topped out. Wispy clouds licked the mountain summit. Wind howled through the conifers. Sweat glazed Shane's brow and cheek and ran down his back from the stiff pace set to reach the top by first light. Shivers took hold of him as he rested in the trees. His hands tingled, then turned wooden, then he had no hands at all. He was sitting there, miserable, when Martinez buzzed past like a humming-bird.

Martinez asked, "Wind blowing up your skirt?"

Shane's manhood was in doubt, so he sprung to his feet. At that moment the sun burst through the trees. The rays were warm on his face. Shane told the sun, "Good mornin'. "

The Newts and Afghans began clearing the summit. They moved by bounding: Machine-gun teams took set positions while the others swept in line to flush the enemy from the thick forest. They bounded one hundred yards, then moved up the machine guns and did it again. Here and there in the forest, trees gave off slow, sad creaks as the stiff wind twirled their crowns. Needle clusters adorned the tree branches, like big green fists on skinny arms. The wind shook those branches, too, giving the forest a quiver that made Shane jumpy.

The first mile in the forest was hard, sweaty business. Get up, run, drop; get up, run, drop. Shane was panting when he came to a patch of bare ground matted with footprints. He called for the LT. The best tracker in the valley, Burch, was laid up at camp. Shane wondered if he was ready to follow sign by himself. He was studying the footprints when the LT appeared.

Shane said, "LT, I'm thinking no one good is up here. Maybe we follow these tracks."

The LT nodded. "Right now, you're Burch." He pointed to the footprints. "Think you can?"

Shane was incandescent. "Yessir, too easy."

The Newts formed a lazy arrow with Shane at the head.

Shane hooked his fingers into a can of Copenhagen, lipped a wad, and told himself, *Slow and steady.* He locked on to the tread and followed it north. The footprints were darker than the bordering soil, and that meant moisture, fresh tracks. There were concentric circles left by black high-tops, or, as Burch called them, "Muj Air Jordans." Shane followed the prints for a mile before finding a copse where the group had halted.

In the dirt were two small divots a foot apart: *bipod legs.* There was a large divot three feet back: *the buttstock.* It was the imprint of a PKM. At ten-yard intervals to the left and right, Shane found knee marks. Shepherds and woodsmen didn't spread out and rest on one knee, but fighters did. Shane was now certain he was on the tracks of a muj patrol, so he kept on the prints.

The understory thickened. Prints braided here and there in the deadfall. Shane followed the tracks past a hummock. A single set of prints hooked right and backtracked to the top of the hummock in ambush, a classic countertracking measure. *Christ,* thought Shane, *these muj aren't playing.* Shane reconnected with the main trail and marched on.

The forest grew black. In the gloom, Shane lost the tracks a few times and clover-leafed to find them again. Reaching a maze of deadfall, Shane paused and guessed at the enemy route of travel. Fifty yards ahead, he saw a straight line in the brambles, just a foot above the ground. There were no straight lines in nature, so this called for a closer look. With his gun at the high ready, Shane approached the position.

That was when he found the enemy camp hidden on the north summit. Shelters and foxholes were shrouded by understory and towering spruce. There were trenches and aiming stakes and positions with overhead cover. The hide was built for fifty fighters, give or take. Sign indicated some had gone north, but Shane lost their path a short distance from camp.

He returned to the search. In the camp center, Shane found a cluster of half-buried boulders the size of houses. Two leaned together, creating an overhang. One side was improved with a rock wall. It occurred to Shane that the stone bunker was the camp headquarters. Inside he found handheld radios and then the big prize: two Soviet mortar tubes. He heaved them out and set them against a tree. He called for the LT and Martinez, saying, "Looky here."

Martinez came up laughing. "Nice."

The LT snapped photos.

Martinez said, "Thermite should do it," and pressed an incendiary grenade into Shane's hand.

Shane pushed the grenade down one tube and watched the mortars melt into white-hot puddles.

The Newts took up positions around the camp and rotated eating chow. Shane wore a triumphant smile as he ripped open beef stew. Tobacco spit hung off his field beard, but he didn't care. At that moment, he was floating. Skillful tracking had led him to the enemy camp and mortar tubes. He couldn't wait to tell Burch when he got back to Holiday.

Just to Shane's right, Sergeant Martinez plopped down against a tree and took off his helmet. He scooped pomade jelly from a tin can and greased back his jet-black hair. He'd picked a strange time for grooming.

Shane said, "Can't see much point in that, Sar'nt."

Martinez ran his fingers through his hair, saying, "Ay bro, I got to keep this Chicano mane tight for my muj girlfriend down in Gorbat. Remember when that sniper pinned us down near the river? That was no sniper, bro. That was my Gorbat chick slinging rocks. She was pissed 'cause I told her she was getting fat. That's the last time I tell her the truth. She's got a hell of an arm, bro, hell of an arm." Martinez scooped out more pomade. "I'm gonna stop and see her on our way back to Holiday, say sorry. No more talking shit about her stretching out that burka."

Shane chuckled and dabbed his food with the tiny bottle of Tabasco that came in all the rations. On the right side of his mouth, Shane worked a wad of chew. He was going to leave it in for the meal and have a nicotine dessert.

Martinez pointed at the bottle of hot sauce. "That's getting old."

Shane said, "I used to put this on everything growing up, especially catfish—that's some good eatin'. But now, I'm sick of it. I suppose it's just habit."

Martinez asked, "Remember the magic sauce the Pagans put on the rice in Barge Matall?"

Shane said, "I do. I was so warm and peaceful after eating it. I could've been back in the womb. Burch tried to get the recipe, but the Pagans told him to get fucked."

Martinez said, "The Pagans were nicer to me."

Shane set down his chow. "What do you mean?"

"They showed me how to make the magic sauce."

"How'd you get them to do that?"

"Me and those villagers, we had some things in common."

"Like what?"

Martinez said, "My mom is from a village outside Mexico City, up in the mountains. When I was a *pobrecito*, she never missed a chance to tell me we were full Aztecs, not a drop of Spanish blood. Now don't get me wrong, my mom is Catholic. She goes to church on Sunday and always wears her cross, but she still carries the Aztec religion inside her. You know, the weird shit, where they worship snakes and kill virgins."

Shane said, "That's trippy."

With a shrewd smile, Martinez went on, "Yeah, bro, I thought that Aztec stuff made for good ink." Rolling his sleeve, Martinez exposed the snake tat on his forearm. "A Pagan saw this one, and he thought it looked just like one of their gods. We had a lot in common. *Primos*, right? So he showed me the magic sauce."

Shane asked, "Just like that?"

"Just like that." Martinez scooped up more jelly. "Well, I had to give him my gold necklace, too. I got the recipe for the magic sauce now. Too bad we don't have the ingredients at Holiday. This tour would be a lot more fun."

When night fell, the high country wind was rollicking in the moonlight, bringing the citrus scent of pine. The platoon bivouacked in the enemy camp. Shane settled into a two-man fox-hole and lined the bottom with pine branches for warmth. He sat on the branches and gulped water from his last canteen, saving a few ounces for the descent to the village.

Then, with the LT standing over him, Shane set his radio on the foxhole brim and switched to battalion net.

The LT asked, "The enemy, you think they went north?"

Shane said, "Yessir," and passed him the hand mike.

The LT reported the camp details to the battalion S2 and concluded, "The enemy's gone north." Newt platoon had only enough water to make it through the night and back to the village. After that, they'd exfil for Holiday in one mass of 190 men and ten jeeps bristling with heavy guns. Things were looking up.

As the night wind tired, the cap'n came over the horn. "Can you confirm direction of enemy exfil?"

The LT said, "Some went north. Their sign fades after a half mile. Too much rock."

"I'm guessing they're heading down the north ridge," said the cap'n. "New mission—follow the north ridge back to Holiday. Try to flush the Egyptian."

It would be a two-day walk. The Newts needed more water to make it.

The LT asked, "Can we get a bird to drop water?"

The cap'n said, "No helicopters available. They're supporting the other battalions down south."

"We've got no water source up here. What's the plan?"

The cap'n said, "Stretch your water. You can build solar stills. Check the field manual."

Solar stills?! thought Shane, they'd be lucky to get a few ounces like that. The cap'n seemed to think this was a survival TV show. And who the fuck carried a field manual? Shane punched the foxhole wall, rubbed his throbbing hand, then punched it again. Shane shook out his arms. After a few breaths, he found self-control.

At 2100, Shane watched the thirty-five Afghans gather around their platoon commander, Nabi. They argued in whispers. Nabi rubbed his potbelly. The LT and Martinez joined the fray and argued with Nabi and each other. After a good bit of back and forth, Nabi waved them away and turned to his men, "We go." The Afghans picked up their rucks and hustled off into the dark. Shane wasn't too sure what to make of that.

Just then, Martinez motored by.

Shane asked, "Sar'nt, where're the Afghans going?"

"Fuckin' quit. They're walking out with the jeeps."

"Quit? So everyone's going back to Holiday but us?"

"We're Newts, bro. First in, last out."

"Fuck me."

18

Summit of Tiger Mountain
Day 181

As the wind picked up, there was radio traffic. Three enemy leaders spoke to each other in the dark, their voices strained between quick breaths. Their signals came from the north. The LT called for artillery, directing it onto Tiger Mountain and the rises overlooking the road into the village. A salvo of Howitzer shells came in and landed in brilliant explosions that lit the dark, revealing the endless and indifferent mountains. The summit flats around Shane quaked. Rocks sloughed off the rim. The understory went aflame. Another flurry of shells landed beside the road. Fires crawled all over.

Shane sat mesmerized by the twisting flames, letting his thoughts drift. A gust of wind raked the forest. Embers cycloned toward the gemmy stars. Shane figured this is how a war is supposed to look, darkness and fire and magnificent terrain. Far below, flashes and tracer streams pierced the dark. Booms shook the quiet hills. It was an attack on the column of jeeps and dismounts heading back to Holiday. Booms went back and forth.

Wild streams of red tracers reached toward the stars. And there was Shane, watching the embers, glowing bullets, and explosions mixing in the dark. As the shooting died, frenzied reports came over the radio. The convoy had taken casualties but fought through. Now they were an hour from Holiday. Lucky bastards.

The morning sun was flecking the tree bark. Most of the fires had run full and fast and died with the daylight. Inside his foxhole Shane spread a map across his knees. He examined the approach to the north ridge and thought of the mission. By marching the north ridge, they were supposed to flush out the enemy. Simple enough. Ideally, there would only be a small group of fighters, perhaps just the Egyptian and his entourage. They'd flee like quail from dogs. The others at Holiday could then pursue. But the size of the enemy camp said otherwise, and the Newts had just lost their thirty-five Afghan counterparts. The solar stills were no help. Shane didn't like any of it.

Shane scribbled compass headings on his hand, shot an azimuth, and picked a summit on the skyline to guide him. The Newts moved out in a wedge formation, everyone behind Shane, the charred grass crunching as they marched through the forest.

Soon Shane came upon a cliff where the north ridge fell away from the summit. He toed the edge and stood with his chest out. The high peaks of the Himalaya lay east, fuzzy looking, the way big mountains do when strong winds whip up their snow. Shane eyed the southern horizon: mountains beyond mountains. He turned north. Far beneath lay the Blue River tablelands, dotted with brushwood.

Shane climbed into a rock outcrop with the wind fanning his neck. He sat with his elbows on his knees and his binos aimed at the north ridge. The march would be a descent, but there were plenty of obstacles; cliffs, benches, and sawteeth ran the spine; gendarmes and chimneys were sprinkled in for fun. He'd need to edge the side slopes once in a while.

After careful study, Shane set off, threading the north ridge, hopping to one side and the other, dodging cliffs and rock statues with the Newts behind him. They scrambled and scuttled and balanced over slanting faces. The sun climbed. The wind fell to a whisper. On they went, descending two thousand vertical feet, before coming to a gully. It was a rotten little thing that slashed down to the mountain's apron.

One by one, the Newts traversed across the neck of the gully, their hands grasping for solid holds, their feet slipping beneath them in the steep gravel. Once Shane had made it across, he looked back to the others, finding Bloome in the middle of the crossing on an outcrop of solid rock. There was a cracking sound and, without warning, the outcrop beneath Bloome gave way. Bloome slid, riding the gravel down thirty feet before coming to a stop. Bloome was unhurt but the rocks kept on down the gully, spinning and bouncing and exploding into dust. The noise was tremendous.

Enemy radio traffic erupted, "Ameriki still here. Ameriki on the mountain. The group is small. They are alone. Avenge Tariq. Avenge Tariq."

Everyone looked at everyone. Shane could have shot Bloome on the spot.

Bloome climbed back up the gully and all the Newts finished the crossing, their faces now tight. They continued down the ridge, the hills growing arid, transitioning from subalpine forest to high desert plateau. The shade was disappearing, too, along with any cover and concealment. Shane halted the patrol and stood, with a field beard, cracked lips, and dirt-smeared cheeks, wrapped in the enormous landscape. Enemy radio traffic had picked up. They seemed to number in the hundreds. The progeny of these mountains were bristling for a fight.

The LT and Martinez came trotting up.

Shane pointed to the sun and told them, "If we keep heading down in the daylight, we'll lose the high ground. The muj gain the tactical advantage."

Martinez countered, "If we move back up the ridge, we'll be out of water again by nightfall."

Night temperatures were around freezing, but the heat still reached into the nineties by afternoon. They'd be crippled in eight hours without more water. The helicopters were in another province, supporting an operation by a sister battalion, so they couldn't bring the necessary help.

This was a quandary, and it was the LT's decision. The LT scuffed his heel on a rock for a while. "Hasty defense. We find cover and wait for nightfall. Let the enemy attack uphill if they want. They can't knock us off this rock. Once it's dark, we regain the advantage and keep heading down."

The squad leaders passed the word. The Newts fanned out on a little rise adorned with hollies and turtleshell rocks that could be used as gun positions. It would have to do. Shane shopped around for a defensive position. Just off the crest, he found a little depression that would give him a head start on digging. Drawing his e-tool, Shane hacked at the schist. It was flaky but still offered plenty of opposition. *Clank clank clank* went his e-tool in the sun.

Around the hill, Shane saw the others going deep. The gathering fight was lost on no man, and decent foxholes would make all the difference on the naked ridge. The Newts now stabbed the rock with complete abandon.

Meanwhile, Shane kept tabs on the enemy radio traffic. The muj had massed in large numbers. The one who seemed to be the enemy commander was breathing hard into the radio, as if climbing a hill. The commander worked himself into a frenzy giving orders and broke into a nasally chant:

O son, one word I have for thee,
Fear no one and no one you flee,
Draw your sword and slay any man,
That lays poisoned eyes on our land.

By late afternoon, storm clouds had gathered over a black massif in the distance. The massif's north face was gilded by shining white glaciers. Ribs of black rock ran vertically between the glaciers, giving the whole mountain a zebra-like appearance. Around Shane, the slopes lay bland, save the little clusters of holly. The sky was clear blue, and the sun cooked his Kevlar. The mujahedeen radio chatter kept up, so the Newts called for mortars, which arced up from their distant camp like angry rainbows, but with no gold at the end—just a burst of iron. Many mortars soon plumed in the hills around the north ridge.

Shells kept falling. Martinez picked a spot for himself about twenty yards from Shane. They moved rocks together, rotating between their positions. Horn-faced lizards darted from under the rocks and flitted off. One lit out so fast it made Shane jump. He screamed at the sudden appearance of another, and chased a third little devil with his e-tool, but to no avail. Shane had just come back when Martinez lifted a microwave-sized rock. A tan scorpion popped out. The creature wasn't deadly, but its sting would send a man down the drain for a while. The scorpion rose, stinger up, primed for a strike on any intruder. Then it changed its mind and scampered into a rock pile.

Martinez pointed to the next rock. "Shane, your turn."

"Shit."

After a good bit of work, Martinez came forward. "I've invented a new weapon to tame the valley. It's called shitpalm. Like napalm, but with poop mixed in." This kicked off a rather thoughtful discussion between Martinez and Shane about delivery methods and the proper mixture of diesel fuel and feces.

A troubled look crossed Martinez's face. He scratched his beard and said, "One ingredient is still missing. We'll need something sticky so the shit clings to everything and burns." A lightbulb seemed to go on under his helmet. Martinez reached into his vest, pulled out a can of pomade hair jelly and held it up with a triumphant smile. "Here's your sticky gel."

Shane remembered when he first arrived in the Stan. He had respected the mujahedeen. He was even fascinated by them. Now Shane wasn't sure. What he did know was that he found comfort in the shitpalm fantasy. He imagined the valley covered in shit, the Egyptian covered in shit, everything brown and ruined.

————

An hour before dusk, the Newts took stand-to posture: everyone behind their gun in a foxhole. The enemy radios went quiet. Not one bit of traffic. It seemed like they'd quit the battlefield all at the same time. Shane rubbed his rattlesnake headband for luck. Maybe the muj ran out of time, he thought. They don't want to pick a fight in the dark. They'll try again tomorrow.

Whoosh. An RPG streaked over Shane with a red ring glowing behind the tip. It could have been a javelin thrown by the devil. The grenade exploded in a tree. Bullets were hitting all around. Shane breathed in relief, but not at the muj having missed the RPG shot. The anticipation was over. No more waiting. They would soon decide who owned this ridge.

The enemy fire had kicked off from the uphill side, the same ground Shane had earlier walked. Shane twisted uphill and fired back. About that time, two more enemy positions joined in from different angles, one within a hundred yards of Newt platoon, the other from a nearby ridge at the same elevation. The effect was enemy fire from 360 degrees; a lead blender, one might say. The enemy commander had positioned his men with great skill.

Newt machine guns punched back. The gunners had dialed up the rate of fire to the maximum setting. Their tracer streams looked continuous, and they nearly buried themselves in brass. The enemy fire intensified; 7.62 rounds cracked and winged past Shane's position. The enemy bullets came in short, controlled bursts, showing discipline. The few gnarled hollies around Shane shook with piercing lead. Ninja leaves fluttered down in the haze. Shane's rifle was suddenly knocked from his hand. It wheeled in the dirt. A round had just hit the magazine.

Slapping a fresh mag in the well, Shane rose and searched for a target. Just a hundred yards ahead, there was a muzzle flash. Then another started up, and then another. His rifle punched into the meat of his shoulder as he rotated between targets. Two more muzzle flashes started up. There seemed to be a thousand muj coming at them. Shane kept cussing himself as he cracked off rounds. He wished he would have dug his foxhole deeper. The enemy was coming in fast.

White light. A searing wave enveloped Shane and slammed him down in his foxhole. The smell of burned hair invaded his nose. Star clusters twirled in his eyes. Then it was dark.

When Shane came to, he was buried in dirt and rocks from the explosion. Someone was standing on his foot. It was a muj, wearing black high-tops and an olive drab fighting vest. Shane lay still, holding his breath, and unsure where his own gun was. Fortunately, his bayonet was sheathed in his vest. The fighter standing on his foot was bound to notice him. Even if the fighter believed Shane dead, he'd sink a few bullets into Shane's brain to be sure. Shane had to act.

He sucked in a long breath, slowly unsheathed his bayonet and lunged forward. The fighter felt Shane move and swung his gun around. Shane saw his face. Under his cheek was a tear-shaped birthmark. In a nanosecond, Shane pushed through cloudy memories. It hit him. This was the teenager from Baz—Habibullah. His mother, the witch, had those awful black teeth.

Just as the barrel came round, Shane stabbed Habibullah's trigger hand. Habibullah howled and dropped his AK. Shane drew back for another stab. Habibullah parried the blow with his good hand. They jostled back and forth, panting and grunting. The teenager was small, but he found the strength of desperation. His hot breath touched Shane's cheek before a rock caught Shane's heel. Shane tipped backward, waving his arms to stay upright. When Shane fell, he mistakenly flung the bayonet over the foxhole lip, then landed on the AK. Shane half-rolled to get hands on the gun. Habibullah pinned him and came down with a knee thrust into Shane's crotch. There was a rush of terrible pain. Momentarily crippled, Shane closed his eyes and readied himself for the end.

It did not come.

When he opened his eyes, Habibullah was gone. Shane dug his M4 out from the rocks and rose. Just to his left, Martinez sprang from a foxhole and sprinted across a gauntlet of open ground toward the retreating enemy. *Holy shit*, thought Shane, *the new platoon sergeant has lots of hate in his heart.* Another explosion hammered the rocks. Shane ducked back into his hole. When he popped up again, Martinez had disappeared in billowing dust.

Enemy muzzle flashes danced all over the hills like the lights of angry fireflies. The fight teetered. Now fifty yards out, the enemy launched a volley of RPGs and followed with another frontal assault. Shane had never seen the enemy do such a thing. As the muj flashed between rocks and trees, the Newts picked up their fire. The assault stalled. One muj fell down midstride. His legs just quit working, and he skidded to a stop headfirst in a bout of spasms. Another dragged him backward. Centering his front sight post on the fighter, Shane jerked the trigger. His tracer bounced off a rock. *Damn, just missed.*

The enemy rallied and tried again. Shane could make out their bearded faces. They were baring crooked teeth and screaming. Shane held down the trigger and screamed back, "*Ahhh.*" His barrel rose as thirty rounds jumped out. Again, the Newts chased back the muj.

Mortal screams came through the dust, just to Shane's flank.

It sounded like Corporal Austin. Shane popped smoke, elbowed out of his foxhole, and low-crawled through the rocks. Forward he went through the maelstrom, unsure who held what ground. It was best not to think too much, just commit, he told himself. *Ping. Ping.* Two rocks shattered into his face. Shane was in someone's sight picture. He chucked a frag, wormed backward, and fell headfirst into his foxhole before his tossed grenade exploded. Someone kept screaming, but Shane couldn't muster the grit to leave his hole.

Shane dumped five magazines and six frags before he called, "Red on ammo." By that time, the enemy was slowly pulling off the attack, as if reluctant to concede a loss. The muj closest to the platoon slunk behind the ridge and raced down gullies toward the villages. They were still too close for mortars, so Shane counterattacked with his last three grenades.

Thunk Thunk Thunk. The frags arced through the scarf of smoke over the battlefield. Explosions cropped up and down a gully. Other Newt grenadiers joined in. *Thunk Thunk Thunk.* Tendrils of smoke drifted up. The enemy reported casualties through their walkie-talkies. The fighter named Habibullah was panting commands. He ordered the others to help him carry away two dead.

Shane heard moaning off to his right. With the roar of the gunfight gone, he recognized the voice of Sergeant Martinez. Shane crept through smoke toward the moaning. He first came upon a corpse half tangled in a holly. A cracked helmet lay in the leaves. It was Austin. Blood leaked from the back of his head. He had shrapnel wounds galore. Branches snapped when Shane yanked Austin from the tree. Shane draped a poncho over the body, the only ceremony that could be rendered. A light wind lifted the edge of the poncho. Shane set two rocks to hold it down.

Bloome arrived and looked at the poncho over his battle buddy. He asked if it was Austin. Shane said yes. Pain and disbelief passed over Bloome's face. Then Shane saw something he didn't expect. There was supreme relief in Bloome's countenance, as if a weight had been lifted. There was even a flash of joy. Maybe Bloome was now liberated from the bully corporal's tyranny.

Shane picked up his rifle and, leaving them, ran at a stoop. Fifteen yards from the tree, he saw Kopeki lying on his back with his neck cocked funny. The lenses in Kopeki's birth control goggles were cracked a dozen different ways. The late day sun glinted off the glasses.

The soul-buying private was dead.

Shane kneeled at Kopeki's side. Rubbing his own singed beard, Shane tried to come to grips with what had happened. He hated seeing guys get torn up in a fight, and not just because they were great soldiers or they were his friends. There was another part: The same great burden had to be carried on fewer shoulders.

Shane kept having that crazy vision about it. Right then and there, it came again. He was climbing the hill, his friends were getting hit, one at a time, falling stone dead in raw silence. He gained the summit and stood all alone. The sky was bloodred. *Focus*, he told himself, *focus*. He was back on the ridge.

A short distance away, Shane found Martinez crumpled on thin brown rocks that looked like dinner plates. Martinez was on his side, cringing. His face was gray, his brown eyes red with tears, but he wasn't crying. Martinez was stoic in his pain. Coughed-up blood freckled his face. A bullet had struck the back of his right thigh, burrowed up through his torso, and exited his left shoulder. Doc Soto was kneeling over him. Ole Doc was working hard, but he couldn't hide the shake in his hand. So many organs had been hit.

In all previous wars, Martinez's wound would have been certain death, but the Newts were fighting in the twenty-first century, and medical care for the American infantry was at its finest. Martinez had a chance if the Newts could get him off the ridge within sixty minutes, the so-called golden hour.

The LT came running and dropped next to Shane, "Shane, get the captain on the horn."

Shane dropped his pack, double-checked the radio frequency, and adjusted the antennae. He passed the hand mike to the LT.

"Attack 6, this is 3-6. We got two KIA and one WIA, urgent surgical. I need a dustoff at my position."

"Can you move the WIA to the jeep road for ground exfil?"

"Negative. He'll be dead on arrival."

"Is the HLZ clear?"

Shane winced at the question. The bird wouldn't come if the landing zone was hot. They were no longer in contact, but the enemy might be waiting. Shane wondered if the officer would lie.

The LT said, "HLZ is clear."

"I need you to think real hard about this. We lose a bird, it's gonna be a bad day."

"Affirm. Send medevac to my position."

The cap'n said, "Standby." The radio was silent for a time. "Three-six, medevac is enroute with Apache escort."

The LT said, "Roger that. Thanks, sir."

As they waited for the dustoff, Shane lent a hand with Martinez. Blood was spurting from the entry wound in the sergeant's thigh. Doc whispered, "Severed artery," as he pinched the wound and stuffed in coagulant gauze. Martinez's blood hit the chemical and thickened into gobs, which oozed into creases between the dinner plate rocks.

Shane pressed the heel of his palm into the wound on Martinez's shoulder. Hot blood poured through Shane's fingers, and before long, he felt Martinez's strength fading. It was strange to feel a man dying and not just see it. Shane pressed harder. Blood kept coming. Shane's arm shook from exertion.

Martinez glanced up, looking despondent. He rasped, "Getting killed is for suckers."

It was the LT who answered, "I've seen worse. Just be cool, Martinez."

"How did I do, LT?"

Martinez was bleeding to death, but asking for the LT's judgment on his brief stint as platoon sergeant.

The LT said, "I'm proud to call you our platoon sergeant. You *are* Newt platoon. Now save your energy, Kermit, don't worry about nothing else."

"Tell the boys I'm sorry. I didn't wanna let anyone down."

The LT asked, "What are you talking about?"

"Now I'm out and you're short another guy. I made a mess." Martinez paused for breath, which he drew in shallow gasps. "Tell everyone I'm sorry." That was the last thing Martinez said before shock took over.

Forty minutes passed before a helicopter came pounding over the platoon, raising a cloud of moondust. The chopper lowered a flight medic on a basket. Shane pitched in as they packaged Martinez on a litter. The litter-straps had to be cinched down tight or Martinez might fall out midlift. Shane ratcheted down the straps while Martinez lay unconscious and limp. Then the chopper cranked its winch. Martinez went up, but the flight medic forgot to attach the stabilizing wire. The furious down-prop spun the basket. Martinez whirled round and round faster than the rotor blades. Shane socked the flight medic in the face, yelling, "Mickey Mouse motherfucker."

The remaining casualties were evacuated with textbook precision.

An hour later, darkness swept over the north ridge. The Newts gathered for the movement to Holiday. Shane made sure to collect Habibullah's AK-47. He tied it to his rucksack and then descended with legs of lead, his steps clumsy, as if his feet belonged to someone else. The one bright spot was his gear. It was much lighter than before. The only ammo he had was a half clip in the AK and one magazine of 5.56. If shit went sideways, he was going to save the last bullet for himself. In the distance, the fires they set on Tiger Mountain were still aglow. The flickering startled Shane here and there, but the walk was uneventful. As Shane climbed the last hill for camp, he kept seeing Habibullah in his mind. He wondered if the teen had been a fighter before they raided his village.

The ravaged platoon entered camp, passing without formation through the open metal gate. Shane made for the ammo bunker to refill his magazines. Then he stumbled for his tent, just wanting to put on clean socks. Outside the tent Shane found Burch sucking on a Lucky Strike. Burch had a radio in his lap and a cooler of Gatorade set aside for the squad boys.

When Shane saw his squad leader, he felt safe again. Funny thing—it was like the kids had been in charge for a while, and Dad had just come back.

Burch tossed Shane a Gatorade and took him by the shoulders. "I heard about the camp. You did real good, little buddy."

Shane replied, "I just did what you taught me, Sar'nt."

"I'm putting you in for sergeant. Already spoke with Top. He said we can waive the time-in-rank requirement for battlefield need."

"That means a lot to me, Sar'nt."

"You're going to be my alpha team leader." Burch pointed toward the north ridge. "Up there, I heard the muj tried to overrun the squad. I know you held the line."

"Thanks Sar'nt. I was so scared I wanted to wrap myself in my woobie and suck my thumb. They got Kopeki."

"I know. I saw his gun. He melted the barrel. That kid went down swinging. That's the way to do it. Few people are lucky enough to die like that."

Shane recoiled at those words. Keeping his eyes on Burch, he tried not to show it.

Burch went on: "You're turning into a real ass-kicker. You're short just one thing: hate in your heart. I'm going to bring it out of you before this tour is through. That's what you want, right?"

Shane fiddled with his rifle, wondering how he would prove himself.

Burch glared.

Shane mumbled, "Roger, Sar'nt." He went to his ruck, untied the captured AK, and handed it to Burch.

Inspecting the gun, Burch said, "Nice souvenir."

Shane said, "There's something else. On the hill I saw one of the muj. It was the teenager with the birthmark, Habibullah. He got away but I got his gun."

Burch pointed to an inscription on the AK's buttstock. "I've seen this before." He translated, "Glory to the guerrilla."

Shane said, "I thought we were fighting the Egyptian. Now it seems we've stirred up the whole tribe."

Burch chuckled then crooked his arm round Shane's neck. He limped forward on his shaky ankle, bringing Shane along. "It's personal out here. We run in and out of these same villages, round and round, switching positions in a never-ending fight. And these Injuns, hell, they wanna make a name for themselves. Nothing we can do about that."

He went on. "We got starred men and politicians with flags on their lapels at the controls of this here goatfuck. They've got their geopolitical designs. You're just the slag, a by-product to be flushed away and dumped in some pit. I say you're the end product. Stick with me and there will be a becoming. A becoming I say. It's right around the corner. That muj with the birthmark will be your trophy."

————

In the days that followed, Shane was plagued by his vision more than ever—climbing that same hill, the boys falling stone dead. Except now the fallen boys all had faces twisted in silent screams. There was Harris, Kopeki, and Austin lying dead in the rocks, and then Kermit Martinez, and just before the top, Burch fell like the rest, the life gone out of him all at once, no groaning or thrashing or last breath.

Two weeks passed before word came about Martinez. The bullet had penetrated his hip, stomach, liver, and lung. He died on the helicopter to Bagram. They'd juiced him with a defibrillator and brought him back to life. He underwent three surgeries and was now back in the States, doing well. He'd be in the hospital for a while. Shane rejoiced. Maybe he wasn't going to be the last one on the hill.

19

Camp Holiday
Day 198

I n late October, Shane welcomed the cold. It came without
warning. Fresh snow dusted the high peaks. Storm King
sparkled with the jewels of early winter. The Newts pointed at
ski lines on the peak and spoke of powder turns. It was all nonsense. They were hankering over ski lines no sane man would
attempt. Shane enjoyed their bravado nonetheless.

The snows kept to the alpine, but that would soon change. To
survive winter and keep up the manhunt, the Newts would have to
stockpile all manner of supplies at Holiday. The plan was for a massive ground convoy to bring it all in. Forty trucks would do it in
one shot instead of repeated runs that the enemy could target. The
Newts would move to the valley entrance and provide overwatch
for the convoy.

As heavy clouds gathered over the valley, Shane was in his tent,
packing for the op. Shane sorted through his seven layers of cold
weather gear, hoping he wouldn't need them all at once. Between
jackets he came upon the last letter from Candy. It had been

months since she had mailed anything. *Surely there's a mix up with mail at Bagram*, thought Shane. After all, his rank had changed. Shane had even tried to call, but with unit phone cards nearly depleted, the LT said the satellite phone was to be used only for life events like births and deaths; checking on a stripper girlfriend didn't qualify. Shane didn't linger on it, telling himself Candy was a good girl. He reminded himself that Candy's dad had served, so she knew what she was getting into.

A call came over the radio, projected into the tent from a speaker box in the corner. Four Afghan workers were missing from camp. They'd disappeared the night before. The missing workers filled sandbags and cooked meals. They were part of Holiday's native labor force, which freed American soldiers to focus on fighting. The workers came from all over the province, but not from the valley itself. They made ten dollars a day, a handsome salary in the Kush, but many had been injured during attacks on the camp.

The Newts were ordered to keep an eye out for the workers during the upcoming overwatch mission. Not much else was made of the disappearance. The workers had probably grown tired of getting shot up and stolen away in the night.

As Shane packed the last items into his ruck, the LT came into the tent and marched up to Shane's cot. "Shane, I need you running comms on this op. You're on detail with me."

Over in the corner, Burch heard the news. He charged up to the LT on two healthy ankles and spat, "I finally get back in the fight and first thing you do is take Shane from my squad? Negative, LT. Shane belongs to me."

The LT said, "Shane belongs to the U.S. Army."

With an edge in his voice, Burch said, "He's mine."

"You must be confused about who you're talking to."

"Look, LT, my squad's already thin."

"I'll give him back in a few weeks."

Burch stood there, revved up, his fists clenched.

The LT said, "Is there anything else, Sergeant?"

Burch kicked an ammo crate and spun away.

Now tasked with RTO duties, Shane stuffed twenty pounds of radio equipment into his ruck and cinched it closed. At dusk, he wolfed down beef stew, shouldered his ruck, and made for the camp gate. In eerie silence the Newts gathered. The sergeants counted heads, pointing a finger at each man and mouthing a number but never speaking. Two men slid open the sheet metal gate, and Burch led the platoon out. First thing they passed was the trash pit. The waste still smoldered from a fire they'd set in the afternoon. There in the smoke was the dim kid, lost in his eternal search for booty. When the patrol filed by, the kid stopped and scanned faces. His eyes settled on Shane. The dim kid smiled and ran up and tugged on Shane's pants leg. Shane marched on without giving the kid a second look.

First they followed the jeep trail, then the river. When the banks grew steep and the trail scarce, they moved back onto the jeep trail. They ranged through the night. When dawn reared gray in the east, Shane heard the river confluence. In the distance, he saw the building they'd stage in. The natives called it a madrassa. The building was a long one-story, made of stone, with a fresh coat of blue paint. A cloister ran the entire length. Two small windows pierced each room.

The madrassa sat off the Blue River Road. For now, it was empty, so Burch kicked in the door. The Newts settled into a great room to await the supply convoy. That afternoon, clouds massed and black tendrils reached down. Then came slanting rain, stinging and relentless, for two straight days. Inside the madrassa, the Newts shifted their sleeping bags away from the leaks in the roof. Mud bogged the road outside the madrassa. The river topped the banks. Word came that the Blue River Road was washed out above Asadabad. It would be another week before the supply convoy could pass.

The Newts remained in the madrassa, smoking and cussing

away the time. Shane passed the nights stoking fire in a woodstove while water sheeted off the eaves.

On night three in the madrassa, Shane pulled guard duty under the cloisters. The rain faded. The clouds parted for a full moon, and just below, the river looked to be molten silver. A pair of headlights bounced down the Blue River Road and veered straight for the madrassa. It was a pickup, moving at a clip. Shane stopped the truck at gunpoint. Burch and the LT came running out of the madrassa.

The driver of the truck flung the door open, thrust his hands in the air and nodded to the truck bed.

Burch aimed his rifle at the man and told Shane, "Check the back."

Peering over the tailgate, Shane saw four headless bodies. Tissue-covered spinal cords poked out from red stumps. Shane gulped and held back vomit. He staggered away to let the river wind wash the stench from his nose. He braced himself against a tree where a murder of crows pranced about on naked branches. Shane's chest heaved as acid climbed up his throat. Shane vomited on his boots in the mud; the crows looked on, and then one came down to pick at the puke. Over at the truck, Burch gazed at the bodies and tapped his fingers on the tailgate. Letting down the tailgate, Burch tugged a body halfway out by the ankles and rolled the legs off the gate and sat the torso upright with the legs dangling just above the ground.

"This was the beer drinking position back in high school," said Burch. "We had heads, though."

The LT said to Burch, "For fuck's sake. Knock it off." Then he questioned the driver. "Do you know these men?"

The driver held up a badge issued to all the Afghan workers at Holiday. "They are yours."

The LT asked, "Where did you find them?"

The driver said, "In the middle of the road." He pointed into the People's Valley. "Just beyond that hill."

The LT asked, "Where are the heads?"

The driver shrugged.

Burch and Shane slid the bodies from the truck bed and set them on the ground and searched them. Shane gingerly combed the pockets of one man, careful not to bloody himself up. Beside him, Burch rifled another body without regard for blood.

In a vest pocket on one body, Shane found a bloody note. He unfolded it and gave it to the interpreter, Lil John, for translation.

Lil John said, "It's in Arabic."

The LT said, "From the Egyptian." Then he asked, "What's it say?"

"'Payment for the mortar tubes.'"

Burch laughed. "Shane, you really pissed him off."

The LT took photos, called in a report to the cap'n, and told the driver to take the bodies to the Afghan police station downstream.

In the morning Shane woke to pattering rain. The low clouds were back, and there were puddles under the cloisters. Outside the madrassa Shane saw the puke-eating crows in the same tree, and beside them a gaggle of elders from the Lowland tribes. Shane tidied his vest, squared his patrol cap, and joined the LT in shaking their hands. Minutes later they led the elders inside the madrassa.

Sitting in the corner, Shane threw in a dip and watched the meeting.

The elders yelled over each other and made grand statements. "Someone will pay for the dead workers."

They raised their fists, while the oldest man declared, "This is not the behavior of our fellow Muslims. This is the work of brutes and outcasts."

The Lowland elders blamed the People, who had ongoing feuds with other tribes in the Kush. The feuds had started over who got to sit on what river. The fighting raged for centuries, but beheadings were new.

The Afghani men circled the LT.

Shane reached for his gun and laid it on his knee.

One white-bearded elder asked, "Why aren't you Americans protecting your workers?"

The LT said, "We can't control everything."

The elder said, "What good are your airplanes? What good are your helicopters?"

The elders huddled to talk among each other. Then the white-bearded elder demanded, "How are the Americans going to make this right?"

The LT said, "We'll find the men who did this."

The elder said, "We will be watching," and turned to leave. He stopped in the doorway and swung back around to the LT. "And another thing—this is a madrassa, a religious school. You are not Muslim. Staying here is not good for you."

The LT glanced at the rain outside. "I need a place that sleeps thirty-five. Shall we come to your house?"

The white-bearded elder glared. "I'll be waiting to hear from you." He charged outside. The others shook their heads and followed him.

When they had all gone, the LT told Shane, "That went well."

Shane spat through his teeth.

The LT knelt beside his rucksack and fished out a satellite phone. He said, "Let's see what Smoky knows," as he dialed the informant. Smoky had been handsomely paid for his Tiger Village intel and had since been eager to help.

The LT pressed the speaker button on the phone and waited for an answer. While it rang, he told Shane, "This sneaky fucker is connected. Not sure what his angle is. And you know what gets me— he speaks great English."

Smoky answered, "Commander."

The LT responded, "Greetings. Where are you?"

"Pakistan."

"Vacation?"

"Family affairs."

"Very well. I'm looking for answers."

"Aren't we all?"

"Four workers on Camp Holiday have been killed, their heads cut off. It looks like the Egyptian was behind it. We're not sure who did the cutting. A bunch of pissed-off elders would like to know."

"I'll ask around."

———

The next morning Shane pulled guard under the cloisters, with a balaclava cupping his face and his poncho liner draped over his shoulders. A gray police truck raced up and skidded to a stop. An Afghan police captain, dressed in full regalia, got out. Three men with the steely look of fighters exited the passenger and back seats. Their rigid body language and shifty eyes said they didn't want to be there, but the police captain insisted that the three men be given an audience with the LT.

Shane led the entourage into the big room and said, "LT, some suicide bombers are here to see you."

The LT glanced at the men, then said to Shane, "Stick around. And try to look mean."

The LT summoned his interpreter, Lil John, who poured chai for everyone. The three men blew at their steaming drinks and gulped in haste. The interpreter made small talk. The three men gave uneasy laughs.

The LT told them, "I know you didn't come here for chai."

One man wore a salt-and-pepper beard. He spoke with authority. "We represent the Malik. He wants to see you about the men who lost their heads."

I'll be damned, thought Shane. The Newts knew about the Malik from intelligence reports that came in red folders. The Malik was a warlord along the Af-Pak border. He lived in a remote valley on the Afghan side and controlled an empire that stretched into Pakistan.

Army intelligence held the Malik as a key figure in Afghanistan's opium exports, but the Malik was not an enemy of the coalition. He'd fought the Taliban during their regime, and stayed on the sidelines during the American invasion. No one went to the Malik's territory, not American patrols or Afghan soldiers or foreign jihadists.

The Malik's reputation was born out of the Soviet war, where he was a ferocious mujahedeen commander. His militia was known for brazen attacks on far-flung Soviet bases. The stories were mostly the same. Hundreds of militia fighters massed in stealth, and then used concentrated fire to overrun small bands of communists. Soviet tanks and helicopters responded hours later and found only fire and Russian bodies.

No one was sure what the Malik looked like. The reports were sparse on this topic, except for the story of one CIA informant, who had said, "The Malik has a bad hand from smuggling stinger missiles into Afghanistan during the Soviet jihad. The Malik was leading his men through the reeds along the Kunar River when a cobra bit his wrist. The Malik said, 'So be it' and stayed on the mission. He floated the missiles across the river on small inner tubes. The Malik never sought a doctor because cobra venom ran through his veins before that night." Shane had laughed when he read that part—these Afghans had the imaginations of six-year-olds.

The three men now in the madrassa were the Malik's envoys. The lead messenger said, "The Malik will host you inside his kingdom in two days' time."

This unexpected announcement left Shane in disbelief. Some of the Army analysts thought the Malik was a tall tale. Now he wanted to see the Newts, or at least, someone wanted them to believe that.

The LT reached for the radio, telling Shane, "The captain needs to hear this one."

The cap'n was on the horn a minute later.

The LT said, "The Malik wants to talk."

The cap'n asked, "Which Malik?" Other village elders also went by that title. *Malik* meant "leader" and "king."

"*The* Malik," the LT said. "*The* Malik," he repeated.

"Where's the meeting?"

"Way, way north. How 'bout getting us some birds?"

The cap'n said, "They'll never fly in this weather. I want you to chase this down. Screw the ground convoys. We'll get second platoon to cover that."

———

Two days later, a faded red Toyota pickup bumped down the road. It splashed through standing water, left the road, and came toward the madrassa. Six battered trucks followed the Toyota. Five police trucks trailed them.

Shane yelled to alert the platoon, "Caravan's a'coming." The Newts emerged from the madrassa and, with nervous chatter, gathered into squads.

The red Toyota stopped in front of the madrassa. The other trucks pulled into a semicircle.

Wearing desert camo, the driver of the red Toyota got out and stretched his legs. He declared, "We will lead you to the meeting site."

Each truck was packed with men. The entourage was maybe two bodies shy of a full platoon. Inside the trucks, Shane saw gun barrels and buttstocks under blankets.

Shane pointed to the weapons. "No need for those."

From under their hooded field jackets, the Malik's men glared at him. Their eyes were black as coal, and they had a wild look about them. Shane had seen the look before, among the people in Barge Matall. Mountain living changed a man, right down to his marrow. Shane was beginning to understand it.

The driver of the red Toyota seemed in charge. He wiped naan crumbs off his scraggly beard and said, "The Malik has enemies outside his territory, but he promises you safe passage once north of Thunder Pass, the boundary of his lands."

The LT looked unconvinced. He nodded to Shane. "See what they're packing."

Shane tossed the corner of a blanket, unveiling an RPG-7 and a brand new RPK.

The owner slapped Shane's hand. Suddenly all the Malik's men coiled up, as if ready to draw. The driver held up his palms, saying, "What cause does the Malik have for an elaborate ruse? This is no ambush. We came in force because the People are all around us."

The Malik is showing off his army, thought Shane. It was hard to say how this would play out.

The Newts chambered rounds: *snap, snap, snap.* They loaded machine guns: *ch-chunk, ch-chunk, ch-chunk.* The LT sent the order down the line, "Mount up." The Newts piled into the five Afghan police trucks.

The convoy snaked up the Blue River Road, driving under slate clouds. The river trees were leafless skeletons. Hard rain came in sheets as they crept north. In a few weeks, the rain showers in the lowlands would turn to snowstorms, and the fighting would slow until spring. But for now, it was just cold rain, which made the truck tires spin and Shane's teeth chatter.

Wet hours dripped by. They reached the last major settlement on the Blue River. The trucks turned north over Thunder Pass and descended full speed like runaway mine carts.

They were entering a region seldom visited by outsiders. The first obstacle was a deep gorge of water-carved limestone. Shane cringed as they drove under its vertical walls, knowing they'd be helpless in an ambush. The cliffs were catacombed and bursting with ferns. The hiding spots were infinite. Water sloshed in the truck beds, soaking Shane's bottom as the cliffs slid by.

At last, the gorge opened. Shane's knuckles once again found their color.

Shane sucked long breaths as they entered a second gorge even deeper than the first. One monstrous shadow fell upon them. The truck engines echoed off the walls. Roaring waterfalls dumped over ledges and pulverized rocks along the road.

Swirling mist found the last dry patch on Shane's back. He resisted the urge to punch the tailgate. Twice they forked left. The walls grew ever tighter until the sky was only a stitch.

No ambush came. The Malik had assured safe passage and kept his promise thus far.

They continued north and passed through one last gorge. On the far end, two giant fir trees hugged the road, announcing their arrival in the heart of the Malik's land. Here was a place of cloud-swept valleys, ghostly summits, and impossible arêtes. After an hour, the Malik's men turned right into a side canyon. The slim road attacked a slope head-on. The trucks creaked and bounced as their tires overcame the rocks. And with each bump, the boys got tossed in the cold metal truck beds. As the trucks climbed, old-growth forests came down. Shane gazed at primordial trees as he shivered against the rain.

Another hour of bumping up the road brought them to a crooked village with no one about. Below the houses, unkempt terraces looked to be blackwater pools. The uninhabited look of the place put Shane on edge. It was the normal scene before a shootout, as people fled indoors for cover.

The driver of the red Toyota swaggered toward the Newts. Pointing to a walled house atop the village, he said, "The Malik is waiting. We walk from here."

The Newts assembled. The Malik's camo-clad men led the way, followed by the Afghan police, then the LT and Shane. The rest of the Newts brought up the rear. A hundred men moved through the village's twisting corridors, the spectacle capped by a smattering of different uniforms. All the while, Shane shifted in his bulletproof turtleshell. He'd just been thrown around in a truck bed for hours, and now his spine cried for an end to the war.

The LT whispered, "Relax," reminding Shane, and maybe himself, to look cool.

The group came to a massive stone staircase leading up to the village's highest house. With guns rattling, the Malik's men climbed the stairs three at a time. Shane followed, doing his best to match their pace, but slippery steps held him back. That was what he told himself.

The Malik's men peered over their shoulders and laughed.

Three hundred steps brought them to the house. Shane and the LT passed through the outer wall, winded and sweating. Four sentries paced the roof. Two black wolf-dogs bristled and pulled their chains. The Newts took positions above the house. They kept barrels on the sentries and dogs.

The Malik's men pushed open a large wooden door. Shane and the LT followed. They came into a room with a floor-to-ceiling window overlooking the valley. An opulent red rug covered the floor. Tasseled lounging pillows lined the walls. The LT sat cross-legged and eased into the pillows. Shane removed his helmet and body armor and dried his hair with a kerchief. Moments later, a man brought in a silver tray topped with chai, flatbread, and sugar cookies.

A silence followed, just the wolf-dogs barking outside and clinking spoons stirring chai.

Outside, someone whispered to the dogs. They stopped barking at once.

The Malik's fighters watched the door.

A bearded man with deep wrinkles around his eyes took two steps into the room. The Malik's men rose, showing respect, the same way American soldiers stood when high-ranking officers entered a room. The bearded man had a charcoal blanket draped over a shoulder. As he greeted his guests, the blanket concealed his left hand. His face was central Asian, his eyes oriental. The flat wool hat of the Pashtuns, called a *pakul*, sat on the back of his head. In a swanky display, the bearded man had it cocked sideways.

He exchanged pleasantries with the Afghan police chief. They grinned at each other, holding up their arms like they were firing rifles. Shriveled fingers marred the man's left hand. *It was the Malik.* Suddenly, the Malik reared back, laughing, with his hands on his stomach. The sound was booming and gravelly, like a big African cat making warning noises. The Malik slashed his thumb across his throat. He and the police commander seemed to be remembering a battle.

Shane examined the Malik's footgear. He sported gray suede high-tops. Afghan elders usually wore sandals or plain leather shoes. Enemy commanders wore black high-tops. Shane had not seen suede. In a land of poverty, those suede high-tops must have been the fancy equivalent of crocodile boots.

Between statements, the Malik paused and studied Shane. The warlord's eyes shifted from his boots to his rifle to his fighting vest. Shane felt translucent, and suddenly very, very young. Maybe the Malik was sizing him up to see if he was indeed the messenger of a superpower. Shane wished he hadn't shaved that morning.

After long introductions, the Malik explained the reason for the meeting. "The four beheaded men are my cousins. They asked for my permission to work at your camp in the People's Valley. Their families were in a bad way; they needed the money. I warned them not to mix with you, but the lure of your money was too strong. Their blood is on your hands as well."

The Malik gazed out the window and went on, "The tribe called the People has long made trouble here. They are squatters and thieves and bandits. We fought them into the highest valley—the land no one wanted. The valley had timber, way up where the clouds met the earth, and the People found ways to harvest the forest."

Shane remembered the log flume on Tiger Mountain. At the time, he told the Newts it was a muj waterslide. The Malik had just disproved his theory. Shane would have to clear that up with the boys.

The Malik said, "The People turned the high timber into wealth and fell in bed with a foreigner, the one they call the Egyptian. He trained them and bought them weapons for a war on us. You see, the People have long wanted revenge for their banishment into the badlands." The Malik put one finger in the air, palm facing inward—showing the declarative gesture of the mountain tribes. "I'm sick of the People. The other tribes are outraged by the be-headings of their fellow Muslims. Everyone wants war. The timing is right. We will use the ancient ways to revenge the killings. I will lead a Lashkar."

The Afghan police commander nodded his head vigorously, but Shane and the LT didn't understand what *Lashkar* meant.

The Malik had a long exchange with the interpreter, Lil John, before he nestled into the pillows. He slurped his chai and gave Lil John time to explain.

"The tribes believe in balance. Long ago, each carved out its own territory in the mountains. They own the resources therein. The tribes jockey for control of land and rivers on their territorial boundaries. Feuds often erupt from boundary disputes. Rules and etiquette govern the feuds. If a tribe breaks fighting etiquette or attempts an aggressive land grab, the others will ally as one force and launch a military offensive against the offending tribe. This of-fensive is called a Lashkar. It's a tool to restore balance among the tribes."

The Malik raised his chin to see if the Americans wanted to join his Lashkar.

The LT nodded yes.

The Malik pointed down to his maneuver plan. Icons covered a topographic map, just like American mission plans.

Drawing arrows on the map, the Malik said, "I've prepared a pincer movement. Three thousand tribal fighters will assemble on the Blue River. The main force will enter the valley straight on and split to capture key villages. At the same time, two columns of tribesmen will enter the People's land from the valley walls on the east and west, take up blocking positions, and then move on the high villages. We will burn their fields. We will execute their Khan and the Egyptian at his side."

Shane cut in. "We want the Egyptian."

The Malik's eyes flashed when he was interrupted. Pointing at Shane, the Malik demanded, "Who is this?"

Shane looked to the LT. There was a moment of surprise on the LT's face.

The LT said, "He speaks for me. We want the Egyptian."

The Malik said, "It's their Khan I want. So be it: I'll bring you the Egyptian. Dead or alive?"

The LT said, "Dead."

"Good," said the Malik. "That is easier. Now let me continue. I need your artillery to fire on the high ridges as the main body advances. At ten a.m., stop the artillery to let the flanking columns pass over the ridges."

The LT said, "The People will fight back. How will we know who's who?"

The Malik said, "Yes, there will be confusion. All battles are shrouded in fog. If you keep your soldiers in camp, all will be well."

The LT said, "So don't fire unless fired upon."

The Malik said, "Very good, Commander. This is ours to settle. And when it's over, I'll bring the Egyptian to your doorstep."

The campaign would start November 26.

———

About midnight, the Newts returned to the madrassa at the mouth of the People's Valley.

Most of the boys ran for their sleeping bags. Shane fished out his winter field jacket and reported for guard duty. As the moon glimmered in the puddles in the road, Shane stood under the cloisters, listening to the river and imagining himself sitting in a college class with blondes on all sides. After a while he decided it was the women's track team sitting around him—the sprinters and long jumpers, that is, not the shot-putters.

The LT emerged from the madrassa, yawned, and stretched his arms. "Thanks for humping the radio. Battalion has a replacement on the way. When he arrives, I'll keep my word and send you back to Burch's squad."

Shane said, "Yessir." At the moment, he wasn't sure that was what he wanted. Scanning the dripping hills once more, he said, "The Malik, you think he's for real?"

The LT said, "Don't know. It sounds too good."

"What's the plan?"

"Well, we could keep this quiet and let it play out, or run it up the flagpole."

Shane turned the choices over in his mind, trying to see the best way. He leaned, spit, and wiped his mouth with his sleeve. "Why not run it up, sir, run it as high as we can? Spin it a little, put a pretty dress on it, say *we* hatched this thing and get some assets behind it. What's one little lie in this big-ass war?"

The LT chuckled.

Shane said, "You'll look pretty good if it goes down like the Malik said."

"Everyone looks good."

"We can be the ones who got the Egyptian."

The LT tugged his pistol holster and thumbed the button over the Beretta. *Click click click click.* He snapped and unsnapped the button, lost in his thoughts. "This is bigger than the Egyptian. This is what we've wanted all along, the Afghans policing themselves."

Shane said, "We'll have a quiet finish to this tour. I'll be happy if we don't see another medevac helicopter."

"So will I, Shane, so will I." The LT thumbed the button on his holster again. "Get the captain on the horn."

Shane called Holiday and spoke with the night RTO. At that very moment, the cap'n was entertaining the battalion commander in Holiday headquarters. The two officers announced themselves on the radio.

The LT said, "Gentlemen, we've been working hard down here. Things are boiling over because of the dead workers." He cleared his throat and stood tall. "I've rallied the Malik and the Lowland tribes. With my help, they've organized a tribal offensive against the People. It will be brigade scale, perhaps four thousand fighters in all. The attack will begin November 26. They'll need our help directing air and artillery support. They've asked for attack helicopters and gunships."

The battalion commander said, "Outstanding, Lieutenant, outstanding. Even the theatre commander will hear about how you're winning this war."

The captain got on the horn. "LT, I want your platoon back at Holiday. Give me the full briefing when you arrive. It's time for the big show." The cap'n paused, and then said, "The colonel has been gracious enough to send his helicopter to get you all. We'll ferry everyone back."

The LT was beaming when he set down the hand mike. He turned to Shane. "I think I just turned on the faucet."

Shane said, "Yessir, it's 'bout time someone did."

It took four chopper runs to get the Newts back to Holiday. Shane slept for two hours and got to work the next morning, improving an observation post for the coming offensive. In the days that followed, Shane heard nothing but good news. The battalion commander created a stir about the grassroots offensive his own men had organized. Central Command was paying attention now, calling it Operation Mountain Lion.

Supplies and munitions streamed into Camp Holiday by nightly helicopter. Up until now, they had been starved for supplies, and it had taken months to organize the winter ground convoy. The situation instantly changed. Provisions now came in faster than they could handle. People from higher headquarters arrived by helicopter, too: intelligence officers, full bird colonels, CIA types in civilian clothes. They crowded the little camp and took over its computers and radios. Four Apaches were moved to Asadabad. A-10 Warthogs were moved to Jalalabad. An AC-130 gunship was pulled from Joint Special Operations Command. All the aircraft were on call for Camp Holiday. The excitement was palpable.

The Newts continued regular patrols and routines, knowing it wise not to switch up operations before a big offensive; even subtle changes could tip off the Egyptian. As the day drew closer, the People carried on with their routines. They gathered at the mosques and bent in the fields. Some collected wood in the hills while others led goats down from high meadows. Rain came as Shane waited. On November 18, an early winter storm swept in and powdered the trees. On November 20, the Newts took sniper and rocket fire. Three days later, the Newts slung lead in a monster gunfight outside Gorbat. It was just the day-to-day grind Shane had come to expect.

———————

November 26 arrived. The high meadows were golden. The Winter Spires framed the morning sun. Shane's breath steamed as the Newts climbed a hilltop on the verge of Holiday. When they crested, Shane moved to the hill's northern flank. He dropped into a foxhole and readied his gear. They would observe the jeep road for the Malik's army, and then direct artillery and aircraft on the valley walls.

Looking through his spotting scope, Shane found the river first. It tumbled along, dark with silt. The jeep road ran parallel. Shane traced the road north to where it disappeared behind a bend, then tightened the scope's tripod to lock the bend in view. Spitting tobacco on the foxhole lip, Shane waited and watched. By 0830, clouds were breaking on Storm King. Shane's spit puddle had become a sizable pool. Then came the echoes of truck engines. Then came the dust cloud. The engines grew louder. A red Toyota pickup raced around the bend. Shane recognized the vehicle from the meeting with the Malik.

Shane reported, "Convoy is en route," to the LT. Damn, they were coming fast.

"Hang it…*fire*," was the command from the Holiday mortar crews. *Thunk Thunk Thunk.* Shells arced into space. The barrage began on the high ridges. Detonations rolled across the valley. A battery of Howitzers joined in. Three-foot shells shook the ground on impact. Fighter planes streaked by and dropped 500-pound bombs on the shoulders of Storm King. Two A-10 Warthogs followed the fighter planes, dropping more bombs and shredding the forest with buzzing chainguns. Then came the Apaches, working in twos. They prowled the ridges and touched up Tiger Mountain with flurries of rockets.

Cheers erupted across Camp Holiday.

Over the jarring explosions, Shane kept eyes on the convoy. Only four trucks had rounded the bend. The gap behind them was at least a half mile. *Where were the rest?*

Shane called for the LT, who came running across the hill and dropped into Shane's foxhole.

Shane said, "Only four trucks."

The LT said, "Where are the rest?"

"You tell me, sir. Just the four trucks. No more dust behind them."

The LT eyed the trucks for a long time. "One of those old trucks broke down behind the bend. The rest are stuck behind it. This is not a good start to the operation."

Shane said, "This party sucks." Through his optic, Shane followed the trucks. They ascended the jeep road to Holiday and circled at the gate.

The LT rushed down to meet the convoy. At the gate, he was joined by the cap'n. The two officers exchanged shouts with the driver of the red Toyota. Shane didn't quite believe his eyes when the trucks turned around and left the gate, heading north. They looked to be leaving the valley. Shane saw the LT stagger away from the gate like he was lost. The LT sat on a rock with his head in his hands. This was not the plan.

Shane fidgeted with his radio. A minute passed before the LT came over the platoon frequency. "The Malik's men just delivered a message." His voice was shaky. "There will be no Lashkar. The Malik will contact us soon. That's all we know." The LT's voice was flat and somber, as if giving a eulogy. "We'll get to the bottom of this. It'll take time to sort out what's going on. You all know things don't go as planned when the Afghans are at the wheel. That's all. Three-six, out."

In the following days, a dark cloud hung over Shane. Victory had seemed certain, and he had allowed himself to think of home: lying with Candy at his hunting camp in the woods, the little diner just south, where hunters came in wearing camo and spoke of trophy bucks over a breakfast of black coffee and grits. Now...well, shit. Maybe more boys would get whacked. In his mind, he felt the weight of a stretcher-laid body as he carried another litter to a medevac bird. And then came the vision of him alone on the hill.

Shane perked up when he heard Battalion was sending a helicopter to bring the cap'n and the LT to a meeting with the Afghan provincial governor. They would be accompanied by two American colonels, the battalion and brigade commanders.

The bird came after dark. Watching it swoop away, Shane hoped the brass would rip off some Afghan heads. Certainly, the gray-haired officers could untangle this mess.

In the morning, Shane hustled to HQ for the battalion's daily radio update. The Lashkar wasn't even mentioned. He stormed out of HQ and found Sergeant Vasquez sitting against a bunker wall, Q-tipping his rifle.

Shane said, "No news on the Lashkar. Is that a good or bad sign, Sar'nt?"

Vasquez replied, "Don't get your panties in a wad, Corporal. The Lashkar is postponed. I've seen the rhythm of the fighting here." Vasquez paused and rodded his gun barrel with a cleaning patch. "The Malik changed his mind. It's too late in the season. Snow will soon close the road. The invading tribes would be trapped. They'd run out of food. The early storm told the Malik it was too late. The Malik knows the mountains. He's going to wait for spring."

———

A day later, Shane spied the helicopter that carried the LT and the cap'n. It weaved through the narrows, flared over Holiday, and landed. The two officers hopped out and trotted for headquarters. Minutes later, the LT called the Newts for a briefing. Shane ran down to HQ with his rattlesnake skin in hand. Everyone soon crowded into the tiny command post. They stood shoulder to shoulder, tapping their boots on the plywood floor.

The LT said, "We met with the Afghan government. We asked why the Lashkar didn't come to fruition. They looked surprised and offended. Then, well, things went sideways. The provincial governor heard rumors that we had killed the four workers."

With a violent swing of his arm, the LT flung papers and maps off a desk. He yelled, "Our friend, the governor. That cocksucker-motherfucker. He said *we* killed the workers to start a fight."

Shane could find no words.

The LT went on, "The brigade commander got hot. He called that politician a crooked motherfucker. So the bad news is we have no answer right now. Brigade is checking with the Afghan intelligence guys to see if they know where the Malik is. They'll check into the other rumors floating around. In the meantime, we aren't going to stand by. This all started in our backyard. We can find the answer here, too."

The next day, Newt platoon mounted the jeeps that had been slung in for the Tiger Village operation. They drove one valley east to call on the Khan from the Omari clan. Gunfights between the Omaris and the People were a monthly occurrence, so the Omaris might know the score.

After a bumpy ride, the Newts dismounted below a stone village. Shane had barely stepped into the village when the tribal leader came running up from the river to greet the platoon. The leader wore a tan vest and a *pakul* so far back on his head that Shane wondered how it stayed on.

They had a meeting right there, in the terraces.

The LT asked the elder, "Have you heard about the Lashkar?"

The elder gave a half smile. "Yes, of course."

"When is it happening?"

"It's not." It seemed like there would be more, but the elder only tamped the *pakul* on the back of his head.

The LT asked, "Why?"

The elder looked confused. "You don't know?"

"Let's just say I've heard conflicting stories."

"It was a ploy."

The LT said, "Whose ploy?"

The elder said, "The Malik was upset about the deaths in his clan. He wanted compensation, but had no interest in a war against the People. So the Malik stoked rumors about a Lashkar to get the People's attention. They caught wind of the coming offensive and paid the Malik for the deaths in his clan. The People even sent some of their teenage boys for the Malik. And that is that."

Shane pondered on that explanation. The four beheaded men

were from the Malik's clan, and the tribes shed blood over childish taunts. The Malik would lose all face if he settled for a payoff after a spectacular insult. He wouldn't back down. The idea was unthinkable.

The LT adjourned the meeting and the elder hiked down to the river again. The LT peeled off his helmet and ran a hand through his sandy hair, looking far, far off.

Shane stood at his side. "It don't add up, sir."

The LT said, "Nope."

"Now what?"

"When I met with our brigade commander, he looked so disgusted with me. I can't tell you how much it hurt to let him down. We have to keep beating the bushes." A proud look washed over the LT. He raised one fist. "We have it in our grasp. We can be the engineers of a lasting peace. Think about it. We can be the ones who subdued the People. We can bring them into the light, even if they come kicking and screaming. We're so fortunate to be in this moment, with this opportunity."

The LT paused, deep in thought. "We've got one more hand to play," he said. "We're going west to Smoky's village."

They turned the trucks around and followed the Blue River Road. An hour of driving brought them to a rickety footbridge. They dismounted and made haste across the bridge, the planks bouncing and swaying underfoot. Once across, they waded through muddy terraces. Every few steps, Shane shook his heels to fling off the mud, but it was back two steps later. After a quarter mile he gave up and just walked, accepting the extra weight. They reached the village outskirts and burrowed uphill through the muck. In a wilted garden they came across Smoky's nephew. The ten-year-old boy served as his uncle's courier. Right now he was playing with discarded batteries and radio wire.

The LT said to the boy, "Quit making bombs, you little shit. Go get Smoky."

The informant's nephew thrust out his palm. The LT dropped in candy. The boy shook his head. The LT obliged with a rupee note and the boy scampered away. Newt platoon took an abandoned house at the foot of the village.

A sawmill buzzed somewhere downstream as they waited.

At last light, the wailing call for evening prayer sounded from the village mosque. Standing outside the abandoned house, Shane watched men file toward the mosque. A cloud caught fire in the last throes of daylight and then it was dark. Shane flipped on his night vision goggles and squinted at the landscape below. A crescent moon had just reared up over the eastern ridge when Shane spied a figure darting through the terraces. The figure moved with grace and speed, in spite of the dark and mud. Shane gripped his rifle as the figure took shape. It was Smoky. Smoky wore a black fishnet shirt. Two bullet scars knotted the skin on his shoulder.

Smoky said, "Your commander calls for me."

Shane waved his hand, saying, "This way."

He entered a dark room where the LT sat. His headlamp was throwing a beam across a map. Shane said, "LT, a muj is here to see you."

Smoky heard the slight and said, "Mujahedeen, if you please."

Shane sat on his heels in the corner while the LT and Smoky caught up. Smoky liked to shoot the shit. He'd just come from tending to a sick relative in Pakistan. As he recalled his troubles crossing the border, the informant reached into his backpack and took out a bottle of vodka. Smoky's Adam's apple bobbed as he gulped the grain alcohol. His eyes misted with booze.

Smoky snapped a Zippo lighter into flame and lit a Marlboro. He said, "I know something you need to hear."

Shane and the LT leaned in.

Smoky said, "A new fighter is stirring the People, a kid from the valley with a birthmark on his cheek. His name is Habibullah. He's got fire in him, and he's good with his tongue. The others look up to him. Loombara has promoted him to lieutenant."

The LT said, "So what?"

Smoky said, "Everyone saw your trucks when you drove to Chinnah, or as you call it, Tiger Village. Even now, you drive them. The mujahedeen commander has taught Habibullah how to make bombs for the road. Habibullah is talking to the others, telling them bombs are the best way against you. Last Friday, Habibullah was in the white mosque in Gorbat. He said to the People, 'Your sons watch you fight. My son watches me fight. Let them see bombs.'"

The LT said, "Let's talk about that later. I've got something else for you. Have you heard about the Lashkar?"

"Yes."

"Why didn't the Malik follow through?"

Smoky whispered, "The Malik," and laughed to himself.

The LT asked, "Why won't the Lowland tribes stand up to the People?"

Smoky glared at the LT and pushed the smoke from his lungs far across the room. He replied, "Who said it was settled?"

"The Lowland tribes did," said the LT. "Some of them are blaming us for the dead workers. This Lashkar needs to happen."

Smoky said, "No, Commander. You are mistaken. You started this war, now your men are dying here, but just because you come here angry doesn't mean you are king. You stare at your timepiece and drum your fingers. 'Hurry, hurry,' you say. Words we've heard before. This matter is not for you to decide. It's not for your army to decide."

Smoky had a long pull on his cigarette and gulped down vodka before he exhaled.

In the corner, Shane shifted on his heels. He had grown accustomed to the vague Afghan rhetoric Smoky was now employing. Yet Shane's temples were tingling with firing neurons. It hit him like a bullet—Smoky had the Malik's deep voice, as if gargling nails. Smoky wore the high-top shoes of the fighters, but they were gray suede like the Malik's. Smoky was leaning back on a pillow, his face in shadow. To Shane, the two men were one and the same.

The LT said to Smoky, "If you all want this to work, do it now, when we can help you."

Smoky said, "Commander, your haste will lead you into trouble." His face came out of the dark corner and half into the light. "The dust will settle soon. We will still be here, the clans and our mountains. You will not. You'll be back in America. You'll forget why you came. In time, you will even forget what you saw here. Your people will forget. Your memories die with the individual. Ours live forever with the tribe. So you must see—you'll find no puppets here. This matter is ours to decide, in our time, in our way."

The old mujahedeen had nothing else to say. He finished his bottle and staggered out the door into the dark.

20

W inter locked up the valley in December. Shane saw snow on trees, white on green, everywhere up high. The white blitzkrieg marched down to the valley bottom. Flurries blasted Holiday. The tents were cloaked in white mist, which hung for weeks. It left nothing for Shane's eyes, only his ears—they registered the locomotive sound of avalanches up the valley. The war ground to a halt against the sweet hush of winter. Shane got rest, as much as six hours at a time. It was glorious. His vigor returned, and the painful click in his knees faded.

On December 20, Battalion sent a new RTO for the LT. Shane returned to Burch's squad. It felt like home. Humping the radio next to the LT had taught Shane a thing or two, but all the Afghan politicking and mind reading was taxing. Shane felt he belonged with the squad boys.

Best of all, Shane's orders for sergeant came through. The platoon assembled in the mist on the landing zone, each man's breath a shot of steam in the cold air. The company first sergeant pinned the rank on Shane's chest while the Newts clapped vigorously. After, Shane took over a fire team in Burch's squad: Private Cassidy and a new guy named Parker were assigned to Shane. They were short one man. Everyone was short on bodies.

On Christmas morning, Shane climbed out of his sleeping bag and opened the tent flap. For weeks, he'd seen nothing but white mist. The sun now penetrated the cloud blanket and fought off the mist over the camp. A billion microscopic ice crystals drifted in the wind. The sun's piercing rays hit the ice crystals, and by midmorning the entire sky looked to be filled with electric glitter. By and by, the boys emerged from their canvas dens for a sunbath.

Shane kicked up a snowball fight to decide who would burn the shit in the latrines. He threw the first ball near the helicopter landing pad. The fight ran up the hill by headquarters. All the Newts joined in. Shane's fire team made a valiant stand outside the bunkers, fighting off attackers on two flanks. Snowballs whizzed every which way, splattering on impact.

As the battle climaxed, Sergeant Vasquez got tagged in the chest by an errant glob of the fine white stuff. That stopped the ruckus. Vasquez made a good show of being pissed about it, even though Shane had seen the grumpy old platoon sergeant throw a ball or two during the clash. No winner was determined. By early afternoon, the white mist repelled the advancing sun. The diamond dust disappeared as the winter shroud came back over camp.

Long days in the camp bunkers gave Shane time to think about the Malik and his Lashkar. Everyone said something different about why it had never come to pass: Winter weather, American deceit, payoffs and deal cutting, red herrings and lies, manipulation and misinformation. The maze of explanations made Shane's head spin. All were plausible, perhaps all were true. He was sure of one thing: For every conversation the Afghans had with the Newts, they had many more among themselves.

On New Year's Day, 2009, Sergeant Burch burst into the squad tent and ordered, "Drop your cocks and grab your socks. Ski patrol, boys. The Raven just crashed south of Gorbat. We got a grid coordinate, gotta go pick up the camera."

The Raven was a small reconnaissance aircraft, more remote-control plane than full-fledged war drone. Shane wondered why someone would fly a drone when visibility was less than a mile, but hell, he was itching for his skis. He donned his snow parka and clunky white ski boots, appropriately named Mickey Mouse boots. Then he shouldered his Rossignol powder skis and sprang from the tent. Snow smothered the hills and caked the pine branches, which sagged under the weight. Low gray clouds blanketed the valley, shrouding all but the river lowlands.

Plunging through knee-deep snow, Shane found Burch waiting at the gate camp. Burch stabbed his collapsible ski poles into the snow and left them sitting upright while he slung his rifle.

Gazing at the snowy hills, Burch said, "What would we have done if that Lashkar were real? I'll tell ya, we'd have been bored shitless the rest of this tour. One can only sit on his thumb and spin so many times."

"To be honest, Sar'nt, I was hoping for it."

"Spinning on your thumb?"

"The Lashkar."

"Why?"

"Safer for us, that's all."

"Safe?"

"Roger, Sar'nt."

Burch swept his arm from north to south. "This is our little war here. We done made it ourselves. We need to finish it ourselves. No one's going to hand over the Egyptian. It's on us."

"I reckon it's good to see things through."

Burch grabbed hold of his ski poles, saying, "Just wait 'til spring. I'm doing my face with black paint, then I'm gonna burn this fucker down." Burch giggled as he clicked into his skis, like he was only joking. "In the meantime, I'm gonna lay some powder turns in this bitch. The muj will see my tracks and know who's king of this valley."

Shane said, "Right behind you, Sar'nt."

At once Burch was skiing downhill from the gate, straight-lining for the river. Shane followed—rifle across his chest—slinging powder with each pivot around the hollies. Keeping his knees together, Shane loosened his hips, rocked through the turns, and bounced over pillow drifts. About halfway down, the slope leveled, then fell away steeply. When Shane saw the drop, it was already too late. He was airborne for a few moments, his stomach coming into his mouth. *Poof.* The landing was wobbly but he kept upright. *Holy shit—combat ski jump.* Glancing over his shoulder, he saw Cassidy and Parker carving figure eights in the slope. Then Shane turned ahead and tucked into a crouch for speed. The wind whistled through his ears while gravity pulled him down.

When he reached the frozen river, Shane cut to a stop, spraying a powder wave over a boulder. He unclicked from the skis and pulled his skins from his assault pack. Then he pressed the skins onto the bottoms and flipped the heel-release lever on his bindings. Now in touring mode, he set out. Burch skied in front, forging a track through deep powder in the riverbed. Shane followed, his breath steaming through the falling snow, his two men behind him. The squad moved in an offset column, winding upstream, carving with the turns in the river and breaking a track that deepened with each passing man.

Gliding through the valley was visceral. Everything passed smooth and quiet and tranquil, the land in winter's cold grip, like even the war had quit the valley. Shane found his rhythm. Engaging his hip flexors, he thrust one ski forward with the back one planted, half-twisting at the torso to get a good push off each pole. The *swish*ing of his sliding skis was almost hypnotic. Willows passed along the banks, bejeweled in hoarfrost. Here and there, the river climbed sheer. Cascades lay underneath. The squad traversed around the drops and side-cut the snow domes where powder had encased boulders.

After a couple hours they edged a shelf of exposed rocks rimed in ice, showing where the last trickle of flowing water had fought against winter's grip. In warm months, this spot was a rapid. Overhead, a footlog straddled the two banks. Four inches of snow clung to the top of the log. Shane recognized the spot where Harris had fallen in the water back in the spring. In Shane's mind, that was a lifetime ago. He wondered if anything had changed since then. He took an azimuth with his compass and moved on. He had no more time for reflection, but supposed it was for the better.

A half mile past the log they found the drone nose down in a snow bank. It had a four-foot wingspan and was equally long from nose to tail. Burch yanked the Raven from the snow and inspected it. "No bullet holes," he said and broke it down, handing parts to the boys. Shane took a control board and the surveillance camera, and stuffed them in his assault pack.

They set off again, heading north back to camp. The snowfall was heavier now, and the tracks they'd set on the way out had just about filled in. Tree branches canted for the ground with their heavy white burden. The patrol made good time on the downhill. Shane kept a steady glide, his eyebrows crusted by ice. They paused below Gorbat to let the stragglers catch up. Down they came. One "whooped" when he dropped over a ledge.

At that moment, a white-bellied owl sprung from a branch. It swooped over Shane with black saucers for eyes and flew downstream, flapping its massive wings. Finally, he'd seen a bird other than a dirty crow. Shane palmed his face to melt the ice on his eyelashes and they were moving again, everything blurred by silent snow. After putting Gorbat behind them, they cleared a bend, and Shane saw Holiday on the hillside, maybe a mile out. He could see no farther in the building flurries.

A single shot cracked through the bottomlands. Falling snow muffled the echo. Parker jerked forward and whipped back and fell with the tips of his skis skyward. It all happened in a blink. When Shane reached Parker, the snow beneath him was already red. Calling "Man down," Shane unclicked from his skis and stomped the bindings on Parker's skis to release them. He grasped the shoulders of Parker's vest and pulled him toward a boulder. Parker's weight was unnatural. The new guy seemed to be made of lead. Shane realized he'd released only one of Parker's skis. The attached one was dragging through the snow. No time for a fix. They had to find cover. Shane post-holed through deep snow, towing Parker backward. He reached the boulder and shoved Parker behind it. While lying on his side, Parker moaned and pedaled in a circle, the one ski still on. He flattened a landing. Hot blood hit the cold snow beneath him and melted little craters in the landing.

Shane seized Parker to stop his thrashing. "Hold still or you'll bleed out."

Private Cassidy skied up behind the boulder and released himself from the bindings. He said, "Fuck" when he saw the blood and twisted around to the enemy and let loose with his SAW, emptying a whole ammo drum.

Shane knifed open Parker's jacket and saw he was shot in the chest, right next to the armpit. Turning Parker on his side, Shane saw no exit wound. The bullet must have been lodged in his torso. It was a fatal wound. Wondering if he'd failed as a leader, Shane unzipped Parker's bleeder kit and ripped open the anticoagulant and the field dressing. Parker had a wild, disbelieving look. His voice was panicky. "I just got here. I just got here," he kept saying.

Sorry, Parker. That don't count for much with the enemy, thought Shane.

The *crack* of the second shot and *zip* of the bullet were simultaneous. The boys were all tucked into rocks and trees and no one was hit. They blazed suppressive fire at likely positions. Shane lifted his rifle and squeezed off ten, maybe twelve shots at a rock outcrop. The falling snow on Shane's gun barrel was instantly water. In the narrow river bottom, the gunfire echoed. It was impossible to pin down the exact direction of the sniper. He was south, maybe on the hill above Gorbat. A third shot puffed the snow to Shane's right. He drew his feet in tight behind the boulder.

Shane risked a peek around the side. From the corner of his eye, he saw Burch rise and ski for the middle of the frozen river. Looking through his four-power scope, Burch stood tall and very exposed. A fourth shot rang out. Burch didn't even flinch, let alone duck.

Burch threw his arms in the air, yelling, "I'm right here. Don't you see me?" Burch pulled his black scarf up to his eyes and fired on a low ridge. "Shoot me, you pot-shot motherfuckers. I want you to!"

Another shot pierced a snow bank to Burch's right.

Shane looked on. Surely Burch was drawing attention away from Parker. It was a noble deed standing there in the open.

"Do it, please, do it." Burch laughed, and before long, his shoulders quivered. His laughing faded into deep sobs. Falling to his knees, he laughed again. "Do it."

Shane realized this wasn't about baiting the sniper. His squad leader had gone manic.

Another shot.

Burch screamed back, "You can't. You won't. You don't have fucking permission."

Oh God, thought Shane, *Burch is about to be the second casualty of the day.* Shane didn't want to see it, so he turned back to Parker. Shane bit the fingers of his gloves and pulled the gloves off for dexterity. Parker lay there, rasping and wheezing from a punctured lung. Shane sealed the hole with Cassidy's help. It didn't take long before Parker's cloudy eyes grew vacant, his panicky voice soft. After five minutes he died, his gun at his side and one ski on. Shane fell back and lay on his elbows in the snow. For some reason, Cassidy kept up the CPR regime, pumping the chest so hard it looked as if he'd break the solar plexus. He bent and pushed air into Parker's lungs, clearly winded from the work.

Shane said, "It's no use, man. No bird's coming in this weather."

Cassidy checked the pulse once more and declared, "KIA." Cassidy lay back on his elbows next to Shane, and for a good while they sat there staring at the body. When Shane and Cassidy got up, they were covered in Parker's blood, which soon froze on their uniforms.

The sniper had withdrawn, or maybe he was maneuvering to another position. Burch was calm again when he pointed to a draw and said, "That sniper will keep picking us off in this channel. If we cut left here, we should come out by OP-1."

Shane nodded.

Four men carried the body at a time, skis in ascent mode. The snow and weight and stiff grade quickly exhausted them, so every five minutes they rotated on the litter. Shane took the back right handle as the draw forked right toward OP-1. As the litter bearers took uphill ski strokes, Parker's blue hand kept sliding out from under the poncho. The last drops of blood in him ran down his arm and trickled off the end of his finger, leaving a trail in the snow. The dull ring of mortars sounded while they climbed. Shells touched every terrain feature and released little powder avalanches. They kept climbing. Shane's diaphragm heaved for air. The frozen blood on his camo chafed him like roofing shingles. The metallic tang stayed in his nostrils. Shane turned queasy and vomited between ski strokes.

They were a half mile from Camp Holiday when Cassidy tore off his bloody clothes in a fit. Cassidy screamed at the hills, threw down his SAW, and turned his skis for the river. He skied away, one man with no gun, rocketing downhill toward God knows what end. Shane took two big turning steps with his skis and pursued.

They'd gone a couple hundred yards when Shane threw an elbow and knocked Cassidy facedown. The snow plumed. Shane wrestled Cassidy onto his back.

Cassidy screamed, "I can taste the blood."

Shane headlocked Cassidy and palmed his mouth to silence

him. The chokehold took effect. Cassidy stopped kicking and went slack. Shane took no chances. He flex-cuffed Cassidy. When Cassidy came to, Shane straddled him and helped him up. Then Shane kept right behind him. They reached the squad again.

Shane said to Cassidy, "Hang in there, man. We'll be partying with strippers by the time this snow melts."

Cassidy snapped his head around. With sunken eyes, he stared at Shane. Cassidy was a thousand miles away, or maybe nowhere in particular.

When they crossed into camp, Shane escorted Cassidy to the medical tent. The litter bearers followed them and set down Parker's body outside the tent. The blowing snow had already covered the body when the helicopter came for Parker in the steel light of winter evening.

Two days later, the wind was howling when the LT came into Shane's tent. Shane and the boys were huddled around a little heater with glowing orange filaments.

The LT took off his helmet. Somberly, he said, "Cassidy has combat stress. He needs to take a break for a while."

Shane reckoned Cassidy was still chained up in the medical tent. He imagined his friend lying alone, staring at the canvas overhead—finding nothing for his mind to focus on except what was already in it. The medics would be talking to him once in a while, as if they knew about head shrinking. By now, Cassidy had to be climbing the walls.

A Chinook helicopter came at the end of the week, dropped pallets, and whisked Cassidy away. He was heading for light duty at Battalion.

Shane sat against a timber wall with snow on his shoulders, watching the bird fade into the cold murk. He wanted a seat on that bird. He wanted a cup of real coffee, and peace, and tater tots.

No, make it a barrel of coffee. He'd down it in one sitting and then watch music videos of packaged girl bands.

It was quiet again, so quiet his ears rang. The winter silence was grand, yet there was something menacing in it. It mocked him. It mocked the dead. It mocked their progress.

Shane sat there, half buried in flakes. Others trundled around camp, stooped, their faces hidden under balaclavas. The platoon sergeant, Vasquez, hurried by with his hood up against the gusting snow. He stopped.

Vasquez asked, "What's eating you, Shane?"

"Cassidy's gone off the rails. I didn't see it coming."

Vasquez took a knee in the snow and slapped the flakes off Shane's gear. Vasquez said, "Sometimes no one does. A guy loses his grip and moves into a black, empty world. That's okay, though. We know what needs to happen. We move him to Battalion. He runs errands for the brass, and he can't make a mess. Or maybe he'll catch the silver bird home." Vasquez paused and flipped the snow off his own hood. "Not a big deal—psychic meltdowns are a by-product of heavy combat. The real problem is the guys who want to live in the fog. They duck back and forth under the rope of reality. They're unpredictable. One thing is for sure: They'll try and drag you into the void with them. And believe me, no one comes back from there."

SPRING 2009

21

Camp Holiday
Day 375

I t was April when the last of the snow melted in the deep gullies. Sergeant Shane stowed away his blood-soaked winter gear. The next time he'd see it he would be unpacking in the States. They were getting short; eighty days left. Shane couldn't see the barn yet, but it was just around the bend. As he counted the days, scorching heat pressed into the land like an iron.

On May 15, a helicopter dropped a flock of new guys at Holiday. Three were assigned to Shane. *Great*, he thought, *my fire team's a bunch of fucking cherries*. The new guys reported to him at the burned holly above the tent. They had close-cropped hair and clean uniforms. Shane stood in front of them, with a shock of brown hair, a bullet hole in his sleeve, and snakeskin across his brown. For a while, he said nothing, and they fidgeted, looking ashamed of themselves.

Finally, Shane pointed at the excess gear they wore, saying, "Drop this, this, this, and this. The side with the simplest uniform wins."

They immediately obliged.

"Do what I do and you'll be all right."

There wasn't a storm or even a cloud for weeks, nothing to cool things off. Summer had bullied away the spring a month early. The People's Valley was a furnace. Down low, the sun bleached the slopes, and Shane poured sweat as he traversed the parched hillsides. The weeks rolled by. Shane kept counting days while the heat blazed on. No cloud dared to interrupt the sun's hold on the land. The high forests dried to tinder. The big north wind whipped up the moondust on the jeep road.

On the solstice, Vasquez distributed phone cards to the squads. Shane got hold of a card with fifteen minutes on it. He waited his turn with the satellite phone, pacing with excitement. He was going to call Candy and tell her he was all right and he loved her, hang in there. Months had passed since she'd sent that letter. *She isn't much for the pen*, thought Shane. At last, it was his time. He raced uphill with the satellite phone in hand and found a quiet spot on the Holiday perimeter. He dialed Candy's cell phone. She was giggling when she answered. A man laughed in the background.

Shane said, "It's me."

Candy said, "Oh, hi, Danny. It's been a while."

Shane asked, "Who's with you?"

Candy said, "A friend, don't worry about it."

Shane asked, "What's so funny?"

"We're watching a movie."

"A fucking movie?"

She was forceful. "He's just a friend and it's just a movie."

Next thing Shane knew, he was screaming. He went nuclear and called her a stripper bitch.

Candy said, "Grow up," and the line went dead.

———

Three days passed. That man's voice in the background lingered in Shane's mind. He'd made a mess of it with Candy. The fight was his fault, he supposed, but she didn't have to be so goddamn coy about that man with her. A mess had a way of growing when two people were apart; it flung its tentacles and grabbed other things and pulled them down and got bigger.

The mess with Candy was front and center in Shane's head when he awoke to gusty wind and tied his boots. He ran for camp headquarters and pulled open the door and sat behind the new computer with internet. He was going to send Candy an email saying he was sorry. Just to make things right, he'd find a jeweler and use one of them rubies to make her a necklace. When he opened his inbox, he saw a message from Candy with no subject line. He pulled in a breath and opened it.

"Fuck you, Danny," was all she said.

There was another email from his landlord. She was a nice old lady with blue hair who rented him a garden apartment for Candy. The landlord's message said, "Last night I stopped by 109. The place was empty. All the faucets were running and the floor was flooded. Contact me immediately."

Shane slammed his fist on the table. Then he checked his bank account. Not a penny left. Not one penny. He never should have given Candy access. Panic surged through him when he thought of his rubies. Candy had set up the safe deposit box.

Shane rushed across the room to the red phone. It was only for the captain's official business. The shift RTO let Shane know it.

Picking up the phone, Shane said, "Cap'n ain't around. I'll make it quick. It's about a girl."

The shift RTO turned back to his blue screen.

Shane called the bank. They said Candy had been by to empty the box and close the account. Vomit climbed up Shane's throat. He swallowed it with a gulp. Dropping the phone, he rose to his feet. The world rocked back and forth. He swallowed more vomit and braced himself on a desk and then staggered outside. The blue sky spun. Shane fell to one knee.

Burch strolled up, whistling, and stopped in front of him. "You look sick."

Shane said, "Candy cleaned me out. She done made off with all my money. She even flooded the apartment I rented for her."

Burch folded his arms across his chest. He shook his head. "I warned you, didn't I?"

Shane felt his face go red.

Burch said, "Lock it up, Shane. We got a mission: The Egyptian is back. I'm about to end this chase."

"Can I sit this one out, Sar'nt?"

"No!" said Burch. "You need this. You'll see."

At 1100, Shane led his fire team to Observation Post 1, their jumping-off point for the mission. The squad was going to observe a muj gathering in a nearby village. A "Snoop and Poop" mission. Word was the Egyptian called the meeting, and it all seemed so easy, so out of place, that Shane thought it just might be real.

Burch stood waiting at OP-1. He'd done his face up in black paint. In the pounding heat, Burch's sweat had already beaded over the paint, run down his neck in black droplets, and stained his shirt collar.

The squad made for a thorny ridge and hit the spine. After climbing one-thousand vertical, they ducked into a train of boulders. Shane dabbed the stinging sweat from his eyes and positioned his three men, mingling them perfectly with the rocks at ten-yard intervals.

Far below was the village, a tangle of huts split by a clear creek. The squad surveilled the target as the sun wheeled overhead, but saw nothing of note. Then at 1400, Burch spied something so funny he almost wet his camo trousers. He bit his lip and buried his mouth in his black scarf to muffle his laugh.

Burch suppressed his laugh just enough to whisper to Shane, "Check out the freak show."

Shane was prone behind an M14, a gun brought back from the Korean era for its range and stopping power. Shane had his helmet off to minimize his silhouette. His warbonnet kept the sun off his forehead. Now Shane steadied his ten-power scope on the show. He saw an Afghan man who'd lost both legs at the knees. The legless man sat in a wheelbarrow. A boy pushed the wheelbarrow down the village trail.

Through his scope, Shane could just make out a scar over the boy's eye. Shane realized he'd seen the boy before. That scar came from a wound that Shane himself had patched up. It was the dim kid pushing the wheelbarrow.

The legless man and the dim kid came to a steep section of trail near the clear creek. The dim kid lost control of the wheelbarrow and dumped it sideways. The legless man rolled out and tumbled into the creek.

Burch slapped his thigh with delight. Just then, two armed mujahedeen emerged along the creek, moving toward the village. Shane thought about the shot, the range, the wind, whether he should take it at all. The fighters slung their guns, waded into the water and wrestled the man out of the current. Shane readied himself for the shot, then paused, undecided.

The AK-toting Samaritans tugged the legless man from the creek and carried him up the steep bank. They slipped a few times in the mud and struggled to their feet and heaved the man upward. They were about to crest the slope when Shane squeezed off a shot. The bullet hit one fighter in the head. Pink brain mist splattered on the legless man. The other fighter let go of the legless man, and the cripple hurtled down the slippery bank. Shane cracked off another shot. At the exact time, the dim kid crossed in front of the second fighter. They both crumpled, killed by the same bullet.

The legless man splashed back into the water. He bobbed downstream for a little while. The current pinned him against a logjam. He flailed his arms in a splashing panic before going under. Shane watched downstream but the man never emerged. If Shane would have waited five more seconds to take the shots, the muj would've gotten the legless man onto flat ground.

Shane said, "Oops."

Burch gave Shane a bear hug, squeezing so hard Shane's back popped. He said, "You've got hate in your heart, little bro. You really do. I'm so proud."

Shane glimpsed his three new guys off to the left. They sat there looking horrified. Shane put one finger to his lips and whispered "Shhh" to them.

Shane's two shots gave away their position. Fighters poured from the village houses, skittering into the woods in clumps as Shane took shots that sent up little puffs of dust around the village. Shane fired and fired and changed mags and fired some more. The others did the same. When Shane could see no targets, he shot at two farmers in a terrace because they were probably bad and who gave a shit anyway.

The enemy kept pouring into the forest. Outnumbered, the squad pulled back, bounding by fire teams from one rib to the next. They did this without speaking. There was only the sound of guns.

Shane had just gotten his men on line for supporting fire when he saw an enemy flanking force to his right. The group had seen the Newts, and were taking firing positions on a hummock five hundred yards distant. Shane dropped prone, aimed his M14, and scanned through the ten-power scope. Barely visible, there was a man standing in the foliage and trees, giving commands to the fighters around him. The man moved back and forth with a slight limp, and a face, an Arabic face. There was something about...*fuck*, thought Shane. It was him. The man from the bazaar so long ago. The Egyptian, now here for the taking. But just then the Egyptian disappeared behind the rise. Shane lost the shot.

Shane radioed to Burch, "I've got positive ID on the Egyptian. We need mortars. The hilltop five hundred yards northeast. Thirty degrees."

Burch said, "Roger," and radioed for a white phosphorus, or Willie Pete, artillery strike on a large stand of dead trees three hundred yards northwest.

Shane didn't know why. "Three-three," he said, "that is not the target. Target is five hundred yards, thirty degrees."

"Affirm," said Burch. "Watch this."

In came the Willie Pete. Hoops of white flame sprang from each bursting shell. After weeks of drought, the Willie Pete barrage ignited a fire in the dead trees. At first, only a few trees burned from the explosions. Soon gouts of fire found each other, turning a ribbon of forest aflame. The enemy attack stopped.

Wind grabbed hold of the flames and blew them across an entire hillside. From there, the flames advanced as a forked orange tongue. Embers flew out for new fuel. Wind ferried them along. The crackling fire found its roar, racing through bands of timber in the drainages on the slope of a gray mountain.

Burch said, "It's gorgeous."

Shane said, "Fuckin' A, Sarge."

The fire followed a ridgeline and, before long, the whole mountain burned.

Burch yelled, "*Go, go, go.*"

Shane screamed, "Burn, you fuckers."

The north wind pushed the fire along. The flames were unstoppable, and the squad was soon on the run to Holiday, out of formation, the fire's heat on their backs. Embers drifted in all directions. In minutes, flames crowned the valley and spread. Here was the sound of hell itself.

Hot days dragged by. The greedy fires ate the timber and choked the hills with smoke. Three separate fires grew into two big fires and those two fires united into one, then all the land was aflame. The slopes turned molten. Charred wood blocked every other smell. Shane brushed soot off his gear. Black snot plugged his nose. Ash mantled his green tent.

Furious, the People said the Americans started the fire on purpose. Their treasured timber was burning. Word spread like the fire itself. The media had a field day with headlines of scorched earth, and the Newts heard whispers: The Egyptian had escaped the flames, and now he had all the People preparing to strike Camp Holiday. Fighters from Pakistan would come into the valley through the high passes. They were going to overrun the camp.

———

A full-fledged assault was at hand. Newt platoon got orders to block muj coming in from the high passes. Every squad had ground to watch. Shane and Burch would go back out, too. Their squad was going to seize a camel-hump hill and observe South Pass for enemy fighters.

Shane was prepping his gear in the tent when the LT stepped in, scrunched his eyebrows, and stomped toward Burch.

Burch looked up from packing his ruck. "What's up, LT?"

The LT said, "The only reason you're still on the line is because we need every swinging dick in the fight. But listen close—you've created a media shitstorm with this fire. Battalion is talking about a court martial."

Burch asked, "What was I supposed to do, blow kisses at 'em?"

"Do not fire Willie Pete again. High explosive is all you get. I'll make sure of it."

Sneering, Burch chambered a round. He rose and strolled for the door.

The LT grabbed his arm. "You're on thin ice with your job, Sergeant. Do you want to make big rocks into small ones at Leavenworth?"

Burch said, "Got it, LT. Should we take water balloons and Silly String with us?"

Shane led the squad to the camel-hump hill after dark. They milled around for a bit, looking for a good spot to set up. Shane found a splatter of hollies and dug a grave-sized foxhole on the left wing of the hill. Burch joined him.

Shane and Burch sat cramped in their foxhole for twenty-four hours, watching the fire and South Pass.

Shane had plenty of time to think, sitting next to Burch. He breathed in the fire's smoke, which reminded him of his hunting camp in the woods outside Tupelo. His thoughts drifted to college. He'd use the GI Bill, maybe go to Ole Miss. Or better yet, Southern Mississippi. That was supposed to be a party school. Pretty girls would sit next to him in class—smart girls, not slutty girls like Candy. There'd be smarty-pants professors and books as heavy as his helmet. Shane wondered if he had the mettle for college.

Shane had to survive the last stretch of the tour, and then home and college would be real. His apprehension mounted each day. Anything could happen in a war. It was all so random, like that little accident with the dim kid. Just an accident, Shane told himself. The thought of having come so far only to be killed at the end was heavy, like Shane carried an anchor everywhere he went.

At sundown on the second day on the hill, wind in the hollies made their long shadows tremble. The sky turned purple before giving way to a glowing night. Shane stood watch silently, night vision goggles down. Burch's fire continued to chomp up the mountain near the crashed chopper owned by the one-toothed marmot. The blaze was a white glare through Shane's goggles, but outside the eyepiece it looked to be a flowing vermillion beast. Wind fed the relentless flames. Every so often shrieks tore through the valley.

Bored with South Pass, Shane peeked at Burch, who scanned the hillsides with his thermal. Burch swept his view farther left until his eyes met Shane's—they were hot coals. Except for those eyes, Burch could have been a ghost.

The two hadn't spoken much on this mission, but Shane wanted to know something, and now was as good a time as any. He said, "We hadn't been in country long when Harris drowned in the river. We hit Baz looking for him. After the mission, you came back sick."

Burch said, "I quit taking my malaria pills. They made me crazy. Doc thought I had it. But I, uh, I tested negative, so who knows?"

Shane wanted to know about the dark house in Baz. *The woman, oh God, the black-toothed woman*, thought Shane. She was so fast, and her awful eyes, with irises as bright as the fire. Many months had passed. The witch was still marauding through his brain.

Shane said, "Doc said when we came back, you were in a daze, going on about witches."

Burch said, "It's foggy now, and it was then."

Shane spit tobacco juice and tongued the wad in his lip, the way he did when thinking. "I saw the old woman's eyes glow."

Burch twitched. Turning deadly serious, he glanced at Shane. "The old woman...I didn't expect her to be that fast. And when she bit my arm, something wild ran through me." Burch rubbed his forearm. "I started having weird dreams after we came back."

Shane asked, "What kind of dreams?"

"Sweaty dreams," said Burch. "I kept having this one where I was lying on a cot in a dark room. The old woman was there in her gray cloak, hovering near the wall, watching me. She had me in a spell, see. I couldn't move. Then she was gliding toward me. I'd wake up yelling and sweating through my fart sack." Burch tugged his black scarf before continuing. "Then I'd go back to sleep. Sure as shit, we'd be together in the room again, me and the witch. Every dream, she glides toward me. Every dream, she gets closer. She reaches out for me with long, sharp fingernails."

Shane found himself leaning away from Burch. Part of him wanted Burch to stop.

Burch's voice trembled just a bit, "In the last dream, she got me."

Shane waited for it.

Burch said, "She touched me. Her hand was soft and warm. She bent down to kiss my cheek. Her mouth was black, and, and, taran-tulas came pouring out. They crawled inside me and I was burning. Big, black tarantulas, they were fast as lighting and—"

"—furry as bears," said Shane. "I remember."

Burch stared at the flames in silence.

Shane said, "That's a good ghost story."

"I wish that's all it was."

Shane wasn't sure what else to say. He'd gotten what he was look-ing for, and now he wished he would have left it alone. He wanted to change the subject.

Shane asked, "Have you heard anything about Cassidy?"

Burch said, "Cassidy needs rest."

Shane said, "I heard when something like that lingers, they call it PTSD." He articulated each word slowly. "Posttraumatic stress dis-order." Shane figured that was too long a name for being jumpy and scared. "Is Cassidy going to be back?"

Burch said, "I don't know. Some guys get swept up in the war tide, but they were never ready. For other guys, death hits too close to home. Their buddy gets whacked and they lose their nerve, their confidence. Or maybe it's the way someone dies. The first time I was here, my squad leader was made of gold. Fourteen karats, buddy. Everyone loved him. That sumbitch seemed to have a force field around him, but the night I got this scarf, the Taliban blew his head off. Clean off. I got my first brain bath."

"Sorry, Sar'nt."

"Don't say *that* to me."

Shane waited in silent confusion.

Burch went on, "So I return fire and touch up this house real good. We go up there and it's bodies all over the place. Good guys, bad guys, lots of bodies. There's a girl among them, couldn't be more than twelve, just a fragile little thing. She caught a round in the heart. Exit wound is the size of a softball. I know it was mine. And she's lying there, faceup. She's got this look and—" Burch tapped his nostril "—and a little turquoise stud in her nose. You know, it's like, a flash of beauty in all that gore. And over her head, she's got this scarf. I lifted it, right then and there. I said I'd take it to the family. But it spoke to me. I could hide behind it. I needed to."

"Hide?"

Burch didn't answer. He rubbed the scarf. "You see shit like I saw that night, and it sticks. There ain't no getting it out. I figure Cassidy feels the same way, you know, something got stuck. Now what will happen to him? I don't know."

Shane understood. Quiet crept into the foxhole again. The wind rattled the surrounding ninja leaves. They couldn't hear the river up that high—just the wind, the same wind that fed the fire.

Shane asked, "How are you, Sar'nt?"

Burch smiled. "The platoon mascot we got at the bazaar, what was it…George. It ran off with your night vision." Burch seemed to flip a switch. He was instantly blank, his words slow. "That little monkey must have weighed ten pounds but I put a dozen bullets in it. Somehow it stayed alive, even with the heavy bleeding. The monkey was looking up at us, wanting someone to make me stop. That monkey couldn't understand why I was killing him. And he wouldn't let go. You know, some creatures struggle so hard to hang on to life. Here's the thing: Once you stop clinging, everything falls in place."

It was silent again. Firelight flickered on Burch's face. Only his eyes were alive.

A memory welled up inside Shane; one that got stuck. He saw the dim kid lying dead on the riverbank, the wheelbarrow lying on its side. Shane's lip quivered. He bit down and held back a sob. "That boy I shot. That boy—"

"—had it coming," said Burch.

"No. No, he didn't."

Once more, silence crept in. Burch leaned back with his thumbs in his belt. "Out here, it's cruel. There's no chance to reset. There's no time to sort things out, to put those experiences where they need to be so you can keep moving forward. You go to sleep with shaking hands and they're still shaking when you wake up. Then more comes in and it swirls around with the first mess. It's all swirling around until your head is one glorious fuckpile. That's when guys come apart, a proper come-apart, like Cassidy. But if you lean into this shit, something good happens. You can mutate. You can be a new species. This place…this thing…this greedy thing. The organism. You can be in it and flow through it."

Jesus Christ, thought Shane. His squad leader needed sleep—not the fitful kind all the Newts got. No, Burch needed a good rest. That would help him pull it back together.

Except Burch's words were clear. His mind was sharp.

Shane didn't want to wallow in the mud with Burch. He tried to tie up the conversation. "I just wish Cassidy was okay. I don't trust the new guys."

Burch laughed.

Broken words came through Burch's radio: First platoon was calling an artillery mission. A few minutes later, shells whizzed over. Flashes preceded the booms. Trees fell in the east saddle. Even at that distance, the explosions jiggled Shane's organs. He prayed the shells hit the enemy.

Shane said, "We drop a lot of bombs on the muj, but they keep coming. They keep fighting. I know we're hitting 'em. You can hear them screaming through the Icoms." Shane flipped up his night vision goggles and rubbed his eyes. "I wonder if the muj get strung out, too. You know, do their wires get all messed up in their heads?"

Shane wanted the muj to be strung out like his friend Cassidy. "We bomb these muj night and day. I think they're going to hear the artillery shells forever."

Burch didn't respond right away. When he did, he looked straight at Shane, almost through him. Burch's eyes were orange in the firelight. "You want the muj to be like us. We are First World children, little buddy. We think we're going to live forever. We suffer from the 'too-much' disease. That's our problem. The war is just another little adventure for us, something to do before settling down with babies and dogs in the suburbs. Combat is an experience, something to be consumed. It will be neatly packaged, well organized, and when you've had enough, you can throw it in the trash and walk away. But you get here and it's ugly and random and no one's in control. It's not over when you want it to be. You can't just walk away when you get tired."

Shane pictured his friend ripping off his bloody clothes again.

Burch went on, "The Afghans don't see it the way we do. They eat dirt and rocks and grow up in war. They don't hang on to life so hard, but not because it's pointless. They just don't expect so much, right from the start. If you go into a fight that way, it makes you a monster. Now I see things the way they do, and I'm shooting lightning from my fingertips."

He paused, eyed the fire. The wind picked up through trees. Shane knew there would be more if he waited.

Burch continued, "Think about life back home. It's a desperate little drama, ain't it? Eating right, exercising, running our kids around, and watering the grass. You see everyone scurrying, trying to drag it out as long as they can. They embrace the fads and get ready for their fucking half marathons. It's like baby cows running from wolves—all panicky and not very fast. Once you stop trying to live forever, it all opens up. That's how those muj come at it. So the answer is no, the muj don't get combat stress. And there's no PTSD clinic in Pakistan for the crazy muj who saw their buddy get wasted. PTSD, all this other stuff between your ears, it's a First World problem."

Shane said, "I know what would mess them up. Send a few hundred muj to a nice flat place in the States and have them duke it out with the locals. Make them stay fifteen months."

Burch said, "How about Mississippi, down in the swamps with the skeeters and your kinfolk? The muj would go nuts in a week."

22

With weeks of spotting artillery, the Newts thwarted the Egyptian's attack on Holiday before it was launched. Now the fires had gone out, leaving the valley black and the trees all gone. There were twenty-nine days left for the Newts. A sense of finality settled in with the days left and the land all black. One morning, the captain commanding the incoming unit flew into Holiday on a chopper, alighted from the side door, and stood there looking disgusted when he saw the Newts in positions. Some wore sleeveless T-shirts beneath their armor. All had withered bodies and faces drawn and eyes like the dead.

Later that morning, the LT gathered the Newts in Shane's tent to explain their final mission. Shane was laying on his rack, reading *Maxim* magazine, as the boys trickled in. He swung his feet to the floor and sat, ready for something outlandish.

The LT stood in front of them, wearing his American flag baseball cap. The LT said, "We've had a tough go of it out here. You all have been heroes, nothing short of heroes. You'll look back on this tour and know it's the hardest thing you've ever done or will do in your life. For that, I commend you."

Great—a pep talk, thought Shane. *Weren't they way past speeches as an effective motivational tool?*

The LT continued, "I know what you guys are thinking. The Egyptian is still on the loose. That doesn't mean we've lost. We can still claim victory if, if, we hand over a secure road to the paratroopers coming in. The new guys are going to pave and widen the road, and before long, the valley will be linked to the outside world. Law and order and aid and troops will come pouring in. We'll beat the Egyptian with civilization."

The LT paced with his hands clasped behind his back. "In the rosiest scenario, the valley will someday host a charming ski resort. We can all come back for a ski vacation. I imagine most of you privates will be shithead snowboarders. We'll have to keep our distance. No hard feelings. But first, we need to control the land around the road. That's where our platoon comes in."

Guard a road? thought Shane. *Guess we've been demoted to JROTC.*

On the night of June 24, the Newts formed a staggered column at the Holiday gate. Sergeant Shane's uniform was full of holes. Dust powdered his wild hair. Shane had duct-taped the toes of his boots to hold the flapping soles. Ragged as he was, he stood with poise on strong legs. He carried only the essentials. He craved silence. He expected the same from the three men assigned to him.

They left the wire and marched north. After two hours, they cut down to the river. Reaching the bank, Shane and Burch built a rope bridge. Then the Newts climbed halfway up the valley's east wall. Without saying a word, they seized an abandoned village girdling a bubbling spring.

The houses gave commanding views of the jeep road 1,500 feet below, all the way from the valley mouth to Holiday. The double-track road was the sole transportation artery in the People's Valley. Rockslides and washouts often made the road impassable. Along some stretches, a momentary lapse in a driver's attention could result in a thousand-foot death plunge.

Newt platoon split into two groups of eighteen men. The LT led Team One. They occupied houses a stone's throw from the bubbling spring, and watched the southern stretch of road. They called their position the Spring.

Shane took his fire team with Team Two. Sergeant Burch led the team. They marched one mile north of the Spring, passing through a rock cleaver running upslope. They slipped into position in a schist outcrop littered with enemy shell casings. Burch called the spot the Brass Pile. From there, Team Two glassed the north end of the road.

Second platoon drew the undesirable mission of traveling the road in armored jeeps. Newt platoon would protect second platoon from ambushes and roadside bombs. The combined presence of the two platoons would create a bubble of safety that the incoming unit could expand for the paving project.

By July 3, the spring thaw was long over. The People's River flowed gentler now. Neon green leaves shaded the water next to the road. Shane and his team had been in their positions for just over a week. Second platoon had run the road four times without incident. Their next run would happen the morning of July 4.

At 1500, Shane listened as the cap'n gave a situation report through the radio. "Enemy fighters have moved into the hills above the Newts. They are staging in stone huts, location RD 1435 6845. They're planning an attack on the second platoon convoy." The cap'n ordered the Newts, "Assault the stone huts and deny an enemy attack against the road."

The mission seemed straightforward. Newt platoon had three simultaneous tasks: Watch the north end of the road; watch the south end; and assault the stone huts. Doing all three at the same time would require splitting into groups of twelve men each. If the enemy attacked one of these small groups, they could wipe them out. For self-preservation, the Newts had to vacate one position and leave the road unguarded.

The LT made the decision at twilight. Shane and Team Two would vacate the Brass Pile. The north end of the road would go unguarded.

A half hour later, Team Two marched into the village. They made their assault scheme and drew water from the bubbling spring for the climb. The platoon sergeant, Vasquez, consolidated positions around the houses. He would keep a squad at the Spring and continue watching the road's south end.

It took two hours for Shane, Burch, and half the Newts to climb to the alcove. Stars winked overhead as Shane rammed the first door at 0300. His men chased him through a maze of dark rooms. Five huts were cleared in two minutes flat. They split again and hit the outbuildings. The combined find was an old Enfield rifle, a bag of henna paste, prayer beads, and approximately five tons of goat shit.

Just beyond the village, Shane scampered up a domed rock and feasted on the views. In the distance, village lights sparkled like galaxies in a mountain universe. Shane realized he might never see mountains like this again. Hell, he didn't want to. After this shit, he wanted to live somewhere flat. Mississippi would do just fine. For now, Shane told himself to take in the scenery.

As Shane stood there in the dark, Burch ascended the rock and stood next to him. Flipping up his night vision goggles, Burch said, "This is prime real estate. I'm gonna get me a time-share in one of these huts and make it my summer love pad."

Shane said, "I'm counting this as the last wild goose chase. Feels good, I suppose."

He didn't say what he was really thinking—that Burch was two people. One minute, he was a beguiling vet, finding humor in the war and caring for the boys like they were his own kids. The next minute he was a sociopath. The good left inside Shane told him to pull back, to break contact and put up a wall.

————————

Just before dawn, the assault force tumbled back down the hill. The LT and his group returned to the Spring. Shane, Burch, and seven others climbed over the rock cleaver and returned to the Brass Pile, arriving just as the vehicles of second platoon rounded the L-shaped spur at the valley mouth. The squad spread out in the rocks.

Shane followed second platoon's movement with his binos. The vehicles were small tan dots in a cloud of moondust. Their engines groaned as they struggled up the rock-strewn lane. Two boulders protected Shane's flanks. When he scanned to his left, Shane saw the three members of his fire team just downhill. Lying prone, they had their weapons trained on the slopes. They were keyed up at the right moment, just as Shane had taught them; when a body was amped all the time, it was easy to get worn down.

Shane worked a wad of tobacco, albeit a much smaller one than usual. He was stretching two cans to the end of the tour. Snuff rationing proved to be a monumental challenge.

For Shane, the end of his first combat tour was one long cringe. He counted down the days, everyone did, and each passed in slow motion. Shane had lost his taste for action. That's not to say he wasn't up for a good gunfight at the end. His concern was his squad leader. Right now, Burch was on the right side of the rope. He could instantly cross to the wrong side. Shane wanted out of the valley before things changed.

Shane scanned the hills above the trucks. He clutched his warbonnet and rubbed the scales for luck. Eight days of rubbing the snakeskin had made hamburger meat of Shane's thumb, but he didn't mind. His lucky headband was going to get him home in one piece.

Binos down. Shane closed his tired eyes to refocus. Binos back up. Nothing out of place. No enemy radio chatter. Maybe the raid on the huts had worked. It looked to be another quiet run of the road.

KAAPOW. Light flashed through the narrow valley. The first truck flipped end over end. The sound of the blast bowled down the valley. Shane knew what had happened—a bomb under the road. Enemy guns clattered before the truck returned to the ground. Bullets raked the convoy. The ambush was perfect. The bomb was placed at the road's narrowest point. The route was now blocked by the first truck. The other trucks were stuck. Down came RPGs.

Shane traced the rocket contrails to the enemy positions on the hillside. They were three hundred yards away.

Shane yelled, "Suppressive fire," as he flipped his selector switch to burst mode. *Blap. Blap. Blap.* His fire team joined in for a mad minute.

The enemy blasted away at the convoy. Shane's men pounded the enemy. RPGs, AT4s, and TOW missiles interwove on their furious trajectories. In the melee, the convoy fired on Shane's position. Fifty-cal rounds cracked by. Shane ducked into the deepest crevice between the boulders. Rounds kept coming. *Ping.* Rock fragments showered his helmet. "Two-six, two-six, you're engaging friendlies," was the call over the radio. Fear quaked through Shane's hands. He imagined being hit by a .50-cal round. He damn sure didn't want to be part of a horror movie. And getting killed by one of his own, hell, there wasn't much glory in that. One could even call it embarrassing.

Knowing his fire team was right below, Shane clenched his teeth, popped back up, and fired wildly.

Down on the road, a second platoon soldier reached the first jeep and screamed through the radio, "They're dead. All of them are fucking dead."

The bomb had killed four as it flipped the first jeep. The dead gunner was half pinned under the vehicle's charred skeleton. An RPG killed two more in the second jeep.

The enemy lost interest in the trucks as the flanking fire from Team Two intensified. The enemy swung four machine guns and two RPGs onto Shane's position. Shane shot back to keep the muj hunkered down, but his men were badly outgunned.

More panted words came through the radio. "Burch, I've got everyone with me. We are coming toward your six," said the LT. The remaining Newts had vacated the Spring to join the fight. They were now climbing through the rock cleaver toward the Brass Pile.

Shane dumped mag after mag into the muj positions—the enemy had set a perfect ambush under their watch, and he was doing all he could to get even. Just to the right, Shane saw Burch pull his black scarf up to his eyes and spring to his feet. Burch grabbed Shane's collar.

Burch said, "No time to wait for the LT. Let's get these fuckers."

Shane said, "I'm with you."

They galloped forward to close the distance. The muj rallied together and broke off the attack, racing uphill through trees along a dry creek with tracers streaming this way and that. Burch charged after them on his long legs, hurtling downed trunks and scrambling boulders and leaping from one rock to another at a pace that would've made fresh troops faint. Shane did his best to keep up.

A few minutes into the chase, Burch turned and said, "Shane, let's eat these bastards when we catch 'em."

The words stopped Shane in his tracks. *I'm too short for this shit,* he thought. He wanted revenge, but not through a reckless pursuit, and he damn sure didn't want to eat anyone. Shane had to slow his squad leader down, but he didn't know how.

"Please, Sar'nt, let's wait for the others."

Burch pointed to his black scarf. "Don't worry—the muj can't see us."

Shane reeled backward—Burch thought he was invisible. Shane had hitched his wagon to the sergeant, and now the crazy bastard was leading him off a cliff. The voice of doom inside Shane told him to stop.

Burch was running again.

Shane said, "Sar'nt, please."

Burch said, "What the fuck, Shane? Let's go, they're waiting for us."

"Who's waiting?"

"The muj."

Shane opened his mouth to plead, but nothing came out. Burch was off again, and Shane was after him. As they raced uphill, Shane's chest battled for oxygen against his bulletproof vest. The vessels popped in his lungs. A bloody taste soured his mouth.

The enemy ran through the trees along the dry creek, trying to widen their distance from the Newts. The muj stopped every so often to fire down. One burst smacked a fat tree next to Shane. A branch snapped and crashed over his shoulders. He fell facedown, rolled onto his back, and scanned downhill to see if anyone was hit. No one was back there.

A shiver ran through Shane: It was just him and Burch chasing the muj through the trees. No one else could keep up. Pine needles pricked Shane's underside when he rolled onto his elbows. His mind churned. He could lay there and wait for the others, right there, behind the fat tree in the pine needles. There was no shame in that. Burch wouldn't even notice he'd dropped out of the race.

But Burch would be alone. Shane hit himself on the helmet to force his mind one way or the other. He hopped back onto his feet and resumed the chase, cursing himself and his damned loyalty.

Shane caught up to his squad leader. Their tree weaving and bullet dodging continued. Just above, the enemy fighters shouted commands to each other. Shane stepped on a discarded radio. One hundred yards uphill, he found a backpack, and then two RPGs. *Shit*, he thought, *the muj are ditching gear.*

The muj were goat centaurs to begin with. Now they were dropping equipment to pick up speed. Their terse commands grew faint. The firing trickled off, and forty minutes after the bomb, the shooting stopped. No more figures flashed through the trees above Shane and Burch. Deadfall and rocks hid the enemy tracks. The fighters were gone.

Burch stopped in the dry creek. He wandered in a circle, crunching rocks and staring at the ground like he'd lost his car keys. Burch yanked down his scarf. Foam fell from his lip. He howled at the sky—a long, doleful howl. Then he ripped off his helmet and slammed it into a rock, baring yellow teeth, cussing the Creator for allowing the muj to best him. The repeated blows cracked his helmet. Burch flung it aside and punched his own face. His bloody fist made sick, squishy thuds.

Shane rested his hands on his knees. His tongue hung from his mouth. Everything came into focus as he eyed the atomic meltdown. The platoon sergeant had warned Shane about the guys who lived in the fog. Burch had built a castle in it. The gate was down, and he was waving at Shane from the battlements.

The rumble of an engine brought Shane back to the present. He craned toward the northern sky.

A call came over the radio. "Burch, we've got an A-10 inbound. I'm giving you control."

Burch stopped punching himself. A sinister smile crossed his face, with bloody teeth and all. He reached for his radio. "Roger that, LT. I've got control of the bird."

A few seconds later, the plane streaked by, flying low between the valley's tight walls. The dark green A-10 had shark teeth painted on the nose.

The Warthog pilot asked, "What do you need?"

Burch nodded at Shane, and said to the pilot, "I've got muj in the trees above me. I'll mark the target with green smoke. Unload everything you've got on the green smoke."

Shane thought it strange that Burch was so absolutely sure about the mujahedeen's position.

The A-10 pilot acknowledged the signal.

Burch reached into his vest and tugged out a green smoke grenade. He pulled the pin and dropped the grenade at his feet.

POOF. HISS. Green smoke billowed out.

Burch had just marked himself as the target. Shane was ten feet away. Blood rushed to his face. His knees gave out. Righting himself, he looked back for the plane. The flying death machine banked to line up on the green smoke. The engine roared. Shane stood frozen.

Shane screamed, "BURCH, GET AWAY FROM THE SMOKE."

Burch clapped his hands together, like he was applauding himself. "LET'S GO OUT WITH A BANG."

Shane sprinted for Burch, wanting to drag his squad leader away. *God, get us out of this*, thought Shane, *and I'll give all my money to First United Baptist in Tupelo.* He skidded to a stop. It was too late. He would be killed, too. Shane ran sideways for a clump of trees beyond the dry creek. Concrete in his legs kept him in slow motion. He cried, "Please, please," as he ran.

Hearing the banshee shriek of rockets, Shane closed his eyes.

His world became fire.

———

The explosions knocked Burch into a tree. His ears rang like he was hugging a cathedral bell. Tree bark and branches covered his body. His black scarf sizzled. He couldn't see Shane through the dust.

The pilot came over the radio, "Lining up for another run."

Burch said, "Roger that, re-attack," and glanced over his shoulder. The A-10 was circling. The plane's green paint blended perfectly with the mountain behind it. Machine guns crackled from above. Green tracers streaked over Burch's head toward the plane. The muj were just two hundred yards uphill.

The war bird adjusted for a new target. Burch could make out the pilot's white helmet as he thundered overhead. The plane spit carnage all over the dry creek. And this time, the Warthog's chain gun buzzed. It pumped out depleted uranium bullets at sixty rounds per second.

Trees shattered. Rocks vaporized. Shell casings poured down and clinked off the cobbles in the creek bed.

The plane circled around for another go. The mujahedeen shot back from the trees. The pilot slammed the throttle forward. A flurry of rockets swished out of the pods. One fell short and detonated in the creek bed right above Burch. Football-sized cobblestones flew every which way. One smashed into Burch's face. His head snapped back and he crumpled where he stood, lying motionless.

The pilot radioed to Burch, "Munitions expended. Target destroyed. Mission complete."

No one answered.

The pilot repeated himself.

The LT came over the radio, "Affirm. Thanks for your help." The A-10 sped north and disappeared. The LT called for Burch on the radio.

No answer.

———

Burch opened his eyes. Everything was cloudy. His thoughts were scribbles. The world slowly returned. The sky was electric over the North Dakota prairie. He didn't remember how he got home. Burch rolled his neck—mountains on all sides. A tiger-striped M4 lay across his chest.

He wasn't home. He was in the People's Valley. He groaned and propped himself to a knee. Charred skin peeked through a dozen holes on his uniform. Blood from his broken nose stained the bib of his shirt. He coughed black grime.

Sergeant Vasquez came running up. He asked, "You okay?"

Burch said, "Good."

Vasquez patted him down for wounds. "Nothing fatal" was his assessment.

Burch asked, "What happened?"

"You tell me."

"I don't remember."

"The Warthog lit up the whole mountain," said Vasquez. He thrust out a dirty hand. "Up you go."

Burch swayed onto his feet. He looked right. Trees were on fire. There was Shane, lying at the base of a burning pine. Two soldiers lifted him. It was only Shane's torso. Another soldier carried Shane's pink intestines like a tangled climbing rope. Pine needles matted the sticky guts. Twenty yards away, two others grabbed hold of Shane's boots and dragged his legs. They piled the body parts onto a poncho.

Vasquez said, "We're calling a bird to evac Shane's body. You need to hop on."

Burch wiped the blood off his face and said, "For what, a few burns? I'm staying."

Vasquez said, "Then rally your squad. We're going to clear these trees and see if the A-10 hit anything besides Shane."

The hills were quiet, save the crackling fires in the battered trees. Burch found his bearings. This was just a training drill, he thought. No big deal. Shane would come back to life once the drill was over. Burch beheld the burning trees and tried to put his finger on something. Every fiber inside him vibrated. It wasn't a bad thing, more like peace, tranquility, like something inside him was purged. Something waited for him up the dry creek, Burch could still feel it.

The Newts divided into squads and marched astride the creek bed. All around, shattered trees bled yellow sap. Burch weaved between the trunks, gun at the ready in the haze. The first thing he found was four dead muj on the creek bank.

Burch stood over the mujahedeen, but not triumphantly, just embracing some measure of retaliation. Rockets had killed three of them. Their bodies were black and crispy, frozen in death throes with their lips burned off, eyes melted in the flash heat of white explosions. The empty sockets were still steaming. Another fighter was hit by the A-10's chain gun. His chest was a red pasta salad, topped by a skinny neck, patchy beard, and disheveled hair.

After a sweep through the trees above, Burch found a fifth body. A depleted uranium bullet, meant for a tank, had burrowed into the fighter's back, splattering his innards over the pine needles. Burch closed his eyes for a moment.

The fighter was a teenager, maybe seventeen at most. His empty eyes were split by a hooked nose. To Burch, the fighter looked like all the other muj except for the tear-shaped birthmark on his cheek. No one could miss that birthmark.

Suddenly, in Burch's mind, the Baz raid came to life again. He saw the witch.

The memory struck Burch like a lightning bolt: The dead fighter was Sadboy. Burch's mind flashed to Sadboy cooking french fries in the courtyard, Sadboy holding a picture of Burch's wife, looking at his wife's jeans and saying, "Sheenz."

Shane had killed Sadboy's father. The witch was Sadboy's mother. Sadboy was a father, too.

Burch looked into the teenager's empty eyes. At that moment, Burch wanted to be at home, cheering as his son ran for six. Even more, he wanted to lay with his wife on the sunny bank of the Little Missouri, all day, just lying there on that old wool blanket with nothing to do.

A spell of dizziness hit Burch. He sidestepped to a rock to brace himself. Images skated through his head. He was all tangled up over Sadboy and Shane. They killed Sadboy because he attacked American soldiers. But maybe Sadboy's attack was just retaliation. Burch could hear the talking heads on TV back home, pontificating about the chicken and the egg. Burch was supposed to block it all out. The platoon sergeant had told him, "All you have to do is take care of your boys and kill every bad guy you can along the way." Burch had only done the second. His little brother was dead.

Burch's knees hit the pine needles. Everything was heaving, and he couldn't slow his mind. Sadboy's war was over but his son was somewhere in the valley waiting for him, the brave mujahedeen, to come home with war stories. Maybe the son would follow his old man and become a muj, too. Just maybe, Burch would kill Sadboy's son on his next tour. In this way, the very act of fighting guerrillas was good job security for a soldier. But all the carnage felt self-inflicted to Burch right then and there on the rocky hillside under fiery trees.

Burch staggered to a burning holly, took off his black scarf, and threw it in the flames.

EPILOGUE

South Dakota

Burch wiggled into a camping chair. He'd put on some weight, most of it due to his spectacular red beard. The ice in his cup cracked when he poured in whiskey. He took a swig. In front of him, there was a windy lake ringed by aspen trees starting to find their yellow. Rust covered Burch's world, but he still saw brilliant color in those yellow aspens. His beat-up silver camper was parked behind him. It was a Tuesday afternoon, and Burch was carrying out his weekday regimen.

His cell phone rang. The caller had a 303 area code. Burch didn't recognize the number.

Burch answered, "What?"

"Hey, asshole. Lock and load. We're going to Balay to shoot people and goats. We step off at 1500 tomorrow."

Burch recognized the voice of the LT. The last time they spoke was on Burch's final day in the Army, three years ago.

Burch said, "Fuckin' A, I'll be half drunk by 1500, but don't worry, my aim gets better with each tip of the bottle." He gulped at his whiskey. "What're you doing?"

The LT said, "I'm in Bowman for a project in the Bakken Shale. Workin' for Halliburton. I'll be in your neck of the woods for a few days. Let's link up."

Burch gave the LT directions to the windy lake.

———

The LT drove up in a dually truck on Thursday afternoon. He wore long hair, but not hippie long—just the hair of a free man.

Burch clenched a cigarette in his teeth, saying, "I like your new 'do, LT. Less uptight. That old buzz cut made you look like a total asshole." Burch swept his hand at the surrounding land. "Welcome to the Black Hills. This is my kingdom."

The LT chuckled. "I like the beard. You could be a fur trapper in 1830. Where're your buckskins at?"

They got down to business. Burch strung together cuss words in ways no normal person could follow. He yanked off his shirt and showed tattoos of dogtags, guns, and bayonets. The LT pulled off his shirt and pointed at a big tattoo on his ribs—it was the snaggle-toothed marmot guarding the crashed chinook above Ghar.

Burch shook his head, saying, "Were you fucking high when you got that?"

The LT said, "It just captured the experience so well."

Burch had two pistols, an SKS, a carbine, and an AR15 in his camper. He readied his arsenal and they proceeded to shoot the fuck out of everything around the lake. Four crows and two raccoons were KIA. One NO SHOOTING sign was damaged beyond repair.

As they reloaded magazines, Burch asked, "What the hell have you been doing, LT?"

The LT said, "I'm a drilling manager for Halliburton. You

know about the Bakken? It's going nuts. We're making money hand over fist."

Burch said, "They're fracking under my parents' land. I got a little something for it." Burch pointed at his camper. "That black stuff helps fund my opulent lifestyle."

The LT smiled and asked, "Are you out here for the week?"

Burch said, "Naw. I'm out here most days. Money's no problem for me. My wife left with my son a couple years back, so I ain't got much reason to hang around town."

———

The cold, biting wind of the northern plains never tired. That afternoon, Burch made for a rocky point on the lake's far shore. Two summers of fishing the lake had taught him where to cast. His reel sang in the wind. With a cigarette hanging from his lip, Burch pulled in a trophy-sized trout. The LT caught a big trout, too, but only after he squatted on Burch's fishing hole. They talked about what the boys were doing. Burch had the scoop on most guys. Some never returned his calls.

Burch said, "Most of the boys got out. They're doing all sorts of different things, some for better, some for worse. Not Vasquez. He stayed in and went back to the Stan. Four fucking tours, man. On the fourth, a rocket killed him. He was inside a big base at the time, one of those safe ones. Heard it was plain bad luck." Burch cast his line. "You stick around the infantry long enough, either your body gets broke or you get dead. Way it is."

Burch remembered a newspaper clipping Vasquez sent him before he died. The article was about Kermit Martinez, the Newt sergeant from LA who was badly wounded on the north ridge.

Burch grinned as he asked, "You remember Martinez, don't you?"

The LT said, "Of course. Super Chicano."

Burch said, "I missed having him around. That old gangster was a funny bastard. A few weeks before Martinez got hit, we were climbing the mountain above Gorbat, thirsty as hell from the summer heat and a week of walking. I had two sips of water left, and I was this close to shriveling up. Thankfully, a cloud rolled over us about halfway up, and it got to raining pretty hard. I looked over at Martinez. He was looking at the sky with his mouth open, tongue out, drinking up the raindrops. At that moment, a big crow flew over and dropped a messy white turd straight in Martinez's mouth. Martinez gagged and swore on the Virgin of Guadalupe that he was gonna waste that crow. He was going to hunt it to the ends of the earth. It would have no peace. I just couldn't stop laughing about the precision of the crow's strike. It was impeccable. That crow must have been the head of the muj air force."

The LT said, "That was a muj bird colonel for sure."

Burch said, "The crow even screamed as he flew off. I reckon he was proud of his successful strike on the Americans." Burch hooked a worm and adjusted his bobber before going on: "I didn't keep up with Martinez after he left Afghanistan. But two years ago, Vasquez sent me this newspaper article about him. Martinez spent a year recovering from his gut wound on the north ridge. His mom was taking good care of him back in LA. Martinez had nothing else to do with his days, so he helped his mom cook tacos. Before long, they got a food truck going. And after a couple years, Martinez had himself a chain of taquerias. I imagine he wasn't the first Mexican to open a taco stand in southern California, that's for sure."

The LT laughed.

Burch explained, "Here's the thing, the newspaper said Martinez had some secret sauce he put on the tacos."

The LT remembered something. He said, "My God."

"He wouldn't tell anyone the recipe, not even his mom. People were crazy about his secret sauce. Before long, Martinez's restaurants caught on with the rich white folks in Santa Monica and Beverly Hills. The taquerias became a big fad. You know how people are in the big cities, always worrying about being in the know. After a little while, that singer chick with the big butt got to talking 'bout it. What's her damn name... J-Lo. She raved about Martinez's taquerias, and even more celebrities came running. Now ole Martinez is swimming in money. He's a high roller, got a yacht and everything."

The LT said, "Shoot, he got what was coming to him." He chuckled. "I remember, we were up on Tiger Mountain. Martinez said he got the magic sauce recipe from the Pagans in Barge Matall. Martinez was full of shit, mostly, so I never thought anything of it. Now Martinez is using the magic sauce in California. Before too long, all of LA will be worshipping bunnies."

The two old Newts kept their hooks in the fishing hole. Another hour passed. The fish stopped biting. They were watching the wind send ripples across the lake when the LT reached into his pocket and took out a rattlesnake headband.

The LT pushed it into Burch's hand and said, "You should keep this."

Burch felt unsteady. He braced himself on a rock. Rubbing the scales, he sat down. "I think about Shane every day."

The LT said, "The fucking A-10 annihilated the whole mountain. That wasn't the way I wanted things to end."

Burch said, "It's all still fuzzy for me. It seems like none of it was real." He kept rubbing the scales. "I've been dying to tell someone this—right after Baz, I got sick. After a few days, I seemed to get over the worst of it. It never really went away. Something was smoldering for a long time. I was slipping and I knew it. But after the last fight, things changed. I got better."

The LT said, "The tour was over."

Burch said, "It wasn't that. Shane was my little bro. I had no reason to feel good after he died. I go digging for what happened all the time. I can see us climbing the hill together, and then nothing, just a huge blank space. Then I see Shane's body in the poncho. It hurts real bad. I know I let him down."

The LT raised one eyebrow. "It's a war. Dudes get killed."

Burch said, "One of the fighters we killed that day had a birth-mark on his cheek. He was from Baz. The night we raided the village, his mom bit me. I knew I was slipping. You saw it, LT. I tell you, I wanted to fucking take their life force and eat it up and get bigger from it. I tried to burn everything."

The LT said, "Burch, you need to go easy on the bottle."

"Hear me out, LT. This is the thing: When we killed that fighter, I got better. It's like the thing that tormented me was expelled. I tried wrapping my mind around it. I talked to a headshrinker at the VA for a year. He was yammering about survivor's guilt and cognitive dissonance and a whole lot of nonsense. All I can say is that valley has some creepy shit going on."

The LT replied, "It's over now. The paratroopers who replaced us got their shit pushed in real bad. I saw it on the news. The Army gave up on the manhunt after their tour, said it was causing too many civilian casualties. No one got the Egyptian. It makes the whole thing seem, well, shit, I don't know."

The two of them found no more words for it. They carried on fishing.

———————

In the light of a pink sunset, they got a campfire going. Trout siz-zled in a pan. Two empty whiskey bottles shattered across a rock. Burch stripped down to his undies and danced around the fire. The LT roared with laughter. They told tales about the Newts and the muj and the Kush. Some were funny. Some were sad. They shared things they'd never told anyone else.

Burch was blackout drunk by 0100. His AR15 was shining in the firelight. The aspen leaves were quaking. The cold was coming on. Burch was at Camp Holiday, so he picked up the rifle, stumbled into a clearing, and shot down the moon.

At dawn, Burch made for his fishing hole again. He whistled as the wind curled the water into whitecaps. Baiting his line, Burch saw the LT unzip his tent, thrust out his head, and puke for a long time. The sound carried far into the Black Hills.

After a half hour, the LT came stumbling up to the fishing hole. His eyes were so red he must have busted capillaries while puking. Burch had done that more than once.

The LT said, "Gotta be on my way. I'll come back again next fall. We can make a tradition of this."

"Sounds good."

———

And he did—four years in a row, the LT came back to the windy lake in the Black Hills, to shoot the breeze with Burch and get wasty-pants. But as time passed the reunions were different. The LT seemed less interested in telling war stories.

During the fourth reunion, they sat on opposite sides of the fire. A midden of beer cans lay at their feet. Off to the left, moon and firelight played back and forth on the lake.

Burch said, "Remember that kid Kopeki?"

The LT didn't answer.

Burch said, "Why you so quiet, LT?"

"I'll tell you. It seems like someone else lived these stories, not me. And part of me wants it to stay that way. Here we are, retelling the tales, rearranging them, tinkering with sequence and facts, playing with what happened. Sometimes things get confused— what happened, and what we *wished* would have happened. Eventually, the only reality is the spoken story."

When he finished, the LT rose and walked toward his dually truck.

Burch followed him. "Where you going?"

The LT opened the door and sat and keyed the ignition. "To find a hotel."

"What's up your ass?"

"Truth is, I can't see the point in any of this. What are you after out here? There's no final score. No one gives a fuck about some dead guys in the mountains on the other side of the world."

With that, the LT threw the truck in gear and sped away. Dust curled up behind him. The taillights disappeared in the aspens.

Burch said, "I do."

ACKNOWLEDGMENTS

Thanks to my lovely wife, Elizabeth, my fountain of great ideas. To my dad, Russ, who read and gave feedback on a hundred early drafts. To my agent, Alec Shane, a consummate professional who gets things done. To Kate Hartson and Jaime Coyne at Hachette Book Group, thank you for your guidance and for having faith in me.

Many thanks to the boys from A Co, 1-32 Infantry, who fought in the Korengal—that's as hard as it gets; to the Rangers of Alpha and Bravo Company, Second Ranger Battalion; Chuck Cigrand; Danny McPadden; Justin Sax; Dave Withey; Jim McKnight; Christopher Cavoli; Tate Preston; Dana Isaacson; Dan Haff; Nic Kenney. And one for the Airborne Ranger in the sky.

About the Author

RAY McPADDEN is a four-tour combat veteran and a former Ground Force Commander in an elite unit of Army Rangers. He earned a Purple Heart, two Bronze Stars, and a medal for valor during his combat tours, which included almost two years on the Afghan-Pakistan border during the height of the conflict. He now lives in Gardiner, Montana.